I0737098

ONCE UPON A CHARLIE

BY

Karen Wilkinson

WIND POINT BOOKS
AN ELECTRON ALLEY PUBLICATION
LORAIN, OHIO

Windpoint Books
Electron Alley Corporation
The Herald Building
732 Broadway Avenue
Lorain, OH 44052

Manufactured in the United States of America

Edited by PaperTrue

ISBN 978-1946266-07-01(eBook)
ISBN 978-1-946266-08-8 (Trade Paperback)

I'd like to dedicate this book to all those people who work with children in rehabilitation centers across the country. While some are paid employees, many of them are volunteers. They all work tirelessly to help bring these children to a place where they can function and fit into the society and take care of themselves on their own. The children range from toddlers to teenagers, and all are well cared for and kept safe from any harm. They come from broken homes or foster homes that have refused to take them in. That is why I am dedicating this book to all those who work in that field, as they work tirelessly at their jobs. Each of them cares greatly for the children that are in their facility, and they must be honored for their hard work. I'd like to thank them for all that they do for the children they supervise. This book is purely a work of fiction, and no child from any of the rehabilitation centers across the country were ever in any danger or harmed as depicted in this book. The people across the country that work with these children make sure that all of the children stay safe and sound. Thank you.

Chapter 1

IT WAS a Tuesday night in May. I was working the three-to-eleven shift. I'm a police officer for the City of Palisades, in Midwest Missouri. There are approximately thirty-five thousand people in the city, from the very rich to the poorest. I've been with the police department for a little over twenty years, and I like what I do. I haven't always seen eye to eye with the Chief of Police, Edward Denault, nor his Personal Assistant, Lieutenant Kenneth Dintzman, or Captain Randolph Eaton, who was pretty much in charge of Police Personnel. And I avoided them as much as they avoided me. The three of them were thick as thieves, everyone knew that. But nobody ever talked about it. It was pretty apparent that something was not right with those three, but no one ever asked any questions.

There are over seventy-two police officers on the force divided into five separate squads. Each squad has their own Sergeant and Lieutenant. Each officer is assigned to a specific sector to patrol, and there are six sectors in all. The officers are also assigned a Department Serial Number (DSN), and depending on which squad they are on, their radio call assignments are given to them. As for the patrol officers, all of our reports are turned in to our immediate Sergeants, who approve them and pass them on to Captain Eaton, who is supposed to have them distributed to the Detective Bureau or returned for further information. As for me, I was on the 'B' squad also known as the 'Boston' squad on the radio. My DSN was 291, therefore I was referred to as Boston 291 on all radio calls.

At ten o'clock p.m., I was on a normal patrol of my sector, when I received a call from the dispatcher.

"Boston 291?" the dispatcher checked. Her voice sounded completely normal, without a trace of inflection as was the case with most dispatchers. They are our lifelines and thus must remain calm at all times.

"Boston 291," I responded immediately to let her know I had heard her call.

"Report to the station to record a missing persons report from Cloverdale," she methodically stated.

"Boston 291, just to confirm, you said to go to the station?" I asked. Cloverdale was in my sector, and we generally went to the location to take missing person reports.

"Boston 291, that's correct. Subject is waiting in the lobby for you."

"Clear. I'm on my way." I turned my car around and headed straight for the station. I was a bit puzzled, as we generally went to the facility for missing reports, but for some reason, this report awaited me at the station. In most cases, I found it best to not ask questions and simply respond to the calls I was given as they were.

Since I was working the three-to-eleven shift, I knew by the time I was done with taking the report, it would be time to head home. So, I pulled into the back lot, which is past the sally port where prisoners are brought in and the arrest report is filed. The prisoners are stripped of all clothing, given orange jumpsuits, and placed in jail cells that are monitored by dispatch through closed circuit televisions. Just past the sally port were the gas pumps used for department vehicles only. It was secured, so I had to enter the code to refill the gas tank. While I was at it, I cleared out the fast food bags I'd collected during my shift. When I was finished, I parked the car in its assigned spot under the canopy next to the other police cars belonging to those who were at the station writing reports or getting ready for their shift change. The police station is a large one-story, square red-brick building, approximately ten thousand square feet. The main floor consisted mostly of offices, the dispatch room, and the detective bureau. The downstairs housed the jail cells, the armory, and the weight-training room for any officer wishing to work out.

As I walked toward the door at the back, my cell phone beeped, informing me that I'd received a text. It was from my sister, Charlie Spencer. She lived in a condominium complex called Garden Terrace.

The text read, *"911 call me ASAP."*

I immediately called her, hitting her speed dial number. "Hi, Charlie. It's me. What's the matter?"

"Oh my God, Cole, I really need to talk to you. I think I may have stumbled on something involving your police department and it's *not good.*" Charlie's voice seemed to be trembling a little.

It was unlike Charlie to panic over minor things. She worked as a school teacher, and I couldn't imagine what she could have possibly 'stumbled on' regarding the police department.

"Okay, first calm down. Now tell me, what's going on?" I tried hard to use my calming voice. As a police officer, we deal with a many different types of situations, and we learn quickly how and when to use the 'calming voice.'

"I can't talk to you about it over the phone, but if I'm not wrong, it's big and really bad. I must tell you in person. There are some things I need to show you. I really need your help on this, I don't know what to do."

Still trying to use my soothing voice to pacify her and get her to relax, I said, "Okay. Okay. Try to calm down. I'll be there as soon as I can. I get off in a half an hour and I need to take a missing persons report here at the station. It shouldn't take me too long; it's another Cloverdale runaway, so I should be able to change and get there soon. Are you home?" In addition to being a teacher, Charlie also volunteered at Cloverdale, helping teach the kids how to read. Spreading literacy was a major ambition for her, and she loved working at Cloverdale.

"Yeah. I got home right before I texted you. And Cole, if you're at the station, be careful!"

"Be careful?" I asked. "About what?"

"I'll tell you as soon as you get here," she said, still sounding uneasy.

"I'll be there as soon as I can. Let me get this report done, and I'll change and drop by. In the meantime, lock your doors and sit tight. I'll get there as soon as I can. Don't let anyone in."

"Thanks, Cole. Don't tell anyone about my call and *be careful.*" I felt something in my gut tighten, but I didn't know why. All I knew was that I needed to reach her soon. She was not the type of person to react this way to just about anything. She's always the levelheaded one.

Saying our goodbyes, we hung up. *Be careful?* I had no idea what that meant nor what compelled her to say that. Whatever she knew had shaken her to the core.

Once Upon a Charlie

I went to the rear entrance of the police station, entered the access code, and walked in down the small hallway. Inside the doorway to my right was the time clock, with all the time cards hung on a rack next to it. The smell of gun oil and sweat always greeted you stepping into the station. The white linoleum floor was recently polished, and there was a bright shine to it under the florescent lights, which lit the entire police department. I walked down the short hallway ending in a T, turned right, and headed toward the report writing room that was connected to the dispatchers' room through a small window. I went to the window to inform the dispatchers that I was there for the report. The report writing room had a simple Formica L-shaped table propped up by metal beams and a few chairs. There was a stack tray in the corner of the table where the basic forms like 'Missing Persons Report' or 'Burglary Report' were kept. Our job here was to fill out the reports and turn them in. I picked up a standard missing persons report form and headed to Sergeant Rodgers' office. He was sitting behind his standard issue gray desk, his hat lay on the credenza behind him. He was a short stocky fellow with a large round face and cheekbones that stood out. He was five-feet-five and probably weighed about 165 pounds, but most of that was probably his beefy upper body with large muscles. He peered up at me through his small brown eyes as I stuck my head in through the door to let him know I was in the station. His office was small and glassed in on all sides.

"Cole," he started, "the lady from Cloverdale is in the lobby waiting for you. Unfortunately, she doesn't have a lot of information on the girl that went missing, so just do what you can, okay? Once you have written the report, just leave it on my desk, and I'll go over it. And don't worry about Captain Eaton kicking it back; I'll take care of that. Just do what you can with what she's got."

"Thanks, Sarge. So, what's up with this? Why is she here and not at Cloverdale? Wouldn't we normally go there? Because that's where all the information should be!"

"I know. But for some reason, the Chief told her to come into the police department and asked for you to come in and make the report, since Cloverdale is in your sector."

"That's odd. Since when does the Chief get involved in this stuff?"

Sergeant Rodgers looked at me and slightly shook his head. "I have no idea. And I know well enough to keep my mouth shut. Whatever the Chief wants, he gets. Since she doesn't seem to have a lot of information, just do the best you can and put it in my inbox," he said glancing at the reports already sitting on the inbox, piled up like a stack of newspapers waiting to go to the trash.

Jeremiah Robinson was sitting at the Formica table. He had smooth dark skin. He wasn't the friendliest of people on the force. Despite that, he was one our best officers. His six-foot ten-inch height made him a looming figure to begin with, but with those neck and arm muscles, he could give any boxer out there a run for their money. He was completely bald, and his complexion reminded me of creamed coffee. He had been a Marine as one of their sharp shooters. He had spent several tours in Afghanistan before joining the Palisades Police Department. He was on the Edward Squad, working the midnight shift.

"I hate these damn reports," he said to me in a deep husky voice.

"I know, me too. I'm about to do a missing persons report, the lady's in the lobby, waiting for me."

"At shift change?" he said, looking at me incredulously. "Man, that's cold. They should have saved it for our shift."

"It's no big deal. Also, when I am done with her, I can go home for the night."

I headed back down the hallway to an intersection that led to the lobby area. When I opened the door, there was a woman sitting in an orange chair, clutching some papers in her hands. I heard the dispatcher's voice through the radio clipped to my epaulet. I turned down the volume enough so that I could still hear what was going on, without disturbing the woman in the chair. I turned to the woman sitting in the chair and asked if she was from Cloverdale, here to report a missing person. She stood up and confirmed it. She was somewhat heavy set and had to look up to see me. Her five-foot four-inch frame was by my estimation about 165 pounds. She wore a simple yellow button-down top, tucked into a pair of black sensible pants. Her shirt was buttoned almost to the top, and I couldn't help but wonder if she had failed to do the top button because of her oversized jowls. There was makeup smudged on her collar. She had curly, mousey brown hair. Her oval face had a lot of makeup on, a great deal too much, I'd say. She would probably be much prettier without that thick eyeliner and dark blue eye shadow that covered the lids of her hazel eyes. She wore red rouge on her cheeks, and I chuckled to myself, thinking she'd make the perfect Mrs. Santa Claus. Her lipstick was a bright red, and she had some of it smeared on her teeth. It bothered me when she talked, and I just wanted to reach out and wipe it away from her teeth.

"Hello. I'm Officer Spencer. Are you here for the Missing Persons Report from Cloverdale?"

"Yes," she said. "Officer, another one has flown the coop as we say down there. This seems to be happening more and more all the time. My name is Barbara Stratton. I am one of the aides at Cloverdale. They sent me here have the paperwork filled out."

Just past the front doors, there was a locked room that was designed specifically for filling out walk-in reports as these. I shook Barbara's hand; they was wet and clammy. I led her to the door and unlocked it, pulling the set of keys off my belt.

"Follow me and we'll get started." I held the door open for her.

The room was barely big enough for three people and had one Formica table occupying most of the space. There were three metal chairs in the room, and I motioned for Barbara to sit on the second chair. I took the chair adjacent to hers. My cell phone rang twice. I picked it up and saw Charlie's name on the caller ID, but the line was disconnected before I could answer it. Again, I felt a knot in my stomach. Charlie's words *'be careful'* rang through me as I stared at the phone.

"Excuse me for just a moment. I need to make a quick call," I told Barbara.

"No problem, honey. I'll wait right here." I noticed that she had placed some paperwork on the table for me.

I stepped out of the room and dialed Charlie's number, but it went straight to voice mail. I couldn't help but look at the phone, as if it held the answers to the questions clouding my mind. I tried her again. Once again, straight to voice mail. I finally gave up and returned to Barbara Stratton, knowing I would soon find out what was going on once I finished this report.

I went back inside to Barbara, and we began filling out the missing persons report. The girl that was missing had gone out for a walk, to 'get some air' as Barbara put it. She didn't have a picture, and we had to fill out the form depending on her memory alone.

"When was this?" I asked Barbara.

Her face scrunched up, which only made her makeup crack and appear dry. I tried not to make a face.

"Well…let's see…I think it was sometime yesterday."

"You don't know for sure?"

"Well…She does this quite often, but usually, she comes home the next day; usually, in the morning, for breakfast you know. I guess staying out all night makes a girl hungry," Barbara said with a girlish giggle that didn't seem to fit her looks or her size.

"Okay, let's get some basics here. What's her name?" I asked, almost like an interrogation.

"Lauren Stanford."

"How old is she?"

"I think she's fifteen now…yes…yes, because we just celebrated her birthday last month."

"Do you happen to know her date of birth?"

"Oh, no. I'm afraid I don't."

"Hair color?"

"I beg your pardon?" Clearly, Barbara hadn't understood the question.

"Do you remember what color her hair is? Or whether it is long? Short? Anything like that?"

Barbara sat still for a moment, her eyes directed at the ceiling, as if by some magical coincidence, the answer would show up there. She closed her eyes a moment, opened her mouth to speak, and then closed it again.

This was like trying to get milk from a bull. I glanced at my watch—ten fifty-four p.m. I needed to speed this up somehow.

"Let's see," she said tapping her index finger on her lips. "I do believe her hair is that one blond color . . . umm, what do they call it? Dirty dishwater blond, I think. Only in her case, it would really fit. You see she rarely washes her hair, and it is always dirty and stringy looking. You know what I mean?"

"Yes. We'll just put that down for now. How long is her hair? Short? Long? How does she wear it?"

"Oh, that's simple. She has medium-length straight stringy hair that goes down to her shoulders. If I remember correctly she just parts it in the middle and lets it go. Sometimes it's a struggle just to get her to brush it. But even that doesn't help. It only makes her hair look dirtier. Oh, I do so wish these girls maintained better hygiene."

"How tall is she?" I tried not to sound as if I were rushing her.

"I don't really know…I suppose, maybe, five feet two inches, if that. She's pretty short."

"Do you know how much she weighs?"

"No, but I can tell you she's a thin little thing. Practically skin and bones."

"Doesn't Cloverdale have this information on hand for such incidents?" I tried not to sound impatient.

"Oh, yes. Certainly. But the Headmaster, Wilson Puckett, has all that information, and his office was locked up and I couldn't get to it. I think he was in some kind of meeting or something."

"Okay, then for the purposes of this form, we'll put her down as 100 pounds. Do you think that's okay?"

"Oh, sure, sure. She can't weigh any more than that."

"We've established that she is a female; is she white or black?"

"White." Finally an answer that did not require a dentist drill.

"Do you recall what she was wearing when she left?"

"Oh my, no. I really couldn't say. I do know, however, that she wears blue jeans all the time. Usually Levi's. And she has these high-top tennis shoes, like the kind basketball players wear. Hers are red, if I remember correctly."

"Do you happen to know what shirt or jacket she may have been wearing?"

"She wears a lot of sweatshirts and usually no jacket. I mean I know its spring and everything, but it's still cold at night. I have no idea how she manages to stay warm all night," she rambled a little.

"Maybe she's staying with a friend? Does she have any close friends in the area that you know of?" I asked.

"Not that I'm aware of. She's a nuisance, you know. So, I can't see any other parent putting up with her for a night. We have a hard enough time as it is with her at Cloverdale."

"I don't suppose you have a picture of her with you?" I was slightly disgusted by the nonchalance and trying not to let my voice betray it.

"No. That's locked up in the Headmaster's office. Like I said, I couldn't get in there."

"Do you happen to know when the Headmaster will be available to speak to the detectives and perhaps provide a photograph?"

"Oh, I'm sure he'll be available to talk to the detectives tomorrow morning. His name is Wilson Puckett. He's been with us for years. If anyone knows how to run a place like Cloverdale, it's him. And I'm sure he'll be more than happy to help you guys out." Barbara smiled and again I couldn't help but notice the lipstick on her front teeth.

"Well, then, here's what we're going to do: I'm going to fill out as much of this form as I can, and I'll turn it over to Sergeant Rodgers. He'll then pass it along to the Missing Persons Division in the detective bureau. If you'll just write down Wilson Puckett's phone number here on the form, I'm sure they will call or come by to get the rest of the information."

"Okay. That's fine. I'm sorry, I wasn't of much help to you, but sometimes, these things just can't be helped. But we wanted to at least get you guys started on looking for Lauren, and hopefully, she hasn't gone too far."

"We will be looking for her as soon as we can. If she happens to come home, please call and let me know, so that we can cancel the missing persons report. Here's my card. Call me if you discover something or once you have all the information. Otherwise, the detectives will probably contact you."

"I'll do that right away if she shows up. But, it's way past breakfast time." She pondered over something for a moment, then added, "Well there's always breakfast tomorrow." She gave another chuckle and it cost all of my willpower not to shudder.

I grabbed the half-filled report and opened the door for Barbara. I walked her to the front door, where she thanked me for my time and apologized for not having all the information. I assured her that it was okay and that we would be looking into it soon. She gave me another lipstick-teeth smile and headed for her car. I checked my watch. It was eleven thirty. I still needed to change out of my uniform.

I went down the hall to Sergeant Rodgers' office. He was still sitting there, looking over and approving reports from the afternoon shift. I handed him my missing persons report, and he looked through it. His eyebrows furrowed, making deep creases on his forehead.

"That's it?" he asked, brows still furrowed.

"Yep," I said. "You told me she didn't have much information, and you were right. Apparently, all the information regarding the residents at Cloverdale are under lock and key in the Headmaster's office. She said he was in a meeting and couldn't be disturbed, so this information was pretty much from her own memory of the girl. I think most of the information is purely guesswork on Barbara Stratton's part."

"Well, I suppose there's enough information on here for me to approve it, but I'll send it to the Captain and have him forward it to Missing Persons, along with a note to check with the Headmaster. What's his name?"

"Wilson Puckett," I answered, checking my watch again. It was now eleven forty-five.

"You in a hurry, Cole?"

"No," I lied. I'd always gotten along well with the Sergeant, but in light of Charlie's warning, I decided not to mention it to him.

"Do I have the rest of your reports from the night?"

"Yeah. I filled them all out. They should be in your inbox."

"Okay, just add it to the pile, I'll go over it later." He sounded super frustrated.

"You know the Captain's going to kick it back? There's nothing on there and you know how he is," I said, more as a statement than a question.

"Yeah, I know. If he does, I'll let you know and then you can go up to Cloverdale and get the rest of the information…provided this Wilson Puckett isn't in another meeting. We'll see what happens. I'll do my best to push it through to Missing Persons and let them deal with it."

"Thanks, Sarge," I said, giving him half a salute.

I glanced at his inbox with the large stack of reports from all the officers. It was going to be a long night for him. He was conscientious if nothing else. He rarely left before he'd read and approved all the shift reports. I knew he was due for becoming Lieutenant and was preparing to take the exam soon, so he made sure all his I's were dotted and his T's were crossed. He was a good man, and he'd helped me out of some tough situations with the captain and the chief.

"No problem. Change and go home. Whatever happens, happens."

We said our good nights, and when I left his office, his head was buried into more reports over his desk.

I walked down the long hallway, past the detective bureau, and straight downstairs to the men's locker room. I tried to call Charlie, but again, it went directly to voice mail. Again, haunted by her *'be careful,'* I consulted my watch. It was nearly midnight now, so I decided to skip the shower and changed into my street clothes. I put on jeans and a long-sleeved t-shirt, then grabbed my shoulder holster and slipped it on. I retrieved my standard issue 9 mm semiautomatic and placed it in the holster. I grabbed my blue windbreaker and headed toward the door. I picked up the radio attached to my belt, detaching it from my shirt, and hurried to the report writing room. No one was there, so I plugged in my radio to recharge and headed for the back door.

As I walked to my blue Ford *Bronco,* I put in another call to Charlie. Yet again, it went straight to voice mail. I revved the engine and let the car warm up a bit, as it had gotten chilly overnight. I turned on the heater, called Charlie once more, voice mail once more. I pulled the truck out of the lot and headed toward Charlie's condo.

The clock on my dashboard read twelve sixteen. Determined as I was, I called Charlie's cell phone again. Voice mail. I pressed the accelerator down and drove faster. I must admit I beat land speed records getting there and even sped through a few stop signs and red lights. Something was wrong, and I needed to get there…she needed me to get there.

There was a large wooden sign with painted gold letters announcing 'Garden Terrace Condominiums.' I drove directly to Charlie's condo, which was at the back of the complex. As I pulled into the parking lot, I caught a glimpse of Jeremiah Robinson pulling out onto the main road in his personal vehicle, and it made me pause for a moment. I knew he was on shift, as I'd just seen him in the report writing room before I got off work. But my mind immediately reverted to Charlie's condo. There were six buildings in all and each had two separate levels. They were all connected by a mutual porch.

As I approached Charlie's building, I became painfully aware that something was terribly wrong.

Everywhere my eyes turned, there were flashing red and blue

lights from four patrol cars that were parked in front of her condo. There was an ambulance and several detective cars parked as well, in front of her place. I pulled my *Bronco* in behind one of the nearer police cars and ran up the stairs. The door to Charlie's condo stood ajar, and there were swarms of people going in and out, like ants from an ant hole. She lived on the second floor. I took the stairs, two at a time, and was immediately stopped by a uniformed officer standing in the doorway with a clipboard in his hands. I knew the kid. His name was Jason Greer, and he'd only been on the force a couple of years. He was about five feet six inches, and with my five feet ten inches, I was able to look over his shoulder to see what was going on inside. He was on the midnight shift, and he looked wired with coffee and excitement.

"Jason, what the hell is going on here?" I asked, trying to keep my panic to a minimum.

Over his shoulder, I saw a patrol officer, a couple of detectives, one of which was my old partner, Chris Bradley, and crime scene investigators taking pictures. I caught a glimpse of what could only be Charlie's body lying on the floor, covered in blood, but I couldn't see her face, as Jason kept trying to block my view. I noticed the door jamb was broken and splintered.

"I'm sorry Cole, I can't let you in. I have orders from Chief Denault. And he said not to let anyone in, especially you."

"What the fuck? What's the Chief doing here?" I yelled at Jason, still trying to see what was going on. "She's my goddamn sister! I have the right to go in there. Now let me in!" I ordered, feeling fury rise up from what had been, till a few moments ago, a bad feeling in my gut.

Jason stared at me with his big blue eyes. His usually bright short red hair was covered by his hat. In spite of his size and weight, I knew I could take him if it meant I got to Charlie.

I took in a deep breath and let it out as slowly as I could, then reaching out, I grabbed Jason by his collar and pulled him toward me, so we were incredibly close, our noses almost touching. I could see the freckles on his face so clearly and fear in his eyes. He had turned a deathly pale.

"I'm so sorry, Cole. But they told me not to let you in. They said if you showed up, we must send you home. And if you refuse, we're supposed to remove you by force." His voice sounded like someone who was being choked, and it was oddly high pitched.

"Just what in the name of hell is going on here?" I looked up angrily and saw Lieutenant Dintzman walk in behind Jason. His voice was loud, his tone severe and angry. The Lieutenant was the Chief's Personal Assistant, and why he was there was beyond me. His uniform fit tightly on his five-foot eleven-inch frame, and the hundred and sixty pounds didn't support his belt. He always appeared angry with his steely gray cutting eyes. Looking at me now, his face was slowly turning red with anger, which I knew would soon turn to a fiery rage if I wasn't careful.

I stared square into the Lieutenant's eyes, while he glared at me with squinted evil eyes. He continued to stare at me and said in an eerily calm voice, "Son, I strongly suggest you let go of that officer. You do realize that you are this close to assaulting a police officer, and I'd certainly hate to have you arrested." He held up his forefinger and thumb to show me exactly how close, but the sarcasm in his voice did not slip by me. He would love nothing more than to actually have me arrested.

I released Jason from my grip and the relief washed over him visibly, as the color returned to his face.

The Lieutenant turned to Jason and spoke to him, ignoring me altogether. "Let him in. We need him to identify the body, that is, if he can. She's been badly beaten, and we need to identify her remains."

My heart leapt inside my chest. Then, turning to me, his harsh eyes boring into mine, he said, "I'm going to let you in. Only to identify the body. You are not to talk to anyone or touch anything. You make the identification and then you go. If you refuse to leave, you will be forcibly removed. The only reason we are allowing you to come in is because she was beaten nearly beyond recognition, and we need to have her identified." His words hit me hard, like a punch to the solar plexus.

Jason stepped aside as I walked through the threshold of the condo. My eyes were immediately drawn to Charlie, as she lay on the floor, brutally beaten and battered. She lay stretched out at an odd angle in her living room. Her eyes were bruised, and one was swollen shut. Through the other, still open, her beautiful brown eye looked dull and lifeless. Her lips were swollen and cut. There were marks around her neck as though she'd been strangled. Her hair scattered under her head was covered with blood, and her nose appeared to be broken. She had taken a single bullet to the center of her forehead, there was gun powder residue surrounding it. There were bruises on her arms and legs. I saw around her neck the cross she always wore and her engagement ring still adorned her finger. The familiar wrist watch that she always wore was a little too large for her, but she loved it, as it was a keepsake from Mother. The Lieutenant was right: she was beaten beyond recognition. I knelt beside her and was reaching out to take her bloody hand, when the Lieutenant stopped me in my track. I felt tears welling up in my eyes as I stared at her. I wanted to pick her up…hug her…try to breathe the life back into her.

"Well?" I heard the Lieutenant say from somewhere behind me. His voice was far and distant, as if it were coming from another place and time.

He grabbed me by the arm and forced me to stand up. I caught a glimpse of Chris who was busy working the scene. He wouldn't meet my eyes.

"It's her. That's Charlie…my sister," I could hardly get the words out.

"Now that the identification has been done, you need to leave now," he said coldly, without a flicker in his voice, as if nothing had happened.

"I need to stay with her. I need to be here for her," I cried out in protest.

"That's not possible and you know it," the Lieutenant said, ushering me out the door.

No sooner was I out the door, that Jason returned to his post.

Through my tears and bubbling anger, I couldn't help but yell at the Lieutenant, "This is total bullshit. I should be allowed to stay in there. She's my sister."

"You know damn well that this is a crime scene and is being treated as such. You have no business being in there."

"Fuck you," I yelled at the Lieutenant. My rage was beyond my control, and I knew it.

"Lieutenant, is there a problem here?" Chief Denault appeared at the door way. He was a bulky man—his stomach stretched the buttons of his shirt and his jowls hung over his collar. His brownish-gray hair was combed over the bald part on his head, hiding it.

"Nothing I can't handle," the Lieutenant replied, "Spencer's here and has apparently been harassing Officer Greer. But I think we can come to a reasonable understanding. I let him in long enough to identify her, and he has confirmed that she is indeed Charlie Spencer."

"Let me talk to him," the Chief said, stepping through the doorway and out onto the stairway in front of Charlie's condo.

"No," I yelled to the Chief. "I want in…I want to see my sister. I want to know what happened."

In a soothing voice, the Chief tried to convince me otherwise. "Why don't we take a walk downstairs, son?"

He grabbed my upper arm and squeezed it hard while directing me toward the stairs. In my broken condition, I was no match for his two hundred and sixty-five pounds. He tugged me along to the parking lot, where I saw the Medical Examiner's van sitting idly, like an old decrepit ice-cream truck waiting for children who'd never show up, waiting to take my poor Charlie away.

As we reached the bottom step, I yanked my arm away from the Chief's grasp and turned to look at him. His face was round, his bulbous and red nose protruding from it.

He look at me, almost through me, with emotionless green eyes, standing no more than two feet away. "Now Spencer, you know you can't go in there. It's a crime scene and only the techs and detectives are allowed in. Now, if we just go on letting anyone in, it would contaminate the crime scene. You know that, right? And besides, you're family and a part of the suspect pool."

"You know damn well I wouldn't kill my own sister. I was at the station writing that stupid missing persons report."

"Yes, but still, you're family, and you're not allowed in. You know that, Spencer."

His tone was condescending, and it pissed me off. His dislike for me was apparent, and my dislike for him was mutual. I glared at his unfeeling eyes. It seemed like there was nothing in him, and I had to wonder if he was even looking at me; if he had any feelings at all.

"Now, I don't know what went on up there between you and Greer, but he was given specific orders to keep you from entering the premises. By me." he spoke to me as if he were a king and I his subject. "He was only doing what he was told."

"Goddamnit, Chief, that's my fucking sister up there, and I have the right to see her. I have the right to know what's going on," I said fighting the urge to sock the man's upper jaw. My hands were already curled in fists at my sides.

For the first time since we began this conversation, I began to see some emotion reflect on the man's face as he burned with anger. "Listen boy, don't you dare talk to me like that! I'm the Chief of Police. You *will* show me the respect I deserve."

I said nothing. When the King gives you a command, you must abide by it, bowing and kissing his ring…at least, that was the way he saw it. And that's the way he ran the police department, but I'd be damned if I was going to bow before him and kiss the ring on his fat stubby finger.

"What you need to do is to get into your car now and go home. I will make sure the morgue contacts you once they complete the autopsy and are ready to release her body. That's your only option officer, because you're not getting into that condo until the crime techs release it."

"Wait," I said, spewing fire, "Why was there no dispatch

call sent out? I spoke to Charlie right before shift change, and she was scared about something."

"Well, perhaps you didn't have your radio on you when the call came in," the Chief shirked at the question.

"No. I did have my radio on. I got called into the station at ten p.m. to file a missing person's report for some runaway from Cloverdale. I assure you I had my radio on the entire time. In fact, I didn't turn in my radio until eleven forty-five, which is when I left. Where was the call from dispatch? I would have heard it, and there was no call made from the dispatch office."

"Look Spencer, this investigation is none of your concern, and you would do best to stay out of it." The Chief's eyes squinted at me—they were cold, hard, and sent a shiver down my spine. "Now, I'm giving you a direct order to go home and stay there."

I was outranked and out-trumped. The Chief beats the officer in any situation.

Angry and frustrated I turned and headed toward my truck, but there was no way I was leaving yet. Something wasn't right here. I was certain there had been no dispatch call to Charlie's address; I'd have heard it. It simply didn't go out. I sat in the driver's side of my *Bronco* and turned on the ignition and heater. I stared at the stairs, watching Charlie's condo, as the detectives, crime technicians, and the Chief and Lieutenant did their crime scene dance in and out of the house—like puppets on a stage. I watched as two men in blue scrubs wheeled a gurney up the stairs and into the house. It was some fifteen minutes later that the gurney reappeared with a black body bag strapped to the gurney. I continued to watch as they placed the gurney into the back of the van and drove away. Anger and despair burned inside me, in the pit of my stomach that had been uneasy since I had talked to Charlie earlier. Something was definitely wrong. I remember Charlie's last words to me: *be careful.* And now she was dead. Murdered. Brutally. And there was no radio call dispatched to her condo. I knew for sure that if there had been one, I'd have heard it. As the tears rolled down my cheeks, I didn't notice it had begun to rain. Even the sky was grieving Charlie's passing.

Chapter 2

I SAT in my Ford *Bronco* for a long time, in the rain, watching the Chief and his Lieutenant, along with the detectives and other police officers, scurrying in and out of her condo carrying various items and boxes I recognized as belonging to Charlie. It was as if they were doing a little dance, out of sync with my life…with Charlie's life…and now my hands were tied and I couldn't to anything about it. I could feel the rage boil inside me, with no outlet whatsoever. I looked at my hands clenching the steering wheel, my knuckles white with anger. I kept going over it, again and again, as I watched them. I couldn't figure out for the life of me how I missed the dispatcher's call to Charlie's address. It made no sense at all. I had to know. I needed to know.

I saw Chris Bradley, my friend, one of the Robbery/Homicide detectives. He was wearing blue jeans, a blue striped shirt with no tie even though it was required by the dress code of the department. His brown tweed sport coat covered his shoulder holster. We had been on the same squad for years before he made it to detective, but we had remained close friends. If anything, I knew I could depend on Chris to tell me what was going on. I sat, watching as rain pattered on my windshield. I knew there was nothing I could do, so I decided to head home.

I called my wife Mia, informing her I was on my way. I asked her to call Charlie's fiancée, Tony DeMarco and to have him come down to our place. She asked no questions and assured me she'd do it. I turned on my wipers, realizing the droplets were coming down harder. I felt hot tears run down my face as I headed home, wondering how I would even break the news to Mia and Tony.

It took me ten minutes to reach home, by which time, the rain was beating down even harder. I pulled my vehicle into the driveway, numb and exhausted from rage and grief. I couldn't bring myself to get out of the car. I stared at our small one-story clapboard house. The walls were light blue with a red roof and dark blue shutters. The front door was made of solid wood with an oval stained-glass window in the center. The separate garage was the same color as the house although rarely used. I took several deep breaths before I attempted to approach the house. Since I had not told Mia what happened, I knew we were all in for a long night.

Mia and Charlie were the best of friends. Sisters, they would call each other. Charlie and I were close as kids. She had always been more of a tomboy than the little girl my mother had wanted her to be. I remembered my mom always trying to dress Charlie up in little pink dresses with bows in her hair, but Charlie wouldn't have any of that. She wanted to hang around with me and my friends. We were only two years apart, and she enjoyed playing baseball more than anything. She liked climbing trees and wading in the creek in our back yard. My mother finally gave up trying with her. If only mom could have seen her now. Charlie was all class and style now. She wore pretty dresses, and while she never put little pink bows in her brown curly hair, she always maintained a pretty, feminine look. Every strand of hair in place. Her clothes always of the latest fashion. She had always been so beautiful, and yet the image of her sprawled on the carpet brought out the tears and anger.

I leaned my head against the steering wheel and took a moment to collect myself. Realizing I couldn't hide out in the truck all night, I finally made for the house. I walked in through the patio's sliding glass door, which led directly into our kitchen. I was soaked to the skin, thanks to the rain and tears, and Mia met me at the door, her face betraying her curiosity, which I wasn't sure I was ready to address yet. She immediately wrapped her arms around me as if she were a shield protecting me from whatever it was that had happened. She was all of five feet tall and weighed a hundred pounds. She placed her head against my wet chest and asked no questions. Her long black hair smelled of lavender and cocoa butter, and I found it very comforting. She knew whatever had gone wrong was bad enough to make me cry. So, she simply held me, and I took refuge in her arms. I held on to her as though she were a buoy in the middle of a torrential ocean. I placed my cheek on top of her head and felt more tears burst forth. How was I going to tell her and Tony that Charlie had been murdered? The mere word 'murdered' seemed incomprehensible to them. Mia and Charlie were so very close, it would break her heart, just as mine had been.

Mia leaned back and said, "You're soaking wet. Let me fetch you a towel."

She left the room only to return moments later with a large bath towel. I dried myself off as much as possible and embraced her again. She was wearing her pink terrycloth bathrobe, and it felt soft and snug against my body.

I said, without moving, "Did you call Tony?"

"Yeah." I could barely hear her reply with her head still

pressed against my chest. "He said he'd come right over. What's going on, Cole? Did something happen at work? Are you okay?"

I shook my head; the words refused come out. My head and my heart were a tangled mess of anger, grief, love and loss. Finally, Mia pulled herself away from me and stared into my eyes. Her deep, almost-black eyes held endless pools of questions I just couldn't answer.

"My God, Cole…what happened? I've never seen you this upset. Why are you crying?"

Before I could respond, I heard Tony's BMW pull up through the drive. His headlights flashed against the front window facing the street. Tony was never one to follow formalities and walked in through the front door after a quick knock. Tony DeMarco was Charlie's fiancée. They had been together for as long as I could remember. His hair was wet from the rain, and his blue windbreaker jacket was beaded with rain drops. He was wearing a plaid flannel shirt with jeans and his standard work boots. He was of medium height with a stocky build. His shoulders and upper body were buff, as he worked in construction and had thus developed much upper body strength. Many people underestimated him from his size. He worked out regularly, and if that wasn't enough, he carried a 9 mm just for protection. You see, he sometimes worked in the roughest parts of town. He had dark brown hair and a lot of it. He wore it long over his ears and his nape. He was involved in real estate but mostly rehabilitated abandoned and foreclosed houses, then selling them for a much higher price.

"Hey," he said on noticing me and Mia, "what's going on? Mia said you told her to call me over? You don't look so good pal. What's up?"

Once Upon a Charlie

Since it was so late, Mia suggested we move to the kitchen table, and she made us all some coffee, so we could talk at the table, which was at the center of the kitchen. Tony and I sat down. After Mia got the coffee brewing, she took a seat next to me and held my hands.

I wasn't exactly sure how to go about it. As a police officer, you never get used to giving families notifications of a loved ones death, but this was different; this was my family. I started to talk, fumbling for words until I finally took in a deep breath and blurted out, "Charlie was murdered tonight."

A deep silence fell across the room. The only sound you could hear was that of the brewing coffee and the rain beating down on the roof and windows. Everyone sat still, lost in their own thoughts for what seemed to be hours.

Finally, Tony spoke, "What the hell are you saying, Cole? She was murdered? Is this some kind of a joke? What on earth are you saying? Who'd ever do that? Tell me this is some kind of a sick joke."

I heard a small gasp from Mia, and she squeezed my hands harder. Immediately, she began to cry, the tears silently rolling down her beautiful cheeks. She made no sound but stared at me, searching for answers I simply didn't have.

"That can't be," she said, as though saying it would make it untrue.

When the coffee was brewed, I poured us each a cup and brought a box of Kleenex to the table. Mia was the first to take one.

"Sonuvabitch, Cole," Tony said, his eyes watering up, "you can't be serious."

I told them about Charlie's 911 text to me earlier that night. And about our brief phone call. And I told them what she'd said. I also told them about the call I got from Charlie, while I was writing Barbara's report—the one that I never got the chance to answer.

"So, that's it? She didn't tell you what she stumbled upon or nothin'," Tony said. I noticed his brown eyes and their green flecks flicker either with grief or anger. I had never known Tony to cry, but tears gradually welled up his eyes and streak down his cheeks.

"Yeah. That's it," I told him. Tears now flowed freely from Tony's eyes, as the realization of what I'd just told him dawned on him.

My conversation with Charlie was still playing in my head. I tried hard to find some kind of clue from it, but nothing struck me.

"It doesn't make any sense," I said to no one in particular.

Tony's brow furrowed and he said, "Well, whatever it was she found out apparently got her killed."

"That's just it, Tony. It makes no sense." I took a sip of coffee, not caring that it seared the inside of my mouth. "There are so many things that don't make any sense."

"Like what?" Mia said, her voice low and hoarse from crying.

"First of all, no call went out on the radio. I had my radio with me the whole time, and I didn't once hear a call go out to her condo. If it had, I would have recognized her address immediately. And then, there was the text and the phone call about how she'd stumbled onto something going on at the police department. Next, there was the call from Charlie's phone to me while I was taking that missing persons report, but it only rang twice, and I never had the chance to talk to her after that. But what's really strange was that when I got there, one of the cops on the midnight shift, Jason Greer, told me that the Chief had specifically told him not to let me in and if necessary I was to be removed by force. Why would the Chief say that? He had to know I'd show up or he wouldn't have told Jason not to let me in. Although they did allow me in just long enough to identify that is was actually Charlie. You guys…" I choked because I really didn't want to tell them, but they needed to know, "…she was beaten nearly beyond recognition."

"Oh my God!" both Tony and Mia gasped in unison.

"What do you mean?" Tony asked, horror etched across his face.

Mia had placed her hands over her face and began to sob uncontrollably, tears escaping through her fingers. I placed my arm around her and cuddled her under my arm to give her someplace for her to let out her emotions.

Tony said, "So doesn't the Chief usually show up at a murder scene, like in the movies and books and stuff?"

"I can't honestly say. We get so few murders in Palisades that I don't know the protocol for it." My head hung low.

"Seems to me, he should be there, what with it being a murder and all," Tony said.

Mia wiped her tears away with another Kleenex and said, "So when they let you in, it was only to identify her? And they wouldn't let you look around her apartment? She's your sister. Surely the Chief knows that."

"So how bad was it…how bad was she beaten?" Tony asked in a choked voice.

"Let's just say it was really bad." I glanced at Mia, knowing she wouldn't want to hear the details.

"Shit!" was Tony's only response. He grabbed himself a

Kleenex and blew his nose and tried to stop the tears flowing down his face.

I shook my head. The tragedy in the whole thing kept circling in my head. The rain came down harder, and in the silence of the kitchen, I could hear it pounding the roof, loud and clear. An occasional flash of lightning lit up the room followed by a solemn roar of thunder.

"So, why did they make you leave? And why did the Chief tell you to go home?" Mia asked, her eyes red and swollen. Her crying seemed like it would never end.

"I don't know Mia. That's just another thing that doesn't make sense. He ordered me to go home and didn't want me anywhere in the vicinity. He even said I was a suspect because I'm family, and family is always a suspect."

"What the fuck?" Tony said. "They can't honestly believe that!"

"That's bullshit," Mia said. "Why would you kill your own sister?"

"I don't know. It's all bullshit, and we all know it," I said the anger rising in my gut again.

Tony looked from Mia then back to me and said in a voice that spewed his anger, "Too many questions, not enough answers."

Again, the house bathed in silence, with the exception of the rain. Occasionally, I could hear cars zooming up and down the street, their headlights bright against the darkness in the living room, as the only lights switched on in the house were in the kitchen. Tony was right...*too many questions, not enough answers*. It was at that moment, I resolved to find Charlie's killer.

As if reading my thoughts, Tony asked, "So what are you going to do about it?"

Once Upon a Charlie

I looked straight into Tony's eyes, vehement rage still boiling in my gut, and said, "You know me, Tony. I'm going to find those answers and find out who the bastard was that killed Charlie. And I am doing it starting now. I know I get, like, five days of bereavement pay, but I also have some vacation time saved up and I'm taking it. Plus, to be quite honest, with the trust fund, I don't need this fucking job. Tony, I may need your help though. Will you have time to do that?" I had started to gain some semblance of composure.

There was no doubt in his eyes when he said, "Oh yeah. I'm with you." Tony too had begun to regain control of his emotions.

"Okay," I said, "I saw my friend Chris Bradley working the case. He's in Robbery/Homicide. So, maybe I'll start with him."

"He's the one you worked with before, on the streets…before he made detective." It was more of a statement than a question.

"Yeah. We were pretty tight back then and still are. If anyone can help me, it's him. I'm sure he's on the case, so he should be able to answer all our questions. I'll give him a call tomorrow. I want to stop by the police department tomorrow anyway and check the dispatch codes, just to see what's on there."

"You need me to come along?" Tony asked.

"No. Not this time. I think Chris will feel more at ease talking to me alone. When I am done, I'll call you and we can go over what he had to say and what was on the tapes. In order to get a copy of the call, you must get the seven-digit number from the Captain, since he's in charge of dispatch. Then, we gotta contact the St. Louis County Police Department and get a copy of the tape, because as sure as I'm sitting here, no call went out."

For the first time since I left Charlie's condo and took all my spirit with it, I was beginning to feel motivated. Motivated with fury, but motivated nonetheless. And knowing that Tony was going to help me made me feel a lot better.

"I think the first thing we need to do is to get into Charlie's condo and see what's the scene there. I'll need you for that. So, I'll talk to Chris, and then, I'll give you a call and we'll go there tomorrow if we can get in."

"Sounds good. You gonna be okay for tonight?" Tony asked with genuine concern in his eyes.

"I'll be fine. I got Mia here," I said, pulling her into a half hug. "How about you? Will you be okay? You're welcome to stay with us tonight. We'll have the second bedroom prepped for you to sleep in."

Tony looked at me with his sad brown eyes and said, "No, but thanks anyway. I think I need some time alone for now." He finished his cup of coffee and stared into the empty cup. "You're right. It doesn't make any sense. But we'll get the answers," he said almost as if he were trying to convince himself, not me.

"And…what about the funeral?" Tony asked, his voice cracking a little.

"I don't know," I told him. "We can't do anything until the medical examiner releases her. I guess they'll let me know. At least, that's what they said. But you know, I want to talk to her anyway—the examiner. I need to know what exactly happened to Charlie and how she died. And I know her, so I know she won't bullshit me."

"Maybe tomorrow, after we go through her condo, we can go by the ME's office too. Big plans for sad times," Tony said looking up from the empty cup.

"Yeah." It was all I could manage.

We said our goodbyes. Tony gave Mia a big hug. She held him tight; she knew in her heart that's what he needed more than anything right now. We stood at the door and watched as Tony drove away, with the rain falling incessantly. I closed the door and turned to Mia. Although she had stopped crying, her eyes were puffy and red from her tears. I kissed each eye like doing so would make them better.

"Cole," she said to me, "are you okay? You want to talk about it and have some more coffee?"

I shook my head and pulled her into my arms, holding her tight against me. She was warm and soft. I rubbed my hands up and down her back. Then cupping her face in my hands, I gave her a long deep kiss that seemed to last forever. Anger turned to passion, and I felt my hands run down her body, pushing her robe off her shoulders and pulling off her pink nightshirt from over her head. I ran my hands her smooth hips and her supple breasts. Our passion merged into one as we headed toward the bedroom. We made love passionately, in a way I hadn't ever before. When it was over, we lay in the dark bedroom, her head resting on my chest, neither one of us saying a word. We listened to the rain fall until we both fell asleep.

~~~

Chapter 3

I WOKE up that Wednesday morning and sat upright with a jolt, startling Mia.

She sat up beside me and said, "It's okay. I'm here."

She wrapped her arms around my neck and held me close. I felt like I had just awakened from a horrible nightmare, only to realize it was all true—Charlie was dead. I couldn't remember the dream precisely as it had occurred…it was a fog of a dream that had crept into my sleep.

We lay back down and I turned to look into Mia's big dark eyes. It was like peering into the depth of a very deep well. It was hard to tell where her eyes ended and her pupils began.

I told her, "No. It's not okay. Charlie's dead, and we don't know why."

I circled my arms around her and held her snugly against me. It was as if we were one person—one soul—woven together in the fabric of love and grief. Mia rested her head against my arms, and I could feel the tears spilling from her eyes. I, too, couldn't help but cry. We lay there together, in silence. I rubbed her arm that rested across my chest as much to her comfort as me. It wasn't until she reached over to the bedside table and got us each a Kleenex that I saw it was six thirty in the morning. My sleep had been fitful and memories of Charlie's condo from last night flashed through them.

Neither of us had slept much and we were both exhausted. I wanted nothing more than to snuggle in the safety of her arms.

Mia stirred and looked up at me. "I need to call into work. Tell them I'm not coming in today. I think I will take some vacation time too. We need to be together in this."

I couldn't help but feel relieved that she was here. She is my rock, my island in the middle of the ocean.

I gazed at her face and said, "You know, you don't have to work at all if you don't want to. We have enough from the trust to live on. Unless you want to work that is. That's totally up to you."

"I don't know, Cole. I'll think it over. Now's not the time for me to make big decisions like that. I'm still too upset about Charlie."

"I know, sweetie. I just wanted to tell you that you've always got that option. I need to go to the station this afternoon and talk to Sergeant Rodgers. I want to check with Chris too, if he is there. He was working the crime scene last night, so I'm hoping he can tell me what's going on."

A quiet spread through the room. I rubbed Mia's wet cheek with my hand and wiped away her tears with my thumb. It seemed to be a useless task; for each tear I'd wipe away, a new one would appear. I handed her another tissue. She sat up and wiped away her tears and blew her nose. Her eyes were still puffy from all the crying. I went to the bathroom and brought a cold washcloth to place over her eyes. I knew that crying always gave her a headache, so along with it, I brought two aspirins and a cup of water. She took the aspirin and the washcloth without a thought. As she lay with the cold towel over her eyes, I massaged her temples, hoping to ward off the inevitable headache before it came.

"That feels so good. Thank you. So, what do I need to do?" She asked pressing the cold cloth tighter against her head.

"I don't know, yet."

I hadn't stopped reeling from all that had happened. There were too many things racing through my head, and I was too exhausted to make them stop.

A small sad smile appeared on Mia's face. "You realize, this is one of the few times we've ever been naked in bed together, not having sex."

I couldn't help but smile. She was right. Neither of us had the energy or the passion to make love. I couldn't help but give a little chuckle.

"Does last night count?" I asked her.

She chuckled to herself, and we both agreed that it did. Only Mia could ever make me smile in my worst moments.

She handed me back the washcloth with a deep heavy sigh.

"You need me to get you some more cold water?" I asked.

"No. But I do want some coffee. Do you?"

I did. She slipped out of the bed and went to the kitchen to retrieve her robe and nightshirt. It was a soft pink robe that made her dark hair stand out and her olive skin look even more stunning. I pulled on a pair of jeans and a T-shirt and went down to help her get the coffee ready. Walking up behind her, I put my arms around her waist while she poured the coffee. Our coffee maker had a setting that started the brewing automatically every morning. The rain had stopped but the sky was overcast with the promise of more rain to follow.

"I'd be lost without you, you know," I told her.

She turned around and kissed me gently on the lips. Her lips were moist, soft, and gentle like the dewy morning petals on the flowers. We stayed that way, kissing and nibbling on each other's ears and neck for a while.

I placed some cream and sugar on the kitchen table. She poured the cream into her coffee, while I added a teaspoon of sugar into her cup. We sat beside each other in silence. I checked the kitchen clock. It was only seven thirty. The phone rang suddenly, giving us each a start. I picked up the handset in an effort to stop the disturbance in the quiet around us.

"Cole." I heard Tony voice from the other end. "I didn't wake you, did I?"

"No. Mia and I were just having some coffee. Neither one of us slept very well last night. I think it's going to be a caffeine-run day for both of us. How you doing? Were you able to get any sleep last night?"

"Naw. I was up most of the night, I guess. Every time I tried to get some sleep, I kept thinking about Charlie and everything we discussed last night. Nothing makes any sense to me."

"I know. You want to come by and have some coffee with us? Mia's not going to work, and I have to go to the station. I want to talk to Chris, see if he can tell me anything useful. He was there last night. I saw him carrying a bunch of Charlie's shit out of the condo. I thought maybe he could tell me what happened."

"You want me to go with you?" he asked, sounding like he really needed something to do to help at this point.

"Naw, like I told you last night, it's best you aren't with me when I talk to him, but you're welcome to join us for coffee."

"I'll be over in about a half an hour."

I let him know that was fine and hung up.

"Tony?" Mia asked, raising her eyebrows slightly.

"Yeah. He didn't get much sleep either, and he's all alone there in that big house, so he's coming over. Said he'll be here in about half an hour."

Mia nodded her head and sipped on her coffee. "Hmmm, I'd better call into work and let them know. Then, I'm going to take a shower and put on some clothes. She finished her cup of coffee but left the mug on the table, which was a good indication that she wasn't done drinking coffee and would be back for more.

She left the kitchen, taking the phone handset along.

After a while, she came back into the kitchen. "I called work. They said I get three days of bereavement pay, so I told them I was going to take my two weeks' vacation time too." She pecked me on the cheek and headed for the shower.

Tony arrived and let himself in as usual, without knocking. He was dressed in a pair of blue jeans and a long-sleeved blue shirt. He had on a jacket, which I knew he was wearing to conceal his gun. His eyes had dark circles around them that hadn't been there just yesterday.

I poured him a cup of coffee and we sat at the kitchen table. I told him about Mia and about her taking the vacation.

He nodded his head slowly and blew on his coffee. "That's good. She'll be around for you then."

I smiled slightly and nodded. "She'll be around for both of us."

"What time are you planning to go see Chris today?" Tony asked, sipping on his coffee.

"First I need to go talk to the sergeant and fill out the paperwork for my leave of absence. I've decided to take as much time off as it takes to get this thing figured out. I know I have a lot of vacation time due, so that shouldn't be a problem. Plus, I'll get my bereavement time. Then, I want to talk to the dispatchers to see who was working last night. See if I can find out anything from them. Then I'm going to talk to Chris and see what he can tell me. He should be able to shed a little light on what's transpired in that condo."

"You still planning on going to Charlie's condo today and can I go with you?"

"Yep," I said as I got up to get more coffee for each of us.

At that point, Mia came back to the kitchen, wearing newish blue jeans that was well-fitted to her slender form. She also had on her Nike tennis shoes trimmed in pink. Her hair was parted down the center with her bangs clinging to her forehead, still damp from the shower. She was so beautiful I couldn't help but stare in admiration. She refilled her coffee cup and joined Tony and me.

"Are you planning on going to the ME's office today?" Mia asked, with a worrying crease across her forehead.

"I guess. I need to find out when they're doing the autopsy. I'll ask Chris about it while I'm there."

"Do you want me to go with you?" Tony offered again.

"Not to the police station. But when I go to Charlie's and the Medical Examiner's office, I'll want you there with me. I figured you may pick up on things that I miss."

"Sounds good to me," Tony said. "Mia, you gonna go to the condo with us?"

"No," she said, shaking her head. "I don't think I can bear seeing it."

Once Upon a Charlie

We all fell silent like the previous night. It was as if a cloud hung over us; a dark penetrating cloud of doom that reminded us of the void left behind by Charlie's death. We all knew that once the Medical Examiner released Charlie's body, it would be time to make arrangements for her funeral. But no one wanted to consider that aspect of the whole situation. The silence felt deafening. No one stirred. No one drank their coffee. Each of us lost in our own thoughts. I finally got up, gave Mia a peck on the cheek, and headed for the shower. I had nothing more to say.

Chapter 4

I WAITED until around one thirty in the afternoon to go to the station, presuming that the sergeant would have arrived by then. I went in through the back door and headed straight to his office. He looked up from his desk with something of surprised look on his face.

"I'm really sorry about your sister," he said, his face turning somber. "No one expected you to show up today, you know."

"Thank you," I said, acknowledging his regrets. "I just came in to talk to you and Chris; see what's going on with the investigation. Plus, I wanted to let you know I will be taking some time off as well."

"Not a problem." The sergeant pulled open a drawer in his desk and drew out some paperwork. "You know you get five days of bereavement pay, don't you?"

I nodded my head. "Plus, any vacation time and comp time I have accrued."

He handed me the forms. I sat on one of the chairs facing his desk and filled out the forms.

"Looks like you have three weeks of vacation time and about a week's comp time. Do you want to take all of it now?"

"Yeah. I need some time off to process this whole thing. I do want to take this leave of absence. None of it makes any sense to me. Why was the Chief and his Lieutenant there? And why was there no radio call to her address?"

The sergeant seemed helpless. "I can't answer that for you. Maybe Chris can. He was the one to respond to the call. Fill out the paperwork properly, and you'll officially be on a leave of absence. Do you know how much time you're gonna' be gone?"

"No. I honestly don't. I just need time to get everything straight in my head."

"I don't see much of a problem there. I'll make sure you receive all the pay you have due. As far as the Chief is concerned, you know how he can be. He has to have his nose in everything, and that lackey of his, the Lieutenant follows wherever he goes." Sergeant Rodgers rolled his eyes, visibly disgusted.

"What about the radio call? I was in the station and I had my radio on the whole time, and I did not hear a call go out to Charlie's condo. It doesn't make any sense to me."

"I wish I could answer that for you, but I honestly don't know. Chris Bradley is here. I just saw him in the report writing room, but I imagine he's back at his desk by now."

"I think I'll run over to dispatch and talk to them for a minute, before going to see Chris."

"Spencer," the Sergeant started hesitantly, "you know this is an open investigation as of now, and he's not going to be able to tell you much."

"I know. But he was there. I saw him. Maybe he can answer a couple of questions *without hurting the integrity of the investigation,"* I said more sarcastically than I had intended.

I left Sergeant Rodgers' office and headed down the hall to

the dispatch room. I keyed in the pass code to enter the room, and the two dispatchers on duty looked up at me in surprise.

As per procedure, there are always two dispatchers on duty. One handles the police calls and the other the fire department calls. I've always had a good rapport with the dispatchers, and they, in turn, took care of me. They were our life line…our calls for safety. I recognized that and made sure they knew it.

Today, Wanda Rumbaugh and Kathleen Walsh were on duty. Wanda was a woman with a dark and exquisite complexion. She wore her hair short, and her almond eyes only enhanced her high cheekbones. The other dispatcher, Kathleen, was approximately thirty-nine years old and had long blond hair that she had pulled back into a ponytail, so that when she turned her head, it bounced.

"We're all really sorry about your sister, Cole," Wanda said with sympathetic eyes.

"Thanks. I really appreciate that."

"What are you doing here? We thought you'd take the day off," Kathleen said with a frown.

"I'm not here to work. I'm taking some time off. I just came from Sergeant Rodgers' office, got all that paperwork straightened out. I was wondering if Chris said anything to you about what they found at Charlie's place?"

Kathleen shook her head in a 'no,' making her pony tail wag back and forth like a happy puppy's tail. "Nope. But the Chief came in he told us not to talk to you about it."

"Godamnit," I blurted out of frustration. "Did he say why?"

"Nope. Just that we weren't supposed to talk to you about it."

Wanda added, "You can check with Chris Bradley. He caught the call last night, so maybe he knows something about it."

"I never heard the call go out to Charlie's condo, and I was hoping I could find out what happened," I told her with an intent look.

Kathleen said, "Check with Chris. Maybe he knows. He may even have the code to get the recording from the St. Louis County. They'd have any cell phone–dialed 911 calls and all the dispatch calls on their servers."

"Do you know who was working the three-to-eleven shift last night?"

Kathleen thought for a moment, which made her pony tail swing to the side. "I think it was Lacy and Dorothy," she said, finally coming to a conclusion.

Wanda agreed and said, "Yeah. We relieved April and Olivia. They worked the midnight shift, and yes, we relieved them."

"Can you tell me if there were any 911 calls to the station on tape here?"

"Not that we're aware of. Besides the Chief came and took the tapes from last night."

"What does the Chief want with the tapes?"

"I guess he gave them to Chris. I don't know," Kathleen said.

"Okay," I said. I clearly wasn't going to get any information from them, especially since they didn't work the three-to-eleven shift. I resigned myself to the fact that I had to talk to Chris in order to get anywhere. I thanked them for their help and left the room, heading for the detective bureau to see Chris.

Once Upon a Charlie

As I walked down the hall toward the detective bureau, I passed Captain Eaton's office. He was sitting at his desk and looked up to see me walk by. Neither of us acknowledged each other. The detective bureau was right on the other side of the Captain's office and was a wide-open space. There were six sets of gray metal desks lined back to back. Chris was sitting in the far-right corner, going through some paperwork. There were two other detectives sitting at their desks as well, but I was intent on talking to Chris, so I didn't bother to stop by and talk to them. He looked up as I walked over and seated myself on the visitor's chair beside his desk. His desk was inundated with enough papers to fill a forest.

"I'm really sorry about your sister, Cole," he said, looking apologetic.

We'd been friends for ten years, so he knew exactly how close I was to Charlie. The extra weight he'd gained from sitting at a desk every day caused his stomach to balloon out, slightly pulling on the buttons of his light blue shirt. His tie was loosened, askew around his collar, and the top button of his shirt was undone. His long salt and pepper brown hair was nothing short of a mess, and his brownish green eyes were telling of his sleepless night. Under normal circumstances, his hair resembled a version of a John Denver's, with his bowl cut. His thick gray mustache with hints of brown showed signs of his age. His round wire-rimmed glasses lay on his desk, and there were dark circles under his eyes.

"Thanks," I said to him in regard to his condolences.

"I pretty much expected to see you today," he said cleaning the lenses of his glasses and wearing them.

"I need to know what happened last night," I told him.

He let out an audible sigh. "You know I can't do that Cole. It's an ongoing investigation. I'm not allowed to talk about it. Plus, you're family. And you know family is always the first suspects."

"Bullshit, Chris. We've been friends for over ten years now. We were partners back in the days when we had two officers to a car. And you're saying, you can't talk to me about it?" I felt a surge of anger building up inside. "Plus, I have an alibi; I was here at the station taking a missing persons report on a runaway from Cloverdale. So, don't pull that shit on me."

Chris remained silent for a few moments. I tried to read his face, but he was so tired that I couldn't tell if it was exhaustion or he was hiding something behind his dark brownish green eyes.

"I know you were there last night. I saw you. And you caught the call, so I know you must know what had happened," I finally said to him trying to regain my composure. He didn't say a word in his defense.

He looked around the open area and leaned in to talk to me. "Okay. First, you have to know that I'm under strict orders from the Chief to not release any information to you."

"What the hell does that mean? Why?"

"He didn't say. All he said was that nobody is to talk to you about the investigation, especially me," as he said these words, his voice was very low, almost a whisper. "Here's what I can tell you, but you can't breathe a word of this to anyone. If you say anything to anyone, I'll deny it all."

I nodded my head in agreement.

He went on, "Apparently someone broke into Charlie's condo and beat and strangled her, then put a bullet through her head. We haven't gotten the autopsy report back yet from the ME, so I don't know what killed her—the bullet or the strangling. The Chief wanted us to remove everything from the condo, including her computer and any papers we could find."

"Do you know when they're doing the autopsy?"

"I think they're doing it today."

I told Chris about my phone call to Charlie right before I started on the missing person's report and then asked, "Did you at least get the seven-digit number for the call that went out over the radio?" All dispatch calls and 911 calls were recorded in St. Louis County Communications on large computer servers. He let out another audible sigh and checked around the room, then turned to me and said, "There is no code, Cole. It doesn't exist."

"What the fuck does that mean. There's always a code." I was beginning to feel the anger bubble up again, but I knew that Chris was doing his best and I didn't want to take it out on him. "There has to be one. Especially in a murder investigation."

"I don't know. All I know is that when I went to the Captain to ask for the code, he told me there wasn't one. Apparently, no call went out."

"You and I both know that someone had to call it in. Otherwise, how would you have known to go there?"

"I understand. But from what everyone is telling me, there is no seven-digit code. It simply doesn't exist. It's not right, I know, but that's what they keep telling me," Chris said, his words dripping with frustration.

"That doesn't make any sense," I said, feeling a headache coming on from restraining all of my rage. "How did you find out about it? What about all the other cops that were there? How did they know?"

"I can't honestly tell you. All I know is that Chief called my cell and told me to meet him at Charlie's address."

"What the fuck is going on Chris? None of this makes any sense."

"Maybe, it's because he knew it was your sister…I don't know. Who the fuck knows what goes on in that man's head."

"Can I at least get into her condo?"

"Sorry. We still consider it a crime scene, and it has been cordoned off. If it's any consolation, you should be able to get in there soon. I think they got all that there was to get from the condo."

I looked at the corner behind his chair and saw six or seven boxes piled one on top of another. "Is that the stuff you took from her condo?" I asked indicating the boxes.

"Yeah. That's most of it."

"Can I at least look through them?"

"I'm sorry, Cole. There's no way I can let you rummage through that. If I got caught, it would mean my badge. But I can promise you that I'll go through it all very carefully. And I'll let you know what I find."

Chris was a hard worker and was known to be true to his word, so I had no choice but to believe him and let it go at that. I trusted him and knew that he would keep in the loop.

"You gonna be at the autopsy?"

"Yeah, I have to. It's my case."

"Will you let me know what happens then?"

"We'll see. You know I'm not even supposed to tell you what I just have."

"That's fine. I understand," I told him, knowing full well I intended to go see the Medical Examiner myself. I didn't bother to tell him that though.

I've known the medical examiner, Dr. Rachael Costa, for years. Since I started working on the force. I was certain she'd be willing to talk to me. I was hoping when the autopsy would be done and that she'll be ready to release Charlie soon.

"Have you gotten any sleep since last night?" I asked.

"Not yet. I have some paperwork to do here, and then I'm leaving and won't be back until tomorrow. If you need me, you can always reach me on my cell phone."

"Okay. Will you at least let me know when the autopsy report is in?"

"I'll try. And remember…you didn't get any of this from me."

I stood from my chair. "No problem, old friend."

I left Chris to do his job and headed for the door to leave. As I passed Captain Eaton's office, he looked up from his desk and said to me, "Chief Denault wants to see you. Oh, and sorry about your sister." There were no emotions in his words, and they were just meaningless hollow gestures of communication. I said nothing in response and headed toward the Chief's office. Any time you go to the Chief's office, you encounter Lieutenant Dintzman first.

"I understand the Chief wants to see me," I said to Lieutenant Dintzman.

"Yes. He knew you were in the station, so he wants a word you. I'm really sorry about your sister," Lieutenant Dintzman said, his voice even and flat like a bad note from a piano.

My instinct was to say, *'shove it,'* but instead, I thanked him for his trite words in the same meaningless tone. He opened the

Chief's door for me, and I walked in. Chief Denault sat behind a large dark wooden desk. He had a gold plated name plate on dark wood on his desk, 'Edward Denault, Chief of Police' as if to announce just who he was to anyone who may come in there. His office was large; the walls had several plaques with pictures of him and celebrated people from the area. He was maybe six feet tall and weighed well over two hundred pounds. His face had a natural red look to it and was covered with pock marks due to acne from years ago, when he was young. His nose was long and bulbous at the end with veins visible along the sides. I knew he was a drinker. It was evident from his physical appearance. His thick neck hung over his collar and his jowls over reached to his tie.

He wore his typical white starched shirt with six stars on each lapel. I never knew what the stars were for, nor did I care. To my surprise, he stood up as I entered his office.

"Spencer, I want you to know that on behalf of the entire City of Palisades, we are all very sorry for your loss." His eyes revealed no emotion as he spoke, and I wondered if he had any feelings whatsoever. He motioned me to sit in one of the two leather chairs in front of his desk. They matched the same dark wood as his desk.

"Thank you," was the only thing that came to mind. I really had nothing to say to the man; we both knew we didn't like each other.

"Well with that said, I want you to know that we will do everything we can to find your sister's murderer."

His face betrayed his words, and I didn't believe a word of it. I knew Chris was working on it and he would do everything he could to track down the killer, but the Chief's words were like an echo in a cavern, hollow and without meaning.

I nodded my head mechanically, as I was still at a loss for words. At this point, I didn't believe anything that came from that man's mouth.

"I know you were back in the detective bureau talking to Detective Chris Bradley. I don't know what he told you, but this is an open investigation and I assume he gave you no information."

"No sir. He didn't," I lied, with a straight face.

He leaned back on his chair and folded his hands across his bulging stomach. "I want to make things very clear to you, Spencer. You are not a part of this investigation, and I will not tolerate you investigating this on your own."

"With all due respect, sir, she was my sister, and I'd like to know what's going on with the investigation."

"I'm afraid that's not possible. Not only are you a family member, but we do not discuss open investigations with anyone. Not even police officers."

I thought for a moment. I counted the six stars on each of his lapels in an attempt to remain calm and respectful.

"I don't understand," I told him, feeling my face reddening as anger reared its ugly head. My hands gripped the arm rests on the chair, almost painfully hard.

He leaned forward and looked me directly in the eyes as he spoke. "You are not involved in this investigation in any way shape or form. You are to stay as far away from it as you can. If you don't, I will have you arrested for interfering with a police investigation. Have I made myself clear?"

The vehement fury I felt for the man only increased even more, and I could feel the anger intensifying within me. It took all I had to speak to him without the anger reflecting.

"Perfectly clear, sir. And just so you know, I'll be taking a leave of absence from work. I've already seen Sergeant Rodgers about it and filled out the forms."

"Then, we are clear."

"Yes, sir."

"Consider yourself warned," he said.

I clutched the arms of the chair so tight, the whites of my knuckles were clearly visible.

"You're clear to leave, now"

In a burst of anger, I stood up, walked out of his office past Lieutenant Dintzman wordlessly, and left the station. I headed home, the rage and hatred running through my veins with each heartbeat.

~~~

Chapter 5

IT WAS around three thirty when I got home. Mia and Tony were still sitting at the kitchen table, talking. The coffee was gone and the dishes were cleaned. I sat down at the table and told them everything that Chris had said to me.

"Something's not right here," Mia's said in a tiny little voice. Her eyes and nose were still red.

"I know but Chris couldn't really tell me anything. Since they're not doing the autopsy until tomorrow, why don't we go over to Charlie's condo?" I said more to Tony than to Mia. "Are you sure you don't want to go with us, Mia?"

"I don't think I want to go there. I'll stay here. Maybe put something together for us to eat."

I wrapped my arms around her and held her, as if scared she would float away from me. She put her head on my chest and held me around the waist, standing like that for several minutes. I knew she loved Charlie, almost as much as I did, and that her heart was breaking as well.

I gave her a long kiss and told her I'd call her later to let her know what we discovered.

Tony offered to drive us both to Charlie's condo, so we got into his BMW and went to the crime scene.

When we arrived there, we parked next to her car, a sporty little red convertible *Mustang,* which was still standing there.

"It will be strange not seeing her riding around in it. She really loved that car," Tony said in a slightly choked voice.

We sat in his car and stared up the stairway at Charlie's condo, contemplating. The 'Crime Scene' tape was still attached in front of her door in a large 'X'.

"We still going in?" Tony asked motioning to the crime scene tape.

"Yeah. To fuck with Denault and all his shit. I need to get in there and see if there's something that may lead us to what it was she wanted to show me."

We got out of the car and climbed the stairs slowly; neither one of us wanted to really see the place. Neither of us knew what to expect. There were no police officers guarding the door, so we continued on. I pulled out my set of keys and found the one to Charlie's condo, but I didn't need to, since the killer had broken down the door. There were splinters by the doorknob and the lock, so I pushed the door open. As much as I wanted to tear down the crime scene tape, I knew that if I did, the Chief would know it was me who did it. Before we went in, I handed Tony a pair of latex gloves and put a pair on myself.

"What's this for?" Tony asked. "Aren't both our prints already all over the place?"

"Probably. But anything we touch may not have been dusted for prints, so I thought we'd better be cautious. This way, we can pick up and examine anything and not have to worry about it. You think you can get under the tape?"

"Hell yeah," Tony said, looking at the large "X" across the door.

We were both able to squeeze through under the tape without disturbing it, although that was a challenge in itself.

Once Upon a Charlie

We closed the door behind us. It was dark in her condo, so I turned on one of the smaller lights and we surveyed the living room. The place was a disaster to say the least. There was black fingerprint dust everywhere. Both Tony and I stood, looking around in complete and utter disbelief at the disorder. Charlie's house was usually spick and span. To our left was Charlie's kitchen that had a pass through with stools outside it, so she could eat at the counter. These stools lay broken in a heap like a marionette gone awry. There were always fresh flowers on the pass through, but the vase was now shattered on the floor, the flowers wilted. Her oakwood kitchen table lay overturned on one side.

In the living room, there was a pool of blood on the tan carpet, matted down and dried. And blood smears on the wall as well. As if she had tried to scratch her way out of the room. Her sectional couch was cut, and the stuffing removed, as if an angry bear had come and ripped it apart. All the cushions were spread on the floor, and her coffee table was upended, its glass broken.

"My God," I heard Tony gasp, but his voice seemed distant.

Most of the lamps were destroyed, with the exception of one standing lamp in the corner. We searched through the rubble resembling a pile of trash, and I couldn't tell if it was from the murderer or from the forensics team. Markers were placed about the house, and Tony and I took great care not to disturb them.

"You search the bedroom, while I search her living room," I told Tony, finally coming back to myself.

Her roll-top desk stood in the far-right corner, but there was no need to open the roll top as it was already opened. The contents of the empty drawers were spread on the desk top; pens and pencils lay like pick-up sticks. I checked the other drawers and they were completely empty. I pulled out each drawer, checking the bottoms in case Charlie had left anything taped to them, but there was nothing. Several papers were scattered through the apartment, and I went through the painful task of reading each to see what was written on them, all the while hoping for a clue as to what she'd come across. Many were notes to herself in her perfect curly handwriting. Grocery lists, items she wanted to buy at local antique stores, ideas of how she wanted to decorate her house. Most of them were useless both to me and the police. I wanted to believe that there was some clue we would find there as to what had happened. There was nothing under any of the drawers and I replaced them with care in the way they had been. I went to the kitchen and went through her drawers and cabinets, yet found nothing. She had a drawer devoted simply to junk, and I picked up each item, inspecting them carefully. I found nothing that would help me. There were a few scraps of paper in there, but again, nothing gave away what had happened. It was hard to draw the line between what the police investigators and what the murderer took or did. All her books were thrown off her shelves and were fallen on the floor in a pile. Tony came back into the living room and stood by the entrance to her bedroom.

"My God, Tony, they even took all her beautiful pictures off the wall," I said to him.

"I know. I don't get it. Why would they need her pictures?" As if noticing for the first time, he looked around the room. The walls were a light-yellow color, and you could see a dust-free outline where the missing pictures had been hanging.

"The real question is who wanted them. The murderer or the police? They weren't of any value except to Charlie, so I don't get it. I didn't find it out here…but did you find her computer in the bedroom?" I asked him.

"No. The bedroom looks pretty much like this." Tony waved his hand through the air. "I went through her drawers and they did leave her clothes, but they took them all out and threw them all over the room."

"Let's go through it again. I can't help but feel there's something we're missing," I said to him. "Damn! I really wanted to find that computer. Something tells me whatever she wanted to show me, it was on there."

"And you know there's a chance that whoever took it will wipe the hard drive."

"I know. Another useless avenue. Did you find any pictures or anything that would give us a clue to what she found out?"

"Nothing. I even checked the closet but they…whoever they were already went through everything in there. They even opened and looked through all her shoe boxes."

I followed Tony into the bedroom. The mattress lay askew on the bed. We lifted it and found nothing. We each took a drawer from the dresser and scrutinized them. I told Tony to take the drawer out and look under it and inside where the drawer sits, in case she taped something in there for hiding.

"Maybe, just maybe we'll get a clue."

Charlie's clothes lay spread out all over the floor like they were tried on and flung away in a woman's dressing room. We checked all the bottoms of all the drawers and came up empty handed. We went to the closet and checked all her clothes…all her pockets…at least the ones they didn't throw on the floor. We went through every shoe. Every shoe box. And again, there was nothing there. They had removed everything from the closet shelf, so that too was bare. I pulled out Charlie's step ladder and checked the shelf and its back in the corner. There was a paper of sorts sitting in the far corner, which appeared to be upside down. I reached for it, but it was lodged in there. I didn't want to tear it. So, I worked slowly at it and finally freed it from its place in the corner. It was a picture of a small girl. She did not look familiar to me at all.

"Bingo," I exclaimed to Tony. "I got a picture. It has to be one of the kids at Cloverdale."

I handed it to Tony. Under the picture was written the name "Lauren Stanford" in green. And then it hit me. It was the girl whose missing report I had filed on the day of Charlie's murder.

The little girl in the picture was dressed in jeans and a t-shirt with a hooded jacket.

"Holy shit," Tony said, peering closely at the picture. "That's a little girl! Do you think there's a connection?"

"I don't know, but she's from Cloverdale. I wrote a missing report on her while Charlie was being killed," I said holding up to the picture.

We both stared in astonishment at the picture, like it would tell us the story of what happened there last night.

"I want to know how they missed that?" Tony asked.

"It was way back in the corner, where the wall and shelf meet, and I can only assume they didn't get the step ladder to check the entire shelf."

"You think it has something to do with her murder?"

"Seriously, I wish I knew. It's just too much of a coincidence that she would go missing on the same night of

Charlie's murder. Apparently, they left no stone unturned in their quest to find out what Charlie knew. But at least we now have a pebble, albeit a small one."

"Yeah and they killed her for it too. And we don't know what this pebble is all about."

"I guess we're really done here." I put the picture in my shirt pocket, and Tony and I got ready leave.

We stared at the wreckage that was once Charlie's beautifully decorated condo. It was like gazing at the bottom of a sunken ship. In unison, we both turned to leave and headed for the door. I made sure to switch off the light I had turned on and opened the door. I took one last look, before I wriggled under the tape and made for Tony's car. We drove back to my house in complete, dark, and ugly silence.

Chapter 6

WHEN WE reached the house, Mia was in the kitchen and she could tell immediately from the looks on our faces that it did not go as well as we had hoped.

"Are you guy's okay?" she asked, giving me a hug and a kiss. She softly patted Tony on the back.

I told her we were fine and pulled out the picture we had found on the closet shelf. She took it cautiously as it were a porcelain doll and studied it carefully. She stared at the picture, transfixed by the image. She read Lauren's name aloud and then mouthed it several times. She turned the picture over and over and stared into the eyes of the little girl. I was beginning to wonder if she had some kind of notion as to where it came from or what it meant.

"Wow," she finally said. "Is this the missing girl you took the report on that night..." her voice trailed off.

"Yeah. That's the missing girl from Cloverdale whose missing person report was filed last night."

Mia let out a gasp and her hand immediately went to her mouth. "It's one thing to know she was missing; it's another thing to have a face to her. Do you have any idea where she is?"

"No," I shook my head.

Tony said, "We're going to see if we can find her though, now that we know what she looks like."

"Yeah, that's definitely a start."

"I made us some dinner," Mia said. "Why don't we all sit down and eat and maybe we can figure something out. I wonder why the police didn't find this."

"It was tucked away really well, in the far corner of her closet shelf. And I guess they didn't see it. But the important thing is we did and we have something to go on now."

Mia had made baked mostaccioli. There were three place settings on the table. I got Tony and myself a beer and a glass of wine for Mia. She gulped it down. I hadn't realized how hungry I was.

Mia set the pan of mostaccioli on the table as I poured her more wine. As we ate, we told Mia about what was left of Charlie's condo. Mia said very little and picked on her food. When we were done with dinner, Mia got up and began to clean the dishes. I went up behind her and put my arms around her, feeling her soft skin against mine. It felt good. It felt safe. She turned around, dried her hands, and cupped my cheeks in her hands and gave me a kiss.

"I love you so much," she said. She put her arms around my neck and gave me a much-needed hug.

When the dishes were cleaned, Mia returned to the table to finish her wine, and Tony and I had another beer. It felt good gulping it down, but it would take more than a few beers to help me deal with the images that were stuck in my head.

At the center of the table lay the picture of Lauren and each of us without much forethought picked it up, one by one, and looked at it. She was small in stature, and her eyes were a green that offset her blond hair. I couldn't help but wonder when the picture had been taken. Obviously, the picture was taken by Charlie, but for what purpose…and why was it hidden in the corner of her closet?

Mia spent the most amount of time with the picture. "She looks so innocent and loving," Mia's voice was quiet—it felt like she really didn't want us to interrupt her thinking.

Tony looked at the picture several times, as did I, and none of us could figure out what it all could've meant.

Tony took a swig his beer. "I know one thing: there's a reason why Charlie took this picture, and until we find Lauren, we won't know why."

"Maybe she was trying to protect her," Mia offered.

I gave that some thought and said, "That could be the case. But protect her from what exactly?"

"That's the biggest question in all this," Tony said. "And why did she run away from Cloverdale?"

I remembered Charlie mentioning that she worked with Marlene at Cloverdale. "That's something we'll need to talk to Marlene about," I suggested.

Once again, the picture came to rest at the center of the table.

"I guess our next step should be to find out the results of the autopsy, which should be done by now," I told them.

Tony took another gulp of his beer and said, "So I guess tomorrow, we're going to the Medical Examiner's office?"

"We can meet here around eleven and we can head out then," I told him. "If the autopsy is finished, I'm sure she'll be releasing Charlie, so we'll need to find a funeral home to pick her up."

Mia blinked her eyes a couple of times to rid them of her tears forming at the corner of her eyes and agreed with a nod of her head. "I think Teitelbaum and Sons is good," she said quietly.

"Yeah," Tony said. "I've heard a lot of good things about them, too."

"Well, I think once they release the body, we'll call them and have them arrange the funeral," I said.

Mia burst into tears at the thought of burying Charlie. I reached over and put my arm around her and held her close to me while she cried inconsolably in my shirt.

"I don't want to do this," she mumbled into my chest.

"I know, sweetie, but we have to. You don't have to worry about anything. Tony and I can take care of it."

"I just can't bear to think of putting her into the ground where it's all closed in and lifeless."

"I know, honey," I coaxed her, rubbing her arm, "but there's just nothing we can do. It'll take some time, and after a while, I think you'll understand it all. Please don't be upset."

That made her cry even harder. Tony got up and picked up some Kleenexes and handed them to Mia, who took several. "I'm so sorry," she said still tucked into my shirt. "I just don't know how to deal with this. I miss her so much, and I can't seem to let it go like you guys can."

"We're not letting it go," I told her. "We just handle things a little differently than you do. That's all."

"I feel so foolish."

"Please don't," Tony chimed in. "I still can't help but cry every now and then about it myself."

"Really?" Mia asked, holding her head up and using the Kleenexes to wipe away her tears.

"Yes," Tony said. "This is hard on all of us. It's just that you're more emotional than we are right now."

Mia nodded her head and blew her nose. It was red from

the tissues and her eyes were getting puffy again.

With the exception of a few sobs from Mia, we mostly sat in silence listening to the sound of nothingness, as Tony and I drank our beers and Mia, her wine.

~~~

Chapter 7

MIA AND I ended up sleeping in later than we had intended. The clock radio on the bedside table read ten thirteen, which was way too late by our standards. We awoke in the same position we had fallen asleep in, warm and safe, embraced in each other's arms.

"Morning," she said in a groggy voice.

I kissed her on the forehead. "Morning, darlin'. As much as I'd like to stay here all day, Tony's on his way, and we must get up. Tony and I have to go talk to Dr. Costa today."

"I thought Chris said they weren't doing the autopsy until today," Mia asked, her voice recovering from the sleepy state.

"I know, but I still want to talk to her. They'll probably do it first thing this morning, and then, I can talk to her after it's all done."

Neither of us moved. We lay together, immersed in our own thoughts…lost in whatever we felt.

It was another ten minutes before either of us got up.

"I'm going for a shower," Mia said as she walked across the room to the bathroom.

"I'll get the coffee going then."

I made the bed and went to the kitchen, thinking about Rachael Costa. We'd known each other for years from when I was on patrol. There were many times when the Homicide

Detective was busy, and so I caught the original murder case. They would have me stand in for the autopsy. She was a tall thin woman, about sixty-three years old, and had no problem speaking her piece when necessary. She was her own person, and no one was going to tell her how she had to do her job. She'd been an ME for well over thirty years. She always said that she'd rather be with the dead than the living. She believed that the dead spoke to her in ways that living people just could not. I had a deep respect for her, and she'd always given me special treatment when it came to results of the autopsies.

By the time, I heard the shower turn off, I had two mugs of steaming coffee on the table along with sugar and cream. Mia came into the kitchen, wearing a pair of tight blue jeans and a solid red T-Shirt that went well with her dark black hair. Her bangs were dried and curled under, but the rest of her hair was wet and shiny.

"Thanks for the coffee," she said, coming around and giving me a kiss on the lips. The scent of her shampoo and body wash was familiar and comforting.

I heard Tony's car pull up in front of the house.

"How you doing Mia?" Tony asked, walking into the kitchen.

She said hi to Tony, gave him a kiss on the cheek, and took the chair next to me at the table.

"I take it we're still going to the morgue this morning?" Tony asked me, sounding a bit tentative.

"That's the plan," I told him.

"All I know is that I don't want to go along. The thought of that place gives me the chills," Mia said, almost with a shiver.

"I used to feel that way too," I said, "but you get used to it beyond a point."

"I've never been there, and I'm a little on edge about it myself, but I want to know what she has to say," Tony added.

"I guess we're going to have to think about Charlie's funeral," Mia said, tearing up again.

"Yeah, I suppose we should. I guess it all depends on when the ME releases her. We'll probably just call Teitelbaum and Son's, like we talked about."

After we finished our coffee, I took a shower and threw on a pair of blue jeans and a blue and white striped shirt.

By then, Mia had already cleared the kitchen table and the coffee pot was ready for the next day's brew.

Mia, Tony, and I had moved into the living room. Mia sat on the couch with her legs tucked under her and I joined her there, lightly kissing her on the forehead. Tony took the armchair beside the couch. We all sat there staring at the blank television. She had stopped crying but there were tissues within her reach. The sadness on her face made my heart feel broken and shattered. I wanted to make everything alright for her and for all of us, but I knew there was no way that would happen so soon. We all knew that the next few days were going to be tough. The three of us sat there lost in our own thoughts, staring off into the distance, where only one's mind can go.

"I guess it's time to go," Tony said apprehensively.

"Are you sure you want to do this?" I asked him.

It took him a moment to answer but he finally relented. "I'm no detective or anything like that, but I'm with you Cole. I'm as committed to finding out who did this to Charlie as you are."

Tony offered to drive, and thirty minutes later, we entered the Medical Examiner's office.

As we entered the building, the smell of formaldehyde assaulted our nostrils. We encountered a guard at the front desk who asked who we were and why we were there. We explained that we wanted to see Dr. Costa about an autopsy. He dialed on his telephone, spoke a few words, and gave her our names. When he hung up, he gave us each visitor badges and sent us down the hallway toward the autopsy room. It was cold and dreary in there, and I wondered how Dr. Costa could withstand the ghosts of those long dead.

Dr. Costa greeted us at the door. She was dressed in scrubs and immediately gave me a hug.

"Cole, I'm so sorry about your sister," she whispered in my ear.

She was a tall thin woman, with brown hair and golden highlights. There were touches of gray in her hair, which seemed to add character to her very pretty face. She didn't look nearly her age. Her bluish gray eyes were penetrating, especially when she was concentrating on something. She was always blunt and got right to the point. And if it pissed anyone off, she couldn't care less.

I introduced her to Tony and explained that he was Charlie's fiancée. They shook hands.

Since it was common practice for a police officer or a detective to be present and watch the autopsy, I asked if she had seen Chris Bradley yet.

"I talked to Chris, and he said you were doing the autopsy today,"

She tilted her head off to the side and confusion spread

across her face. "You're talking about your sister, Charlie, right? I did the autopsy last night," she said.

Now it was my turn to be confused. "Wait, what? Chis said you were going to do it today. She was just murdered two nights ago. I don't understand."

"Apparently, Chief Denault wanted it done last night, and they called me in from home to come do it. It couldn't just be any doctor. Why he wanted me in particular, I'll never know."

"Since when do you answer to the Chief of Police?"

"I don't normally, but I decided I'd go ahead and do it this time. I guess I was feeling generous last night. But I certainly gave them a piece of my mind about getting me out of bed to do an autopsy for him."

"But Chris told me you weren't going to do it until today."

"Well, he told you wrong, because both Chris and Lieutenant Dintzman were here to view it." My mind was racing through all the lies I'd been told.

"What the hell is going on here?" I looked at Tony. He looked just as confused as I was.

"I wish I knew. All I can tell you is that I got a call from your Chief last night, requesting an immediate autopsy to be done by me. Like I said, I was feeling generous, so I told him I'd do it. But I wasn't happy about it and I let him know it too."

"Did he say why it needed to be done last night?"

"Nope, just that he wanted it done immediately."

"And why was Lieutenant Dintzman there? He doesn't attend to autopsies," I said.

"You got me. All I know is, Chris, the Lieutenant, and the Chief showed up here, I did the autopsy, and they left."

"This makes no sense."

"Sweetie, I learned a long time ago that police officers and their procedures make no sense. And I doubt they ever will."

I shook my head in an effort to clear it and to get back to the reason for our visit.

"Do you want to see her?" Dr. Costa asked.

I looked at Tony whose eyes grew wide and he looked rather pale.

"Let's talk first," she said, apparently sensing the dread by the expression on Tony's face.

"Here's what I got," Dr. Costa began. "First, she was pretty beat up. She was pretty much disfigured beyond recognition. There was a lot of bruising all over her, but her face was particularly horrifying. Her eyes were swollen and her cheek bones were broken. For that matter, she had broken bones all over her body. Her arms, her wrists, her ankles. Looks like she may have tried to fight back, because I found some defensive wounds. But whoever did this to her was simply too strong for her to fend off. There were no signs of rape or forcible entry, so there's a plus. At least, they left that unscathed. She was strangled to death, as there were petechia marks in her eyes and around her face. It appears to be manual strangulations and not ligature. But, here's the interesting part: she was shot in the middle of her forehead with a low caliber .22. And it was at close range, because there was gun powder residue on her forehead. I say low caliber, because there was no exit wound. I sampled the gun powder residue too." She pointed her finger to the center of her forehead to indicate where Charlie had been shot.

"Not that I'm questioning you or anything, you've been doing this for over thirty years, but how can you tell she was strangled to death and that the bullet didn't kill her?" I asked her.

"Well, the bullet wound was definitely postmortem. I could tell by the fact that there was so very little blood around the entry wound. Her larynx and hyoid bones were broken as well. So, the strangulation occurred before the bullet even entered her brain. It rattled around in there, but I was able to recover the bullet. I have it right here." She held up a small evidence bag that held a small bullet. It was mangled and unidentifiable.

"So, you're saying she was shot after she had already died?" Tony asked, still examining the bullet.

"Yep. That's what I'm saying."

Tony handed back the evidence bag to her, and she placed it on her desk.

"Yeah, this doesn't make a whole lot of sense to me. Only the killer would really know why. But I agree, it is strange," Dr. Costa said.

"You said she fought back, was there anything under her fingernails that you could get DNA from?" I asked.

"I did clip off her fingernails and bag them, so we won't know until the lab report comes back. I was waiting to see if you'd show up before I sent all this out to the lab along with the blood work. If you want to see her, I can arrange that, but I have to tell you it's not pretty."

Again, I consulted with Tony. "I want to see her. I need to see what they did to her," Tony said to Dr. Costa.

We went into the cold autopsy room, where four empty metal tables were lined up, awaiting some other poor family members going through what we were. Dr. Costa opened one of the drawers that held bodies.

"I cleaned her up as much as I could, but it is still going to be bad. I'm just telling you so that you can prepare yourself."

There was a long white sheet that covered Charlie from head to foot. Dr. Costa pulled the sheet back far enough for me to see her face, throat, and where Dr. Costa had started the 'Y' incision for the autopsy. I automatically reeled backward and felt all the life drain out of me. Even though I had already seen her at the crime scene, it was still a shock to see her here under the lights of the morgue. She was badly beaten in the face, and you could see the red marks on her neck where she was strangled. The bullet wound stood out in the mass of bruising.

"My God, they brutalized her. She didn't deserve this. No one deserves this kind of brutality," I heard Tony say as tears rolled down his cheeks.

She looked at us with pity, a look I'd never seen on her face before, as she covered Charlie back up and slid her back into her little pit of hell.

"Let me know what funeral parlor you're going to use, and they'll make arrangements to pick her up."

I could barely speak through my own tears. I looked over and saw that Tony was crying profusely as well. I wiped my tears away and looked over to Dr. Costa.

"We'll probably be using Teitelbaum and Son's Funeral Home. I'll give them a call and have them contact you."

"That would be fine. I know them well, so it shouldn't be a problem there," Dr. Costa assured us.

"Just in case, if anyone asks, we were never here," I told her.

She nodded her head. "I won't tell them about what we discussed."

"Thanks Doc. There's something going on here that's all screwed up, and Tony and I are going to find out what. But they can't know I was here."

"Not a problem." Dr. Costa gave me a big hearty hug before we left. "You take care. If I find anything out, I'll call you on your cell. Nobody has to know."

"Thanks Doc, no problem," I said hugging her back.

I'll be ready to release the body to the funeral home tomorrow," Dr. Costa said.

The words 'funeral home' hit me like a head-on collision. Suddenly, all this was coming to me, like great waves from every direction, and I felt like I was being swept away by the tide.

"I'll call you tomorrow. Thanks, Dr. Costa. I appreciate your help."

We said our goodbyes and headed to Tony's car. Neither of us spoke. Neither of us wanted to.

We were half way home when Tony finally broke the silence. "Well, from what Dr. Costa said, at least she fought back," he said in a shaky voice.

"Yeah," I said. "But unfortunately, she lost."

Chapter 8

THE FOLLOWING morning, I called the Teitelbaum and Son's mortuary and set up arrangements for them to pick up Charlie. I then called Dr. Costa and let her know they would be coming to pick her up sometime that afternoon.

Tony, Mia, and I had made arrangements to talk to the funeral director, William Teitelbaum, that morning. We arrived a little before eleven o'clock.

William Teitelbaum was a tall thin man with perfectly barbered brown hair. He was dressed in a dark blue double-breasted suit with perfect creases down the length of his pants. His blue eyes were sympathetic. He showed us to a conference room off to the side of the chapel.

"First, let me say how sorry I am for your loss," he began. "Let me assure you that we will take good care of your loved one. May I offer you some coffee or anything else to drink?"

We all declined his offer graciously.

"We have picked up Charlene Spencer from the Medical Examiner's office this morning." He passed me a small yellow envelope, and I opened it. "These were her effects that the Medical Examiner sent with her.

"Charlene is her given name, but she goes by Charlie. I'd prefer for her to be referred to as Charlie during the service."

"I understand, and that won't be a problem. In fact, when

we type out the obituary and make the prayer cards, we can always put it as 'Charlene (Charlie) Spencer'."

That was fine with us.

I poured the contents of the envelope out on to the table. There was the gold cross that Charlie wore all the time, along with her engagement ring, a watch, and some earrings. I heard Mia sharply inhale at the sight of the items that we were so accustomed to seeing Charlie wear.

"Now, Mr. Spencer…"

"Please call me Cole."

"All right then, Cole, I'm sure you've had the chance to view her body."

I nodded. "Yes, I have."

"If I may make a suggestion, I recommend a closed casket. I don't believe there is a way that we will be able to make Charlene look like the woman you knew."

I felt a lump rise in my throat as I spoke, "I understand."

"That being the case, I see no need to pick out something for her to wear, unless you'd prefer a particular outfit for her."

Mia began to sob and cry relentlessly. There was a box of Kleenexes on the table, and I handed one to her. I placed my hand on hers and gave it a squeeze.

"Obviously your wife was very close to Charlene too," William Teitelbaum said and reached out and placed a hand on her shoulder.

Between sobs, Mia told him to call her by her first name. "I can't bear to think of her being buried without any clothes. She was always dressed so fashionably and the thought of her being buried in nothing…" Mia broke out into tears again.

Mr. Teitelbaum responded, "I completely understand and

that won't be any problem. I'll just need whatever outfit you choose brought to me sometime today."

Up until that point, Tony had been very quiet and had fixed his gaze at the table. He finally broke his silence and said, "I'd like for her to be buried with her engagement ring. It's there with her belongings."

"And the cross," I said.

I opened the envelope and handed Mr. Teitelbaum the ring and the cross.

After much discussion, we decided to hold the funeral on Saturday, nine a.m., with no viewing. Since the funeral home already had a chapel, we decided to hold the service there. We picked out a mahogany casket with gold handles and a soft silk lining. We decided that since we could not have an open casket, we would gather pictures to put around the room for those who knew her. We picked out several Scriptures to be read during the funeral. We selected prayer cards for those in attendance. Mr. Teitelbaum said they would post the funeral and its arrangements in Thursday's paper. We decided to bury her in the cemetery that was on the grounds of Teitelbaum and Son's.

When all was said and done, it took us two and a half hours to complete the funeral arrangements. We left the mortuary and told William Teitelbaum we'd make sure to drop off the clothes to him later that day. When we finally left, we were all numb with grief, trying to gain some semblance of control over our emotions; but that was not to be.

We had taken Tony's car to the mortuary. Before we got in, I turned to Mia to pull her in for a comforting embrace.

"Tony and I are going over to Charlie's apartment to find something for her to wear. Do you want us to drop you off at home or do you want to come?" I asked her.

Mia stepped back from the hug and placed her hand on my cheek. "There is no way in hell I am going to let you two men pick out something for her to wear. No offense, but I'd rather go with you."

We all gave a chuckle. Mia had somehow gained control of her emotions, but she was still on the edge, and it was up to me to prepare her for what she was going to see at the condo.

I thought it over and grasped her hand. "That's fine but you need to be ready for what you're going to see in there. The police tore the place apart, and there is blood everywhere. Are you going to be able to handle that?"

Mia drew in a large breath and held it for a moment, before releasing it. "It's that bad, huh?"

Tony said, "Yeah, it's bad."

I looked into the deep dark pools that were Mia's eyes as she thought about it—considering it…wondering if she had the strength to go there.

"I'll do it," she finally said. Somewhere from the whirlpool of tears came bravery.

I grabbed her and held her for a little longer. We all got into Tony's car and headed for Charlie's apartment.

Charlie's red *Mustang* was still parked where we'd last seen it, and Mia asked what was going to happen to it.

"We'll probably end up taking it back to the house. We're going to need to clean out the condo at some point, so we can redo the carpets and repaint it so as to sell it." I wasn't really thinking that far in advance, so I just said the first thing that came to mind.

"I'll get some of my men to help with that," Tony said. "But that won't be until much after the funeral. We have some time."

As we walked up the stairs toward the condo, I noticed that the yellow X was gone. In a way, it was a relief because that meant that the police wouldn't be back.

I pushed the door open and examined the splinters on the side of the door. It would need to be fixed, so that we could secure the house. I walked in before Mia. The place looked exactly like Tony and I had left it the other night. "Are you sure you're ready for this?" I asked Mia.

Slowly, she nodded her head and stepped over the threshold. Mia immediately gasped, placing both hands over her mouth as she surveyed the disaster before her. "Oh…my…God…What have they done?" Her shock took the form of tears at the sight of the wreckage that was once Charlie's condo. "They ruined it. They destroyed it!"

I grabbed Mia and whirled her around to face me. "Mia. Breathe. Why don't we go into the bedroom and find something from her closet for her to wear? It's not as bad in there. It's a mess, but no blood."

Mia stood stock-still. Unbending. Unable to move as she looked at the living room. It was all Tony and I could do to get her away from there and into the bedroom.

"My God, Cole what did they do?"

"Most of that was from the police investigation team."

"But they took everything. It was such a beautiful room, and they took everything. Why?"

"I don't know. They were looking for evidence."

Once Mia was under control, I got her some toilet paper to blow her nose on. And once again, she seemed to gain some semblance of control over herself. We went to Charlie's closet that was filled with clothes. Most of the clothes were scattered around the room, but there were still a few left on the hangers. We each took a section and began looking for something for Charlie to wear.

"I've got it," Mia said pulling out the sequin blue gown that Charlie had worn at our wedding. She had been Mia's maid of honor. "This is perfect. Remember how beautiful she looked in it when we got married? I still remember how resplendent she looked walking down the aisle before me." Mia was lost in the memory for a moment as she stared at the gown.

"What's this?" I heard Tony ask. He was checking the other side of the closet. He held up a large white bag on a hanger. "It's heavy."

We took it out and placed it on the bed and opened the bag. It was Charlie's wedding dress.

"That's stunning," Tony said with gasp. "I didn't even know she bought it," Tony said, "she never mentioned it to me."

Mia spoke up, "It was supposed to be a surprise. I remember when we went shopping and she first saw it. She looked like an angel in it. Her hair fell over her shoulders in such a pretty way."

We stood and stared at the beautiful dress as if it held a sort of magic to it—an enchantment. It had quaint sparkling buttons down the bodice with silk spaghetti straps. The front was laced with a fine intricate pattern that ran down to the waistline, where the dress opened up and spread out with a fine silk pattern that would form pleats only when the dress was worn. There was a three-foot train on the dress that buttoned up in the back for after the wedding—during the reception.

Tony stared at the dress in astonishment. "Maybe…we can have her buried in this?" His voice cracked up when he spoke.

Mia jumped right in, "No Tony. That wouldn't be right. But I do have an idea. Maybe, we can talk to Mr. Teitelbaum and they can lay her on top of the wedding dress, and we can bury her in the blue one."

Tony continued to stare. "She'd have made such a beautiful bride." Tears formed in his eyes.

Mia went to him, held him, and let him cry on her shoulder for a while. She slowly guided him back toward the living room. I took the wedding dress, wrapped it back up in its plastic bag, and hung both the blue dress and that over my arm and carried them to where Tony and Mia stood. Tony was wiping away his tears as we left the condo and headed for his car.

As we were walking down the stairs, I heard one of Charlie's neighbors calling out to me. I turned to talk to her.

"Mrs. Mower, hello." I said to her. She was a small woman, about seventy years old, and had short gray hair. Her husband had passed away several years ago, which is when she moved into the complex.

"I just want to tell you how very sorry I am to hear about Charlie. She was such a wonderful person and always so helpful to me."

"Thank you. I certainly appreciate hearing that. Her funeral is on Saturday at nine a.m. Teitelbaum and Son's funeral home."

"I certainly hope they catch the guy who did this to her. It was awful. Simply awful. I heard all this banging and screaming, and I wanted to go over there to help her, but I was too scared. So, I called my son and he told me to dial 911, but I guess by the time the police got here, it was already too late. I can't tell you how sorry I am."

"It's okay Mrs. Mower. And thank you for your condolences."

"I'll try to get my son to drive me to the funeral, seeing I can't drive anymore. Damn cataracts."

"It's okay if you can't make it. I understand. And thank you for calling the police. If you had tried to help, you probably would have been hurt or killed yourself."

"Yes dear, you're probably right. What can an old woman like me do to help in such a case?"

"Mrs. Mower, would you mind if I came over sometime to talk to you about what happened and what you heard?"

"Why certainly, Cole. You're always welcome in my home. I don't know if I can be of any help to you or not. I told the police everything I knew already."

"Well, maybe we can have some coffee and talk about it real soon," I said to her.

"That would be lovely. And again, I'm so sorry."

"Thank you."

Mia and Tony were already waiting for me inside the car. I told them that she had made a call to the police the night of the attack.

"I thought Chris said there were no calls that night," Tony said.

"Apparently, he lied." I scowled.

Once Upon a Charlie

We drove back to the funeral home and found Mr. Teitelbaum.

"Hello," he said to us as we entered the lobby of the mortuary. He shook our hands. "It looks like you've found something for her to wear," he said almost as a question.

"Yes," I told him and handed over the dresses.

Mr. Teitelbaum gave me an odd look. "What have we here? It appears that we have two dresses?"

Mia said, "We want her to be buried in the blue dress, but its her wedding dress in the white bag. She was supposed to get married in September. We were wondering if you could perhaps lay her on top of the wedding dress."

"What a wonderful idea. Yes, that can certainly be arranged. I've already had the hair dresser in and she was able to wash out and brush Charlene's hair out, so it looks very nice. I will have them dress her and lay her atop the wedding dress. What a very nice touch. I'm so sorry Mr. DeMarco that you lost her before you were able to see her wear it."

Tony nodded in response. I think he was afraid his tears would betray him again.

"Okay. Then, I think we're all set for her funeral. I do have to ask you, though: would you like to have a private viewing of Charlene before the funeral?"

"No," I told him. "Tony and I both had seen her before she got here, and I think we'd all prefer to remember her as she had been alive. We will arrange for some pictures to set up around the casket for people to remember her by, though."

"That's perfectly acceptable."

As we left the funeral home and headed back to our house, there was complete silence in the car. No one spoke. Each of us lost in our own thoughts. I couldn't help but remember my conversations with Mrs. Mower. I decided another trip out to see Chris was in order after the funeral.

~~~

Chapter 9

THE FUNERAL day brought us a bright beautiful morning with lots of sun and a few wispy clouds. It was the kind of day Charlie would have loved. Both Mia and I got up early and showered. I wore a dark blue suit with a light blue shirt and a blue and white striped tie that matched the suit. Mia dressed in a black dress, with white piping along the sides and the front. The dress flared out at the waist and reached her knees. She wore a pair of leather high-heeled shoes that she only wore on special occasions. By the time we were finished dressing and sitting at the kitchen table, Tony arrived, dressed in a black suit, a white shirt, and black tie. He poured himself a cup of coffee and joined us at the table.

We arrived at the funeral home just before eight o'clock in order to greet those who were coming to the funeral. Mr. Teitelbaum showed us to the parlor where Charlie's casket was set up. The Chapel was larger than we remembered. There were white chairs set up in neat rows with an aisle down the center. Charlie's mahogany casket had a wreath on top of it—white carnations and pink roses, a 'Rest in Peace' ribbon across the middle. It sat on a dais in front of the chairs. Off to the left was the podium where the preacher would give the service. The room was filled with flowers, and the aroma of all the flowers sent in by well-wishers was almost overpowering.

They were beautiful, and we walked around reading the cards to see who had sent them. We all knew that Charlie was very popular but we didn't really realize that she knew so many people. To the right of the dais, there was a room for us to hold a reception after the funeral. The great many flowers filled that room as well.

Mr. Teitelbaum introduced us to the minister who would be doing the funeral. His name was Reverend John Dryer, and he was a tall thin man. He appeared to be in his late fifties and his head was mostly bald except for the half-moon of gray tuft circling his head. He wore black horned glasses around his neck on a chain. We shook hands all around. His hands were soft and smooth and his grip was gentle. His gray eyes were soft and understanding. As if he knew our pain.

"I've added a few other Scriptures aside from the ones you've chosen if you don't mind my taking the liberty to do so," Reverend Dryer said.

"I'm sure whatever you've chosen will be fine," I told him. I was in no state to make decisions, and I assumed he knew what was best under the circumstances.

I told him, "There is one thing I'd like to request though. Even though her given name was Charlene, she always went by the name 'Charlie'. I was wondering if you could please use that name during the funeral."

"Certainly, I'd be happy to do that," Reverend Dryer agreed.

A large number of people had already begun to arrive, and the room filled up quickly. Tony, Mia, and I stood by the casket and accepted condolences from those who entered the room. Many were from Cloverdale. Many were simply friends she had made along the way. I felt numb inside and found myself lost in the pictures that were placed alongside the casket, trying to release my mind of the horrible sight of her face when I last saw her. I too wanted to remember her like she was alive, and I wanted to completely erase the memory of her beaten face from my mind. The pictures of my beautiful sister with her long curly hair running down to her shoulders and a smile that melted your heart. Her skin, soft and tan and her eyes, big and brown with long black lashes. She looked beautiful in whatever she wore. And her heart was so loving and compassionate that no one could help liking her. I felt a stinging in my eye as I stared at the picture, the tears beginning to roll down my cheeks. I missed her so much it hurt in every corner of my being. Mia stood beside me with her cheeks quietly streaming with tears. Tony stood on the other side of Mia. I saw him staring at Charlie's picture, I wondered what was going through his mind. This loss brought a pain too unbearable for us all. We stood as stoically as possible while we greeted well-wishers who then took their seats. I had filled my pockets with Kleenexes, and I knew both Mia and Tony had done so too, but it seemed there weren't enough Kleenexes in the world to wipe away our tears that day. Many in the crowd were crying as well, and it took all I had to remain in that place, beside the beautiful mahogany casket; even in death, she was beautiful as she was in life.

As the chairs begun being occupied and it got closer to nine o'clock, Mr. Teitelbaum showed us all to our seats in the front row. When the Reverend appeared at the podium, the room fell silent. A melancholic silence that seemed to bring the world around us to a standstill. A silence that I found myself lost in. I barely heard the Reverend as he spoke.

"Psalms 119:50; *This is my comfort in my affliction, that your promise gives me life,"* he began.

I could hear Mia crying softly to herself, and I swiftly handed her a tissue. Tears were shed by both Tony and myself.

The Reverend went on and talked about Charlie and how popular she was.

"She volunteered at the Cloverdale Rehabilitation Center, helping children to learn reading. She taught children at the library to read as well. She was a teacher at Crocker Elementary School and loved her job. She was dedicated to children and to teaching them a better way of life. She was always there for them. Just as we are here for her now."

I wasn't sure how he knew all that and could only attribute it to our conversation with Mr. Teitelbaum. The room was filled to capacity and many people were crying along with us.

The Reverend gave a quick sermon and added a few more Bible verses in it, but I could only hear half of what he was saying. My tears and my angst kept me from truly understanding what he said. He concluded the service and told those in attendance that there would be a short graveside ceremony. He walked down the center aisle, and Mia, Tony, and I followed as the pall bearers brought the casket down the aisle.

In turn, each row of seats emptied and followed us out into the sunlight and to the gravesite.

There was a green tent set up with white folding chairs under it. Mia, Tony, and I took our places at the first three seats in front. The pall bearers had placed the casket at the gravesite, and the Reverend waited until everyone was situated before he began the ceremony.

"Romans 14:7-9; *For none of us lives to himself, and none of us dies to himself. For if we live, we live to the Lord, and if we die, we die to the Lord. So then, whether we live or whether we die, we are the Lord's. For to this end Christ died and lived again, that He might be Lord both of the dead and the living.*"

It was as if my ears had suddenly opened and I could hear the Reverend. I was no longer numb…simply sad and miserable. I held Mia as she cried. They had brought a stunning picture of Charlie out to the gravesite, and I found myself staring at it. Memorizing it. Wiping out the awful picture of her from the the morgue. The Reverend went on to say a few more words and ended with a final Scripture:

"Ecclesiastes 3:1-2; *For everything there is a season, and a time for every matter under heaven: a time to be born, and a time to die; a time to plant, and a time to pluck up what is planted.*"

The Reverend finished the graveside service with the *Our Father* prayer. We all waited as they lowered the casket into the grave. Tony, Mia, and I each threw a rose on top of the casket. Those in attendance followed suit.

Reverend Dryer announced that a reception would be held in the room to the right of the dais, and anyone who cared to share their condolences were welcome to come. Many of the people gave each of us a hug and told us how sorry they were or how much Charlie would be missed. Turning around, I saw both Chief Denault and Lieutenant Dintzman standing across the grave. I also saw Chris Bradley standing at the side, waiting for his chance to speak with us. Sergeant Rodgers was also in attendance. Many of the people I recognized were from Cloverdale.

Mia, Tony, and I headed back to the Chapel for the reception.

Mr. Teitelbaum stopped me for a moment, gently tapping on my arm. "Would you like to use the flowers in the Chapel to cover the grave?"

I could barely speak but I managed to tell him that would be fine. There simply wasn't enough room in our house for all the flowers.

He told me he would take care of it once the reception was over, and I thanked him solemnly.

As we entered the reception area, I was amazed at how many people were there and the amount of food that had been brought by well-wishers. We spoke to as many people as we possibly could. The Chief and Lieutenant both attended the reception as well, which surprised me. I spoke to each of them briefly and thanked them both for showing up.

As the reception neared its end, many people hugged us and said their goodbyes. Everyone we spoke to said that the funeral was beautiful and we thanked them all, one by one.

A thin woman of medium height, dressed in black approached me. I assumed her to be around my age. She had short blond hair styled in a bob. Her face was long and her nose was pointed and sloped. I could see she'd been crying. She had what appeared to be a rumpled tissue in her right hand and gave me a big hug and held herself close to me. I couldn't remember where I had seen her before, but I had seen so many people that day, the faces and names were starting to run together.

She whispered softly in my ear, "I don't know if you remember me nor not. My name is Marlene Dillman, and I worked with Charlie at Cloverdale."

Upon hearing her name, I immediately recollected who she was. We had only met a few times, but she was a wonderful person—full of love and care for the children at Cloverdale. "Yes, I remember you. Charlie spoke very highly of you."

I could hear her sob several times. She continued to hug me, whispering in my ear, "I have something I need to talk to you about. It's about Charlie's death."

She pulled back from the hug and took my right hand in both of hers, as though we were shaking hands. Tears welled up in her eyes, making the blues of it look like a pool. Her voice was low. She said, "Take this. It's my name and telephone numbers of where you can reach me. Call me day or night. But I know you're a police officer and that you want to know what happened, and I may be able to help." She slipped the crumpled paper into my hand, and I immediately covered it with my own.

I placed the paper in the outer pocket of my suit, and she gave me another hug. As we hugged, I looked up and saw both the Chief and the Lieutenant watching us. I dried her tears with my thumb.

"Thank you," I said to her. I was puzzled and I'm sure Marlene knew I was, but we went about our business as if she were simply offering me her condolences.

"I have to leave now. Please don't forget."

"I won't." I watched as she walked out the Chapel doors.

It was after five when we finally got home from the funeral home. We were all amazed at the number of people who showed up the for the service. While I hadn't got a chance to talk to Chris, I planned to as soon possible.

"What are we going to do with all this food?" Mia said, kicking off her high heeled shoes and flinging them under the table.

There were casseroles, mostaccioli, seven-layer salads, as well as various other kinds of salads. Our kitchen table and counters were covered with various casseroles and dishes.

"Wow," Tony said, surveying all the food. He picked up the aluminum foil covering one of the dishes. "This looks like a tuna casserole." He lifted another. "Marconi and Cheese."

Most of the casseroles had been partially eaten by the guests, but many were left intact.

"I don't think this is all going to fit in our refrigerator," Mia said looking around the kitchen.

Tony said, "I can take some of it off your hands, but I'll leave the tuna casserole to you.

Mia began looking through the cabinets in search of storage containers and lids to put the food in. "We can split a lot of this up," she said, mostly to Tony. "We could eat for a month on all this stuff."

She found the containers she was looking for, and we began filling them with separate casseroles—half for us, half for Tony—not the tuna casserole though. It took close to an hour for all three of us to go through all the food and separate it into containers. Afterwards, Mia washed all the dishes.

When she was finished, the lonely tuna casserole sat on our kitchen table. It appeared that nobody liked tuna casserole. Even though Charlie and I had grown up on it, I had lost my taste for tuna. We all stood and started at the casserole as if it were some foreign object that had landed there by accident.

Mia finally broke the silence. "Someone went through all the time and trouble to make this, and I'd hate to throw it away. But none of us likes tuna casserole."

Tony said, "Why don't you pack it up and I'll see if anyone

in my crew likes tuna. If so, I'll give it to them. Otherwise, I guess we'll throw it away."

No one moved. It was as if no one wanted to touch it. Finally, Mia brought out a large container and filled it with the casserole and sealed it with a lid.

"It's all yours, Tony," she said, handing him the container.

"I think I could use some wine right about now," Mia said plopping down at the kitchen table.

Tony and I fully supported the idea. So, we took out a bottle of Arbor Mist White Zinfandel, Exotic Fruits and poured us each a glass. We sat at the table in silence as we each drank our wine and held up our glasses to Charlie's memory.

"I suppose we'll need to write Thank You notes to all the people who sent flowers and food," Mia said staring into her wine glass. "And I need to return these dishes back to the rightful owners."

"Oh yeah, I forgot to tell you," I said, "Mr. Teitelbaum gave me all the cards from all the flowers and from the people who sent us food." I still had my suit on. Reaching into my pocket to retrieve the envelopes, I came across the note from Marlene Tillman.

"What's this?" Mia picked up the crumpled paper and unfolded it. "Who's Marlene Tillman?"

"She used to work with Charlie at Cloverdale," I told her. "She came up to me during the reception and handed me this piece of paper, telling me to contact her. She said she had some information related to Charlie's death."

"That's odd," Mia said, still looking at the paper.

"I know she gave me all these phone numbers to contact her at, so I'm going to give her a call the first chance I get," I said. Mia handed the paper to Tony who studied it with great care. He checked the front. Then, he checked the back. "She gave you no clue what it was about?"

"She said she had some information for me, but she slid it into my hand like she didn't want anyone to notice it."

"Well, this whole thing is full of oddities," Tony said, handing me back the paper.

I agreed with Tony. So did Mia. We sat at the table, drinking wine and talking about Charlie, the funeral, and how well it went. It wasn't until after eleven o'clock that Tony finally left. I guessed he just didn't want to be alone with his thoughts. We had offered him to stay over, but he insisted on going home. We were all tired and exhausted from the emotional roller coaster of a day.

Mia and I slowly made it to the bedroom and changed out of our good clothes and lay beside each other in bed. I wrapped my arm around her and she lay on her side, rubbing my chest. There was little left to say that hadn't already been said while at the kitchen table. We wallowed in the peace and comfort of each other's arms, until exhaustion overtook us, and we both fell into a sound sleep.

~~~

Chapter 10

THE FOLLOWING Monday I received a call from Miles Kuhns, the attorney who handled both Charlie's and my trust fund. He worked in one of the largest law firms in the area, which dealt with everything ranging from trusts, wills, investments, divorces, and criminal cases to any other actions that would require an attorney. Miles Kuhn not only handled the trust fund our parents set up for us, but he also created the wills for both Charlie and me. He wanted to meet with Tony, Mia, and me for the reading of the will and discuss Charlie's trust fund. Since Mia hadn't returned to work yet, I made the appointment for Wednesday, ten in the morning. When I got off the phone with Miles, I called Tony and informed him about the appointment. He confirmed he would be there.

While I was on the phone with Tony, I also asked him if he wanted to go over to Charlie's condo to see if there was anything salvageable after the police department seizing almost everything. Plus, I wanted to secure the door and pick up her car, so it was not simply sitting idle in the parking lot where it could get damaged or stolen.

"Do you want to go with us?" I asked Mia. "We're going to bring her car back, so you can drive that back here. And then, we can get all her clothes out of there too."

"I'll go," she said, sounding apprehensive. "I need

something to do to keep my mind off everything that has happened, and I'll feel like I'm doing something."

Tony showed up just after one in the afternoon, and we decided to ride over in the *Bronco* while Tony drove his BMW. I put some boxes in the back of the truck in case we needed to box things up.

The day was cloudy and gray, and the overcast sky promised of rain. Both Tony and I found a parking spot relatively close to Charlie's place and we made way to her unit. I swung the door open. We all stood at the threshold gazing at the destruction that was once a finely furnished home. I looked around, and there was no change in the place since the last time we were there. I heard thunder roaring outside, sounding like it came from behind us. Slowly, we entered the house one by one and looked around.

"So, what are we looking for exactly?" Tony asked, surveying the devastation.

"Anything salvageable," I told him and Mia both. "Mia, why don't you start in the bedroom and start gathering up her clothes. We'll take them and place them at back of the *Bronco*. Check her drawers for any jewelry or anything intact that we may want to keep."

I turned to Tony. "Why don't you and I comb through the living room and kitchen? I'm sure there are dishes and stuff we can pack and take with us. Take your pick. I brought boxes for her dishes and crockery."

Tony chose to go through the kitchen and began opening cabinets and drawers methodically. "Looks like they didn't touch any of the stuff in the kitchen. There are lots of dishes and silverware and a bunch of pots and pans."

Once Upon a Charlie

"I've got some boxes in the *Bronco* if you want to start packing them up," I told Tony.

He went down to the *Bronco* and brought the boxes. Within minutes, he was busy packing the utensils up.

"Why don't you put the dishes and the pots and pans all on the kitchen table and on the counters, for now."

I started going through Charlie's desk. Other than the contents the police technicians had strewn across the desk, there was really nothing of interest.

Mia came out of the bedroom. "I put all her clothes on hangers and arranged them on the bed in neat piles. I went through her dresser drawers, and apparently, the police had already gone through them. I took what clothes she had in them and folded them back up and put them with the rest of her stuff. I did find this picture at the back of one of her bedside table drawers. It was way back there, and I almost missed it." She handed me a photo of a small girl who appeared to be about nine or ten."

She had dirty dishwater blond hair, and it looked uncombed and entangled. She had bangs and wore light blue glasses covering her green eyes. Charlie had her arm around her, and they were both smiling, although the small girl's smile appeared forced, as if she didn't want her picture taken. There was a small blue first-place ribbon in the girl's hand.

"Who is she?" Mia asked. "Do you know her?"

Shaking my head, I replied, "Probably one of the girls from Cloverdale she worked with. Let's hold on to this." I placed the picture in my shirt pocket and continued going through the desk.

"Oh my god," Mia said, walking over toward the kitchen, "it's Charlie's purse. Look what they did to it! They threw everything out of it and emptied her wallet of all the pictures and credit cards. Why would they do that?" She stooped down and looked at the assortment of pens, pencils, Kleenexes, lipstick, and more scattered there.

I walked over to where Mia stood and looked down. "Standard police procedure," I told her. "They have to take everything they think is important to a murder investigation."

"How would the pictures help? They were just pictures of the kids she worked with. What good will that do?" Mia was completely enraged over what the investigators had done. "Isn't it bad enough that they ruined her entire house, they had to take everything in her purse…her pictures…her money? What good is that going to be in finding the killer?" She was now yelling as she went through the stuff lying on the floor. "This is absolutely ridiculous!" She stood up and surveyed the room with her hands on her hips.

"Look what they did to her beautiful coffee table! Oh my God, they broke her beautiful orange crystal candy dish. Look at that. There's candy everywhere." She bent down to pick up the broken pieces and I watched her carefully, hoping she wouldn't cut herself in her blinding anger.

I could hear the thunder getting louder outside as if it was being fueled by Mia's rage.

From the corner of my eye, I saw Tony starting to make his way over to Mia, but I held up my palm, motioning him to stay back. "Give her a minute. She needs this," I told him softly.

"Don't we all," Tony said, nodding, as sadness spread across his face.

The two of us stood and watched as Mia ranted and raved.

I knew that Mia had a temper, but I'd never seen her this livid before.

"And what about her bedroom!" Mia was practically shouting at this point. "They took all her clothes from her dressers and threw them everywhere. I don't even know what's clean or what's dirty. I don't give a shit about police procedures. They had no right going through all her drawers and throwing everything on the floor. What the fuck is going on here, Cole?"

"We don't know what happened exactly. She may have interrupted a burglary in progress, and the guy beat her up," I said, trying to calm her, but I knew it was useless at this point.

"That doesn't give the police the right to destroy her condo. Look at all this. It's all ruined. Charlie's beautiful place is nothing but a wrecked dreadful mess, and we don't even know why."

I saw a tear escape her eye and I immediately went toward her. I took the pieces of the candy dish from her, placed them down, and held her in my arms. She wrapped her arms around my waist, holding on tight as if she were drowning. She didn't cry. She seemed too angry to cry. Lightening flashed across the sky, lighting up the room for a moment, and thunder reared its ugly head as we stood there holding each other.

"Once this is all over, we'll get the stuff back," I told her.

"It just makes me so mad," she screamed into my chest. She pulled her head back and looked up at me. More gently, she said, "Why did they have to take her pictures too? It's not like Charlie had a bunch of expensive paintings or anything. They were beautiful pictures and they took them away from her…from us. It just really pisses me off."

"I know. Me too. But Chris is working the case, and you know Chris will do everything he can to find the killer. Plus, Tony and I will be looking for the killer too."

"But the Chief said you had to stay away from the investigation," Mia said, frustration dripping through her words.

"That's okay. I don't give a rat's ass what the Chief says. We're going to find out what happened come hell or high water."

At some point, Tony had edged closed to us but did not disturb our hug.

Tony looked down at Charlie's purse as well. "Don't worry Mia. We're gonna find him. You have my word."

I heard a small knock on the door. I slid out of Mia's arms and went to the door. I looked through the peephole before opening it. It was Mrs. Mower. I opened the door.

"Hello, Cole," she said in a quiet voice, trying to peek at the house around me.

"Hello, Mrs. Mower. What can I help you with?"

"Well…Cole, the last time you were here, you said you might want to talk to me and I was wondering if you wanted to talk to me today, seeing's how you're here and all."

I immediately remembered that conversation and thought it be the perfect time to gain some information from her.

"Yes, that would be great. I'd most certainly like that," I told her. "It would be best if we did it at your place though, because as you can see, Charlie's place is a real mess, and I don't think you'd want to see it. We need to load up the cars with some of Charlie's stuff and then we'll be over right away."

"That's fine, honey. Do your friends want to come along? I have some freshly baked cookies, and I have a fresh pot of coffee brewing. Please come along whenever you like. I'm not going anywhere."

I thanked her and told her we'd be over in a bit.

"I didn't know you talked to her earlier," Mia said.

"Yeah. The other day when we came to get something for Charlie to wear, I ran into her. She told me she had called 911 the night that Charlie got murdered."

We grabbed what we could of Charlie's clothes and put them in the truck. It was beginning to rain, and streaks of lightening lit up the sky. We left the dishes and the crockery on the counters with a promise to come back with more boxes to cart them home.

"So, you think we may be able to get some answers from the neighbor?" Tony asked with a knowing look on his face.

"That's exactly what I think. As you may recall, Chris told me there was no 911 call made that night. The last time I was here she told me she had dialed 911 the night Charlie got killed."

"I do believe it's cookie and coffee time then," Tony said as we walked toward Mrs. Mower's door.

There was a shared balcony along the front of the condos, while each unit had its own balcony in the back.

We walked to Mrs. Mower's door and knocked lightly on the door. Mrs. Mower came to the door. We were instantaneously overtaken by the smell of freshly baked cookies. Her condo was the exact opposite of Charlie's. Her furniture was threadbare and old. The tables were made of oak and she had two table lamps on each end of the couch. On the wall opposite the couch was a flat screen television and on the coffee table lay a remote for the television along with the *TV*

Guide. She had put on some lipstick and fixed her hair. She was wearing a pair of synthetic navy-blue trousers with a long-sleeved flowery shirt that she had left untucked. Introductions were made, and she told us to call her by her first name, Evelyn.

She stared at Tony for a moment and pointed a bony index finger at him. "I know you. You're Charlie's fiancée. I used to see you coming and going all the time."

"Yes ma'am. I was Charlie's fiancée."

"Oh, come now. There's no need for this ma'am business. I told you, just call me Evelyn. And you," Evelyn went over to Mia and placed her hands on each of Mia's cheeks. "You're such a beautiful woman. I'm telling you, that Cole is a lucky guy to have someone so beautiful. And I'll bet you're smart too."

Mia blushed. "Well, I'm not sure about being smart or anything. But thank you for your kind words."

"I have cookies and coffee all set up on the kitchen table if you'd care to join me. I'm also cooking some beef stew for my son, Eugene. It's his favorite. He's such a good boy. He takes really good care of me."

We all followed her into the kitchen. In the center stood an old oak table with six chairs placed around the table. The chairs were all spindle chairs and they looked worn. There was a white table cloth on the table and a plate of delicious-looking cookies of different varieties. She handed us each a small plate and began pouring us steaming cups of coffee. There was sugar and cream by the coffee set next to the cookies.

"It's a real shame about Charlie," Evelyn said. "You said you wanted to talk to me, but I don't know what kind of help I can give you. I've already talked to the police and told them everything I know. But I suppose you already know that, being a policeman yourself and everything."

We each took a cookie from the plate.

"If you'll excuse me for just a moment, I need to stir my stew." Evelyn got up from the table and stirred the contents of the large silver pot that was set on the back burner of the stove. "Almost ready," she said returning to the table.

"Beef stew is Eugene's favorite, so I try to make it for him as much as possible. There's always plenty left over for him to take home and heat up later. I don't suppose you've ever met him. He's a good boy. He really takes care of me. He went to Harvard, you know. He's got a Master's in Accounting and works for this big accounting firm downtown. I can never remember the name." She put her index finger over her lip and looked up as though she'd find the answer in the ceiling. "I think its Tobin, Mackey, and Mower…umm, or something like that. Anyway, he's the one that got this condo for me to live in, and he helps me pay my bills and manages my money for me. I'm on a fixed income, you know. Oh!" She stood abruptly from her chair, stirred the stew, and left the room saying, "Let me show you his picture. He's such a handsome man too. He has a girlfriend, but she works long hours."

As we waited for Evelyn to return to the kitchen, we all stared awkwardly at each other. I shrugged my shoulders while Tony shook his head. The cookies were good; I happened to pick out a peanut butter cookie. I placed it on my plate and took a sip of my coffee.

"Here it is," Evelyn said as she walked back into the kitchen, picture in hand. "This is his graduation picture. Did I tell you he graduated from Harvard? And with honors too."

She handed me the picture. Eugene was wearing a black graduation gown with a red hood and a cap—the kind with a tassel. He had dark hair and brown eyes. He had a strong face with a turned-up nose. It appeared like his ears stuck out from his head farther than normal, but that could've been from the cap. He wore round wire-rimmed glasses and looked like an accountant.

"I keep his picture on my bed table, so I can see him every night before going to sleep and each morning when I wake up. Such a handsome young man. He's dating this beautiful young lady. Anna her name is. She has beautiful long blond hair that she curls up nice and pretty. They've been dating for two years now, and I do hope that they will get married someday and have babies. She's a bank manager for some big bank downtown. I guess that's where they met. I know they've been contemplating marriage recently," she said, then whispered, "Eugene told me, but I don't think I'm supposed to know that. He probably wants it to be a surprise, and he's so afraid I'll say something ahead of time."

She got up from the table and stirred the pot again.

"Wait," she said, and it startled us all a bit as she left the table again. "I think I have a picture of them together. I'll be right back," she trailed as she went off into the unknown room again.

We waited patiently for her to return to the kitchen. She held an eight-by-ten black photo frame and handed it to us.

"This is Anna and Eugene. Don't they make such a wonderful couple? This was taken last year on Valentine's Day."

"She really is very pretty," Mia said handing the picture to me.

Once Upon a Charlie

Eugene looked much like his graduation picture, only he was dressed differently. In front of him sat a beautiful young woman with blond hair curled up at her shoulders. She had deep blue eyes and long lashes. Her makeup was perfectly done, with just a touch of blush. They were both smiling, and her teeth were pearly and perfect. I couldn't help but wonder how many years it must've taken to get them that straight. They looked like the 'perfect couple,' the kind you see in Ralph Lauren commercials and magazines. I handed the picture to Tony. We all complimented Evelyn on how wonderful they looked.

"A perfect match," Evelyn said, as Tony handed her back the photograph. "Let me put this away before I forget."

We watched Evelyn leave once again. We all looked around the table, ate a few more cookies and drank some more coffee.

Tony leaned toward me and Mia and whispered, "That woman could talk to a dead deer on the side of the road."

We all snickered quietly, to not let Evelyn notice.

On Evelyn reentering the kitchen, she stirred the pot once more. We all took a sip of our coffee almost simultaneously in an attempt to not laugh at Tony's jest.

"It would be so wonderful if they got married. I'd love to have some grandbabies sometime soon."

"Yeah, kids are a lot of fun," Tony said, grabbing another cookie from the plate.

"He's my only child, you know. I wanted more, but my husband only wanted to have one child. He wanted a boy to carry on the family name. It would just be so wonderful if Anna and Eugene got married."

Once again, Evelyn got up and stirred the stew and turned

the burner flame low. "I think it's done. Now, it just needs to sit and stay warm until Eugene gets here."

Evelyn sat down at the table and looked at me, "So you said you had some questions for me?"

"Yes, I do. It's about the night Charlie was murdered. You told me that you called 911, is that right?" I asked, hoping that she wasn't confused about all that went on that night. I pulled out my notepad to take notes.

"I most certainly did," she said proudly, as if pressing those three numbers on the telephone had fulfilled all her civic duties. "Well, first I didn't know what to do. I heard all this banging and yelling and screaming. For a minute, I thought that I should go over and help the poor girl. But I'm just an old little lady. What could I do? So, I call Eugene and told him what was going on, and he's the one who told me to dial 911."

Mia spoke up quickly before I had a chance to say anything. "It's a good thing you didn't go over there. You could have been killed yourself."

"That's exactly what Eugene said. He told me to call the police and stay inside. But it was horrible. I felt so helpless. All that screaming and banging."

"Do you remember what time you called 911?"

"Let me think for a moment…I think it was right before eleven o'clock—maybe ten forty-five or so."

"Did you see anything or anyone?" I asked.

She was quiet for a moment and pursed her lips. She took a moment to look around at each of us before she answered. Her voice was barely more than a whisper, and she put her hands around her lips, as if scared that someone else was going to hear what she had to say. Her eyes were moving back and forth as she spoke, "I saw this really big black man in the parking lot. Now I'm not prejudiced or anything, but it's just that I've never seen him before."

"Do you remember what he looked like? Or what car he drove?"

"He was tall and completely bald, and he was dressed all in black. Why if it weren't for the headlights that pulled into the parking lot, I'd never have seen him."

"What about his car? Did you see the car he drove?"

"Oh, my heavens, no. There's so many cars coming and going all at hours of the day and night…there's just no way for me to tell which one was his."

"What time did you see him in the parking lot?"

"Oh, my I think it was ten thirty…or around then, because I was just about to get into bed. I will tell you this. I do remember seeing a police car out there in the parking lot, and the Chief and some Lieutenant was there too."

We all shared glances at each other around the table.

"When did you see the police car?"

"It was just before I saw him. I thought that one of the neighbors called the police on him because he was…" she cupped her hand on the side of her mouth again as if it were a secret, "…black. We don't get too many of them here."

"So, did the police officer talk to this man you saw?"

"Yes. They talked for a little while, and then the police car went around to the side parking lot. But that man was still here. He didn't leave."

"Is there a chance he lives in one of these condos?" Tony asked.

"I don't think so. I know most people who live here, and I've never seen him before."

"So, let me get this straight. You saw a black male in your parking lot around ten thirty, and then fifteen minutes later, you heard the 'screaming and banging' from Charlie's apartment." The thunder clapped a moment after lightning lit up the sky, almost emphasizing my words.

"Yes. That's exactly correct. And after that, I called Eugene and he told me to call the police so I dialed 911."

I reached in my wallet and pulled out one of my cards and wrote my cell phone number on the back of it and slid it to Evelyn.

"If you remember anything else, please call me. It's very important."

She gave me a half smile and promised to do so.

We thanked her for the coffee and cookies and headed out. "What are you going to do with Charlie's apartment?" she asked from behind.

"Tony here does rehab work on old homes. He's going to get it fixed up again, and we're probably going to sell it."

"Please keep in touch," Evelyn said as she opened the door for us. She gave us each a hug, and we left silently out the door in single file.

I handed Charlie's car keys to Mia. "Here, you drive her car back to our house and I'll drive ours."

We gathered in a small circle around Charlie's car.

"So, what do you think?" Tony asked looking up at Evelyn's condo.

"I think we have a problem," I said looking at both of them, "We have a big problem."

"Yeah, what she said doesn't exactly match what Chris told you, does it…" Tony said it more as a statement than a question.

"No. It doesn't," I said, beginning to wonder if I could trust Chris anymore.

We all got in our cars and to head home. We needed answers, and the ones we were getting were just not good enough.

~~~

Chapter 11

I SLEPT restlessly as Evelyn's words kept swirling, round and round, in my head. I tossed and turned all night, until I finally got up around two thirty in the morning and went to the living room to look over my notes from our talk with Evelyn and the two pictures we had found in Charlie's apartment. I couldn't make any sense out of what Chris had told me and what Evelyn had said. Both accounts were poles apart. Yet, I knew Chris was my friend and he wouldn't lie to me. So, does that mean Evelyn was just a senile old woman who didn't remember things very clearly? But she seemed so sharp at the time we talked, and there were the pictures of the little girls we found. What did it all mean?

Mia walked into the living room and stood in the long pink T-shirt dress that she wore to sleep. Her hair was askew from the pillow and her eyes were tired. "Are you okay?"

"Yeah. I'm fine," I told her.

She walked over to the couch and sat on the edge of the cushion next to me. "What's bothering you?"

She knew me well. "I was just going over all that stuff that Evelyn told us and was comparing it to what Chris told me. It's just doesn't add up. Not to mention the two pictures we found."

"I know. But I also know you'll figure it all out, too. That's what makes you such a good cop. You figure stuff like this out."

I shook my head and flipped through my notes again. "I'm going to go see Chris tomorrow and see what he has to say. He told me no 911 calls were made, and no radio calls went out, but then, how did all the police get there? I can't see any reason why he would lie to me about it."

She put an arm around my neck and gave me a hug. "Who knows? Maybe Evelyn was just confused. Maybe you misunderstood what Chris said to you. You were pretty upset the day you talked to him. I'm sure by tomorrow after you talk to him, you'll have it all figured out."

I turned toward her and gave her a peck. "Why don't you go back to bed? I'll be coming back to bed soon."

She gave me a quick smile. "Okay. But don't stay up all night. You need to get some sleep."

"I know."

She kissed me on the cheek and went back to the bedroom.

I shut my notepad and followed Mia. She was right. If there was any hope of me figuring this out, I needed to get some rest.

The next morning it was still pouring, and the skies were gray with clouds, which only served to match my mood. I glanced at the clock on the bedside table and the large blue digits read six forty-eight. I could hear the coffee pot brewing in the kitchen, and the aroma wafted through the air and tickled at my taste buds. Mia was still sound asleep. I got out of bed and headed for the kitchen to wait for the coffee to finish brewing. I stared out the patio window and watched blades of grass bend under the rain. I sat down at the kitchen table with mugs for our coffee as well as the cream and the sugar.

Once Upon a Charlie

By the time the coffee was done, Mia had come out from the bedroom looking much like she did last night. Her hair looked like she had teased it on one side, and her eyes were still droopy from sleep.

"Good morning, sweetie," she said and gave me a kiss on the lips. They were soft and warm and it felt good.

"Coffee should be ready," I told her.

"Were you able to get any sleep at all last night?"

"Yeah, a little. I came back to bed right after you, but it was still a fitful sleep."

"I'm sorry," she said, her eyes filled with innocent honesty.

"It's okay. It's not your fault. You didn't do anything."

"I know. I just feel bad, because you didn't get much sleep."

I poured us each a cup of coffee, and we sat at the table and drank our coffee.

"So, what's your plan for today…besides seeing Chris?"

"I think I'm going to call Marlene Tillman from Cloverdale before I leave and see what she has to say. I'll see her after I talk to Chris."

We each took a sip of coffee. Mia said, "I have a big day ahead of writing thank you notes to all the people who send flowers and food for Charlie's funeral."

"I'm sorry, baby. I should really be there to help you with that," I told her.

"Don't worry about it. I really don't mind. You do what you have to do. I'll take care of those."

"Yeah, but there are so many to write."

"I don't mind. Really. It'll give me something to do for today, and it kinda makes me feel closer to Charlie in a weird way. Does that make sense?"

"It actually does. You'll be doing something that Charlie herself would do if she could. I understand."

"Oh, and don't forget, tomorrow ten o'clock. We have an appointment with Miles Kuhn."

"Oh my god. I'm so glad you reminded me. I completely forgot. My mind's been wandering in so many different directions that I've lost track of days and time. I'll make sure Tony remembers too."

I went in and showered, hoping that it would wake me up a little more. I dressed in a pair of jeans, a polo, and tennis shoes and headed back to the kitchen. Mia was still sitting at the table, drinking her coffee and doing her best to wake up properly. It was just after nine, so I decided I'd get an early start and head toward the police station to see if Chris was there. Before I left, I called Marlene Dillman at Cloverdale to see if she'd be in later that afternoon. She said she would and that she was fine with seeing me any time I got there. She told me to just ask for her at the front desk, and they would page her. I gave Mia a kiss on the lips, told her I loved her, then grabbed my cell phone and keys, and headed for the *Bronco*. As I was getting into my truck, my cell phone rang. It was Tony.

I picked up the phone and heard his voice. "What's going on today?" he asked.

"Well, right now, I'm headed to the station to talk to Chris again. And then, I'm going to Cloverdale to talk to Marlene."

There was a slight pause before he said, "You want some company?"

"Sure," I said. "Let me talk to Chris, and then we can meet at my house or yours. Whichever one you prefer."

"I'll meet you at your place, and we can go over in my car."

He always offered to drive. I often wondered why, but I took it for what it was worth, because his BMW was certainly more comfortable than my *Bronco*. "That's fine."

I pulled out of the driveway and headed for the police station, still mulling over all the things that Evelyn had said and comparing it to what Chris had.

I parked in front of the police department and walked in through the front doors. The dispatchers buzzed me in and I headed straight to the detective bureau. I found Chris sitting at his desk with a cup of coffee in his hand. He looked much more rested than the last time I saw him, but the stack of papers on his desk seemed endless. His tweed jacket hung on the backrest of his chair.

"Good God, Chris, you're looking sharp today." I took a seat beside his desk.

"Yeah. I finally got some sleep. I'm inventorying all the stuff from your sister's place, so hopefully, we'll be able to give some of it back to you sometime soon."

I nodded my head. "Listen bud, you said that there was no code for the tapes from the night of the murder, is that right?"

Looking a little wary, he said, "Yeah. They told me there was nothing on the tapes and that there wasn't any dispatch. Why do you ask?"

"I was talking to one of Charlie's neighbors, and she said that she called 911 the night of the murder. So, I'm figuring if she called 911, then there ought to be something on the tapes."

"Did she call using a land line or a cell?"

"I honestly don't know. She's pretty old, so probably through a land line."

"Well, there you have it. She probably had a false memory

or something or maybe she imagined it. Maybe, she's all messed up in her head about what happened that night."

"I don't know, Chris. She was pretty sure she dialed 911." Again, I was beginning to wonder just how much I could trust Chris. I considered mentioning the two pictures we found in Charlie's apartment, but then thought better of it. I wanted to keep that to myself until I knew exactly where I stood with Chris.

"Well, all I know is there's no 7 Digit Code from St. Louis County, and there were no phone calls on the dispatch tape."

"I don't know, Chris. Something's not right here. Did you guys talk to her?"

He let out an audible sigh. "You know, you're not supposed to be involved in this case in any way, shape, or form, so I don't know why you're talking to Charlie's neighbors." He sounded like he was losing patience.

"I really don't give a shit if I'm not supposed to be involved. I'm not letting this go. Something's not right, and I want answers. Did you speak to this lady or not?"

Another sigh. "What's her name?"

"Mower. Evelyn Mower."

Chris started rummaging through the papers on his desk and pulled out one. "Yes. Looks like one of the patrolmen canvasing the building talked to her. And it does say in here that she claims to have called 911, but there was no call on tape."

"What about other neighbors? Did you guys talk to them? Did any of them call 911?"

Chris took off his glasses and laid them gently on his desk. "Look, that's all I'm going to give you. I wasn't supposed to even tell you what I just did. Just go home and leave us to work on the case. That's what we do. And besides, you've been ordered to not get involved, and that came directly from the Chief. So, stop investigating this and leave it be. You're going to get yourself in some deep shit over this. Just stop already."

I stared into his eyes and could see he meant what he was saying. I knew that my one source at the police department had just been cut off. I got up to leave.

"Cole," I heard Chris call after me, "I'm sorry. But I can't afford to lose my job. You just don't know what's going on here, and if you keep sticking your nose in this business, you're going to get hurt. So, stay back."

There was really nothing I could say to that. I wasn't going to cease my investigations, but Chris' words rang in my ears like a church bell. Did he know about the corruption within the police department and what it was? I gave him a solemn nod, and walked back to my car. It was still raining and the droplets felt good on my face.

~~~

From there, I went to Cloverdale to see Wilson Puckett. I decided to put off my visit with Marlene until I was with Tony. Also, I wanted a chance to talk to him about Lauren Stratford. I entered the front door and found the receptionist.

"May I help you?" Her voice was happy and carefree.

"Yes. My name is Cole Spencer, and I'd like to talk to Wilson Puckett if he's available."

Her brows furrowed together and her face turned grave. "Do you have an appointment?"

"No, I don't. I'm a police officer with the Palisades Police Department, and I came by to discuss the case of Lauren Stratford with him. I received the missing persons report on her, and I'm here to follow up on that."

There was a long pause, and her frown was still in place. "Well, let me see if he's available."

I could hear her speaking on the phone but couldn't hear the conversation. When she was finished, she put the receiver down and looked up at me with a hint of surprise in her eyes. "His secretary, Mrs. Brenda Turick, will be with you shortly. If you like, you may have a seat while you wait."

I sat on one of the chairs and leafed through an issue of *People Magazine,* but it couldn't hold my interest, so I placed it back. I only had to wait a few minutes before Mrs. Turick arrived. She was a tall heavy-set woman, but not what I'd call fat. She had blond hair, tied in a topknot, and there was a pencil balanced behind her ear. She wore pink horn-rimmed glasses that made her bright blue eyes look magnified. Her face was round and her cheeks were large as was her chin. She wore very little makeup. She looked like someone I probably wouldn't notice on the street.

She was very pleasant when she greeted me. She held out her hand to shake mine. "You must be Cole Spencer."

"Yes ma'am!"

"I understand that you're here about Lauren Stratford."

"Yes. I took a missing report on her, and I was wondering if I may speak with Mr. Puckett as a follow up to the report."

"Certainly. Please follow me to his office. It's right up these stairs." She led the way past her desk and into Mr. Puckett's door.

She knocked gently on the door, stepped inside, and announced my presence.

"He says you can go right in."

She closed the door behind me. The room was large, with an oversized desk and a great deal many file cabinets against the wall on the right. The colors on the wall were sober, and it gave a somewhat peaceful appearance.

"Mr. Spencer, it's so very nice to meet you." He stood and came around from his desk to shake my hand. He had a strong grip. He was a large man, taller than me by a few inches and had a barrel chest and a rather large stomach that hung over his belt line. His dark complexion resembled cracked asphalt, as it was filled with many lines and crow's feet.

"Always nice to meet one of our finest, as I always say," he said, returning to his cushy chair behind his desk. "Please have a seat," he said. "Now, tell me, what can I do for you?"

"Well, it seems that when Barbara Stratton came in to make the report, she did not have much information. She told me it was all kept in your office. I was wondering if perhaps you've heard from Lauren or if she's returned to Cloverdale."

"Yes, I like to keep the files under lock and key. Privacy Act and all, you know."

"I understand. Have you heard anything from her or about her?"

He pulled out a file from his desk drawer and placed it on his desk. "I'm afraid not. She's neither returned nor have we been able to find her despite our best efforts. There was a detective here about a week ago, following up as well. A…a Chris Bradley. Said he was a detective with the force. That's why I'm surprised to see you here asking about her."

"Well, it's what I do. And since I didn't get much information earlier, I thought I'd come by and check on her."

"I'm sorry, but I believe your trip has been in vain. I gave most of the information to Detective Bradley, and I know he's working very hard on the case."

"Well, that's good to know. Chris and I go back pretty far, and he's one of our best detectives, so I'll just leave it to him to investigate it. I'm sorry I bothered you."

"No. Please don't be sorry. We always welcome the police to stop by and visit, you know. talk to the kids. They do so enjoy that."

"Thank you for your time. I certainly appreciate your seeing me on such short notice."

"Not a problem. If you ever need anything, please feel free to call."

We shook hands again. "Thank you. I'll see myself out." I left, but why did I feel like I was being lied to?

I walked down the stairs and bid farewell to the receptionist. I also thought about going to see Marlene Dillman, but I knew Tony wanted to be there for it, so I headed toward my *Bronco* and drove home.

Chapter 12

BY THE time I arrived at home, the rain had stopped completely, and there was a promise of sunshine in the sky. I entered through the back door and found Tony and Mia sitting at the kitchen table, talking. Mia was drinking a soda and Tony had a beer bottle in his hands.

Mia got up from the table to give me a much-needed kiss. "Did you find out anything from Chris?"

"Hell no. He told me to keep my nose out of the investigation, and if I didn't, I could get hurt…whatever that meant."

"Did he say anything about the 911 call from the Mower lady?" Tony asked, chugging down the rest of his beer and setting the bottle aside. He was dressed in a pair of jeans and a shirt with the rolled up sleeves.

"Chris did say that, according to one of the patrol officers canvassing the area, Mrs. Mower said she had made the 911 call. Chis also said there was no record of any such call and that they talked to the other neighbors and canvassed the area, but he wants me out of this whole thing. His exact words were 'you're going to get hurt,' that is, if I keep sticking my nose in this case."

"So, what does that mean?" Tony asked as he got up to throw away the empty beer bottle.

I felt Mia's arm wrap around my waist and it was comforting to be near her. I laid my head against hers.

"I don't know. Whatever it is, Chris knows something but is not talking. We've pretty much been cut out of that aspect of our investigation."

Mia said, "I can't see what's so dangerous about investigating her murder. That doesn't make any sense to me."

"Me neither, but that's what he said. I guess now we should go see Marlene Dillman up at Cloverdale and see what she has to say. Mia, why don't you tag along with us?"

"I haven't finished the thank you notes yet," Mia said. But she was clearly torn between wanting to come and staying at home.

"It'll keep. I'll help you finish them tonight after we come back home."

A smile appeared her face and she agreed to come with us.

We all piled into Tony's car and headed for Cloverdale. It was only a ten-minute drive, but the place was huge and was situated on a bluff overlooking the Mississippi River. The institution sat on forty acres of land and had many buildings that made it difficult for visitors to locate the office. Fortunately, because I'd been there before earlier that day, I was able to give Tony directions to the office. There were at least six red-brick square buildings that looked like dorms. And then, there were several buildings that looked like colonial houses. It still took us a while to find the same office I had been to earlier.

We followed the sidewalk up to the building and went in. There was a large picture window covering the back wall and overlooking the river. There was patio furniture set up just outside the windows. There was a small woman sitting at the counter situated at the front of the room. She appeared to be about thirty and had subtle African American features. She had brown hair that was cut short and the sides were pulled back with combs. Her name plate stated her name to be Rachael Wright.

"Good afternoon," she said. She had a wide smile and her teeth were a brilliant white. "How may I help you?"

"We're here to see Marlene Dillman," I told her. "She asked us to come to the front desk and that you could page her."

"I most certainly can. I know she's come in today. I just saw here a few minutes ago. Let me call her office. May I have your name please?"

"My name is Cole Spencer. Marlene told me to come by because she had some information for me."

Rachael picked up the phone, dialed a four-digit number, and apparently received an answer from the other end. I heard my name being mentioned as Rachael spoke softly into the phone. After a minute, she hung up and looked at us.

"She said she'll be up in a minute. Please feel free to have a seat while you wait."

We all stood. It only took a few minutes for Marlene to appear at a side door that appeared to lead to a conference room.

"Cole," she said, recognizing me immediately. "I'm so glad you came." She gave me a hug. "And may I ask who your friends are?"

I introduced her to both Tony and Mia and explained how Tony was helping me with the investigation.

"I hope you don't mind me bringing them along," I said.

"Oh, no, no. That's absolutely fine."

I let out a small sigh of relief.

"I'm glad it stopped raining. We need to walk over to one of the dorms, and I forgot to bring my umbrella today."

I was curious as to what we needed to see in the dorms.

"Please follow me, if you don't mind."

We traveled as a group, down the sidewalks, until we reached one of the three-story red-brick dorms. The steel door had a lock on the outside, so Marlene brought her keys out and unlocked the door. We filed in—a single line—while Marlene held the door.

"We like to keep the doors locked," she said walking ahead. "It gives the children a sense of security that no one from the outside can just walk in. We only need to go up one set of stairs." Our steps echoed down the stairway. Once again, Marlene opened the door to another steel door that had 'Second Floor' written on it, and we all entered and waited for Marlene, as she made sure the door was closed securely. The hallway was filled with several doors leading to dorm rooms. Some of the doors were open, whereas others were closed. Each door was numbered. Marlene led us to dorm number 136. The door was closed, so Marlene knocked on it softly and then spoke to the door.

"Michelle? I have some people here I want you to meet?" She phrased it as a question rather than a statement.

Marlene turned to me and said, "Why don't you go in alone? I'm afraid it may frighten her to see all of you at once."

Marlene turned back to the door and spoke again. "Michelle, I'm bringing a friend in. I think you might like him."

She twisted the door knob, opened the door, and we stepped into the room. I did not know exactly what to expect.

Once Upon a Charlie

It was a typical dorm room with a bed on each side and two desks and two matching closets. There were laptops on each desk, but both were turned off. The only window in the room was a large window with wire set inside the panes of glass. The window was divided into four equal squares.

I glanced around the room, and had it not been for Marlene walking up to her, I may have missed Michelle altogether. She was sitting on her bed in the corner, her knees pulled up to her chin and her arms wrapped around her legs. She was wearing some kind of black stretchy pants and a dirty T-shirt. Her long hair was dirty and fell across her face as though she were using it as a shield to protect herself.

Marlene turned to me and spoke softly, "I don't expect you to be able to cure her or to really help her. But I thought maybe meeting Charlie's big brother may bring her out of her shell. She's been like this for several weeks. She isn't the first one we've had who's been in this state but none to this extent."

"What's caused this? Do you know?"

"I honestly have no idea. There are times when some of the police officers come over and take the kids out for ice cream or pizza. She had gone with a Lieutenant Dintzman, and she's been like this ever since she got back."

I showed Marlene the pictures we had found, and Marlene held them delicately in her fingers. "Yes, this is definitely Lauren Stanford, and this other one is Tina Little. Where did you get these from?"

"We found them in Charlie's condo while rooting through her things," I explained to her.

"Well unfortunately, none of us know what happened to Michelle. As for Tina, she's still here. And we usually don't have much problems with her, although I must admit that she's isolated herself from people to some extent."

"What do you mean by that?"

"Well, she used to be quite outgoing and happy. But now, it's almost like the air has been blown out of her bubble, if you know what I mean."

I nodded my head in response. "Have you had many runaways lately from the home?"

"As a matter of fact, we've been reviewing that, and there has been an increase in the number of girls that have run away from the home. But we just can't figure out why."

"Hopefully, we'll be able to figure that from her.

Marlene and I stepped closer to the bed. "Michelle? This is Charlie's older brother. His name is Cole. He wants to talk to you. He's a police officer."

Michelle immediately started shaking violently back and forth.

"How old is she?" I asked Marlene.

"She's only 15."

I moved closer to the bed and sat down on the side of the bed. "Michelle?" I tried to get her attention. "I was Charlie's older brother, and I'm not going to hurt you. I won't even touch you."

Again, her head shook violently back and forth, only this time she said, "No, no no!"

"No what, Michelle?" I asked her.

"No police."

"Has she said anything about the outing she went for with the Lieutenant?" I asked Marlene.

"No. As soon as she got back, she came directly to her room and has been this way ever since. The only time she comes out is to eat now."

I tried again. "Michelle you really liked Charlie, didn't you?"

I heard a mumble from her, but it was unintelligible.

"Did the Lieutenant hurt you when you went with him?"

Again, the violent head shaking.

I looked at Marlene. "I'm afraid I'm not getting anywhere. She's obviously afraid of police officers, and my being one is not helping at all."

"I'm afraid you're right," Marlene agreed.

"I have an idea, if you don't mind. I think that maybe if my wife Mia could come in and give it a try, she'll open up more to a woman rather than a man."

"We have a female psychologist on staff here, and she's been working with her. But she hasn't gotten anywhere either. I'm ready to try anything at this point."

I stepped out into the hallway and called Mia over. I explained the situation as well as I could, and Mia was more than willing to help. I stood at the door beside Marlene and watched as Mia tried to reach Michelle.

"Hi Michelle. My name is Mia, and I am here to help you."

Another mumble came from Michelle. Again, it was unintelligible.

"Did someone hurt you, Michelle? Did a policeman hurt you? Is that why you won't talk to Cole?"

We could hear Michelle begin to cry. Deep heavy sobs. Her shoulders bobbing up and down. Marlene grabbed a box of Kleenexes off the desk and handed them to Mia.

"Here, Michelle. I have a box of Kleenexes for you."

"No," Michelle said in a surprisingly commanding voice.

"Do you think maybe you want to talk to me about what happened to you?"

Again, the violent head shaking. "Kill me!" Michelle said, and this time, it was clear enough to hear.

"I'm not going to kill you. Who's going to kill you, Michelle? We're here to help you. Nobody's going to kill you," Mia tried again. "You're here in the safety of the rehab center. Nobody's will hurt you in here."

"Police," Michelle said, putting her head back between her knees.

Mia tried to get Michelle to talk several times but in vain. We all finally gave up.

As we left Michelle's dorm room, I turned to Marlene. "Was she physically hurt when she came back?"

"No. She had a thorough medical check-up, and health wise, she was fine. I just don't know. None of the other kids came back with any problems whatsoever. Only Michelle."

"Let me know if she says anything. I'm really worried about her. You said you had some information for me. Can you tell me what that is?" I asked Marlene.

"I just wanted to tell you that Charlie was facing some problems with some of the kids here and getting them to open up to her, which was extremely unusual for her. The kids just loved her."

Marlene thanked us for talking to Michelle. Then, she led us back to the main office, and we left Cloverdale, feeling empty and unsettled.

~~~

Chapter 13

JUST HOW long does one have to wait before returning to normal life once they've lost someone so close, I thought to myself as I laid in bed next to Mia.

The clock read six thirty-eight in the large blue digits. I laid with my hands clasped behind my head, my fingers interlaced. I could hear Mia's soft breathing. It was rhythmic and somewhat hypnotizing. She lay on her side, her back to me, the covers drawn up to her chin. We were supposed to meet the attorney later that morning. It was a Wednesday. The sun was beginning to peek through the curtains. Mia had plans of going back to work the following Monday, but I could tell her heart wasn't in it. She was still crying about Charlie, but she always tried to hide it from me. She'd cry in the bathroom, or sometimes, she'd sob herself to sleep. I tried to talk to her about it, but she wouldn't. I told her it was okay to cry in front of me. But she said she didn't want to, because she was afraid it would weaken me as well. She was, in fact, correct in that assumption, and there were many times that I found myself crying while driving someplace to buy groceries or pick up something we needed. I knew there was no shame in crying, but I suppose as a police officer, it somehow made me feel weaker. I could smell the aroma of coffee, and I knew it had finished brewing. Knowing that if I lay there long enough, I would dive into my negative thoughts and start to cry, I pulled myself out of bed and went to the kitchen to get some coffee.

I got out the coffee mugs, sugar, and cream and poured myself a cup of coffee and sat down at the kitchen table. I couldn't help but wonder what the attorney was going to go over with us. Certainly, he would be reading the will. And apparently, Tony was included in the will. I thought about Tony then, who lived in a big house, all alone, and wondered how often he cried. I wouldn't dream of asking him, but I still wondered. We all missed Charlie so very much; sometimes, it was hard to remember she was gone. I thought about the little girl from Cloverdale and knew that Charlie would know exactly how to handle that situation.

I found it interesting that Mia was at least able to get her to talk. Her words however haunted me. *"No!"* she had said and shaken her head so violently. But what bothered me most was when she said, *"Kill me!"* I didn't know what she meant, but who would kill such a sweet little girl like that? My thoughts wandered to how Michelle was doing as I stared into the mug at the black liquid. As if, maybe, it held the answers I was looking for. I drank some more coffee and got up to refill my cup. When I turned back to the table, Mia was walking toward the kitchen. I filled a mug for her, mixed in her cream and sugar, and placed it on the table gingerly.

"Hey babe," she said in a hoarse sleepy voice. "Why didn't you wake me up?"

"You were sleeping so soundly that I just let you be."

She came over and gave me a kiss on the lips. Her eyes were still drowsy, and her hair was messed up from bed. I pulled her into a big hug. She felt warm in my arms, and I didn't want to let go. There was always an element of safety with her in my arms.

"So today, we see the lawyer at what…ten o'clock?" I asked, as Mia took her usual seat next to me at the table.

She took her coffee mug, and we sat at the table, trying to relax.

"I guess it's the reading of the will," Mia said, blowing on her coffee.

"I suppose. I know she had the same trust fund I had, because it was divided equally between us. I know she bought the condo and the car, and if I remember correctly, she invested the rest. I guess we'll find out today."

I took a sip of coffee and tuned my gaze to Mia, who asked, "So, what do you think about the whole thing with Michelle yesterday?"

"I don't know. I'm not really familiar with kids, so I really don't know what to think," I replied.

"Well, I sure hope Marlene and her people figure out how to get Michelle out of her shell, so she can tell them what happened," Mia said shaking her head. "It's just so sad."

"I know. I just keep thinking about it. I can't seem to shake it off."

"I know exactly what you mean. I feel the same way."

We finished the remaining coffee and showered together. I loved washing her beautiful, long black hair. The bathroom immediately filled with the warm scent of lavender as I ran my fingers through her tresses. Once her hair was shampooed, I washed her with her favorite cocoa butter bath wash. I ran my hands all over her and she turned to face me. I brought my lips to hers and we kissed deeply yet softly, our tongues doing a dance of their own inside our mouths. I rubbed her all over, feeling her breasts and her nipples. Still deeply engaged in the kiss, Mia wrapped her arms around my neck and her legs around my waist so I could enter her. We made love in the midst of familiar fragrances that made Mia smell so good.

By the time we finished, the hot water had run out, but neither of us noticed. The love was pure and simple as we'd come together body and soul.

When we finally got out of the shower, it was just after eight thirty, and we needed to get ready for the attorney.

While Mia did her hair and makeup, I called Tony. "Hey," Tony said into the phone.

"You remember we're meeting that attorney today, right?"

"Yeah. I was just getting ready to come over. Are you guys ready to go?"

"We're almost done. Mia's doing her hair and makeup. And I'm getting dressed. So, by the time you get here, we'll be ready to go."

"Do you know where his office is?" Tony asked.

"Yeah. We've been there several times. That's no problem. I'm assuming you're going to drive?"

"Sure. It's downtown, isn't it?"

"Yep."

"Okay. I'll be over in about fifteen minutes or so."

"We'll be ready by then."

As I put on my clothes Mia came into the bedroom.

She came out of the bathroom looking her finest. "You look nice," she said giving me a once over.

"I was just debating whether I should wear a tie or not."

Mia stood back and looked me up and down again. "I think you look fine just like that."

I informed her of Tony picking us up in fifteen minutes and she promised to be ready by then. I left the bedroom to go down, clean up the coffee mugs, and prepare the coffee pot for the next brew. By the time I was done, Mia came into the kitchen. Mia looked extremely beautiful as per usual. The delicate necklace she wore definitely accentuated the dipping of her neckline in her dress.

"You're gorgeous," I said.

"You always say that. Even when I'm in my PJ's," she said with a chuckle.

"Well, it's true," I replied, walking over to her and holding her hand. "Tony should be here anytime now."

Since the attorney's office was downtown, we left about forty minutes before our appointment in case of traffic or construction. We reached his office fifteen minutes early. The receptionist was a heavy-set blond woman, who wore a lot of makeup. She was called Christine Conley according to her nameplate. She had on one of those headsets which come with an attached microphone.

"May I help you?" she asked with a small pleasant smile. It was evident that she was used to this job where she had to be polite.

"Yes. We have a ten o'clock appointment with the attorney Miles Kuhns," I told her.

"Let me ring his secretary. May I have your name please?"

"My name is Cole Spencer, this is my wife Mia Spencer, and the gentleman here is Tony DeMarco. The appointment was for the three of us."

"Okay, then. Why don't you have a seat and I'll buzz his secretary to let them know you're here."

And with that, she dismissed us.

We made ourselves comfortable on the elaborate furniture in the waiting area. We did not however have to wait too long before a woman came out from the hallway on the left and introduced herself.

"Cole Spencer?" she enquired. She was a beautiful woman with dark hair and brown eyes. She had an exotic quality about her face and in the way, she moved. She was about five feet five inches and very thin.

We all stood up at the mention of my name.

"Hello. My name is Reanna Mitchel. I'm Mr. Kuhn's secretary." She shook each of our hands with her long slender fingers with pretty fingernails that were perfectly manicured and painted a pearl pink. "If you'll follow me, I'll take you back to see Mr. Kuhn."

She walked swiftly down the hallway, gliding across the plush carpet in her stiletto heels like she'd done it all her life. She was dressed in a tailored business suit, and had a string of pearls around her neck that matched the pearl buttons. After passing several doorways, we finally reached Mr. Kuhn's office. His door was shut, so she knocked lightly and opened the door. She announced our arrival and opened the door all the way.

Mr. Kuhn was a tall man with sharp features. He was in shape and fit but not muscular. He had short gray hair, neatly trimmed above his ears and collar. He had a genuine smile and he greeted us at the door as we entered, shaking each of our hands. His fingers were long and well-groomed.

"Please have a seat," he said. We each took a chair in front of his desk. He went back to his desk and sat down on his large office chair. He then turned to his secretary and said, "Reanna, please bring me the Charlene Spencer file."

She was gone and back, all within seconds, and she handed him a large accordion file, then left.

"Please forgive me here. I only want to make sure I have all your names correct," he said, opening the file and pulling out a large white envelope within another file. Then he looked up at us in turns.

"As I understand, you are Cole Spencer. You were Charlene's brother. Is that correct?"

"Yes."

He pointed to Mia and said, "And you are Mia Spencer, Cole's wife. Am I correct?"

"Yes," Mia said in a small voice.

"And that leaves you," he pointed toward Tony. "You are Anthony DeMarco and were Charlene's fiancée."

"Yes, sir. That is correct."

"Okay, then. Now that we have the names straight, I am going to explain a little about what is going to happen here. This is what we call 'the reading of the will' and the distribution of assets. Charlene left an extensive will involving all three of you to some degree or another. If you have any questions anywhere along the line, please feel free to interrupt me. Sometimes it's hard to understand the legalese in any legal document, much less a will. Do any of you have any questions?"

We all indicated that we did not, and he began to read the will. Once we got past the 'being of sound mind and body' portion, I was lost. The will was very thick, and I glanced over at Tony who was frowning slightly. I could tell he was just as confused as I was. Mia had little or no expression on her face, as she worked for a law firm. And I knew that while she didn't do wills, she certainly understood the language. Every so often, Mr. Kuhn would look up with arched eyebrows to see if we had any questions.

My head was swimming in a sea of legal terms I didn't understand, but I had no idea how to phrase a question to him.

"I can already tell you're lost in all this," Mr. Kuhn said. "Once we get through the reading of the entire will, we will be able to talk about the assets and the distribution of the assets as Charlene intended. That will be much easier for you all to understand."

I felt a unanimous sigh of relief come from all of us, which gave Mr. Kuhn a bit of a chuckle. "You're not the only ones who've been through this. Just be patient and allow me to read the entire will, and then, we can discuss the assets and Charlene's wishes."

It took him more than half an hour to read the entire will, but once he was finished, he placed the will back down on his desk and turned his eyes to his audience.

"Let's talk assets first," he said, "—it was Charlene's wish to liquidate all her assets upon her death, so it would be easier to distribute. Cole, as you're aware, she was given her share of the trust fund from your parents account at the age of thirty, just as you were. Charlene chose to purchase the Condominium at Garden Place. She also chose to purchase a new car…if I remember correctly, it was a Ford *Mustang* convertible. She then opened a high yield savings account for five hundred thousand dollars, which left approximately four million two hundred and fifty thousand dollars in her trust account. She then invested the remaining trust money into a stock portfolio. Now, while she did lose some of her money when market crashed, she was a very wise investor and had the investment company spread her investments into multiple stocks. A couple of those stocks did very well, and she recovered nicely. So, upon her death, I contacted the investment company, Chambliss, Oliver and Pantano Accounting Investment Firm and had them liquidate all her assets. The trust account originally had five million dollars, but after the purchase of the condominium and the car and the savings account, she had approximately four million two hundred and fifty thousand dollars that she invested in the portfolio. Add on her earned dividends from the portfolio, and that brings you up to eight and a half million dollars."

"That's the investment return?" I asked.

"Yes. And now here's where we get down to business as far as the distribution of those funds is concerned. She has allotted one million dollars to The Literacy Foundation, one million dollars to Cloverdale Rehabilitation Center, two million five hundred thousand dollars, plus the condominium and any furnishings and artwork go to Anthony DeMarco. Which leaves four million dollars that go to Cole and Mia, plus the car. This amount does not include the funds from the savings account, because she added Cole's name to the savings account, which has a balance of the original deposit, because she was only living off the interest she got from it. I have a check for each of you which I will distribute to you at the end of our meeting. Any jewelry or clothing or personal belongings she has requested to go to Mia. She also has remaining debt of twenty-seven hundred dollars on her American Express credit card, which Cole will need to take care of using the money from the saving account. I will make sure that the Literacy Foundation and Cloverdale Rehabilitation Center receives their portions in Charlene's name, so you need not worry about that.

I could only speak for myself, but I was completely shocked at the amount of money Charlie had. And I could tell by the looks on Tony and Mia's faces, they too had no idea.

The attorney continued, "Do you have any questions?"

Still stunned, I told him I did not and so did Mia and Tony.

"Of course, there will be papers to sign, and then I will distribute the checks to each of you as well as the title to the car."

We spent another hour, signing papers and going over questions that grew like seeds in our brains now that the shock had worn off. He answered them politely and patiently and spent as much time as he needed with us to make sure we had no more questions. Mr. Kuhn recommended I should now update my will and that I contact the accounting firm Charlie had used, once I decided what I was going to do with the money.

It was almost two o'clock when we finally left the office. We rode the elevator down in silence and walked to the car without any of us speaking. It was as if the reading of the will and the distribution of assets had put a punctuation mark on Charlie's death. It was like there's nothing left to say. We didn't speak again until we got into the car, and even then, the conversation was the bare minimum. We each had a part of Charlie and now that was the final end to her life. All that was left now were the memories.

~~~

Chapter 14

AFTER WE reached home, Tony hung around for a while. I grabbed two bottles of Bud Lite from the refrigerator and poured a glass of Arbor Mist, White Zinfandel for Mia, and we all sat in the living room, drinking. Mia and I sat on the couch and Tony took the overstuffed armchair facing us.

Tony took a swig of his beer and looked up at us. "She gave you a lot of money. Do you know what you're going to do with it?" He seemed to want that answer for himself as well.

"Well, I already have the trust fund from my parents, so I'm probably going to invest a lot of it with that, but maybe keep some aside for us," I answered shaking my head back and forth trying to fathom having that kind of money.

"Are you going to keep the condo?" Mia asked Tony, sipping on her wine.

"I'm not sure," Tony said. "I'd hate to give it up, but I have that big house of mine and all. Plus, it needs a lot of work done, since the police department tore it apart." The disgust in his voice was very apparent. "I'm definitely going to send my men in there to get working on fixing the place up. I just need to figure out exactly how and what I want in there."

"I know. I can't believe all this. I'm having such a hard time wrapping my head around it all," I replied. "If we plan it right, neither one of us will have to work after this."

I glanced at Mia to see her reaction. "But if I quit my job, I wouldn't know what to do with myself. It's just too much to take in right now." Mia said.

"I know," Tony said. "It's like putting a stamp, on Charlie's death."

I asked Mia, "Do you want to quit your job? If so, that's fine, otherwise you can maybe go back to school and get a degree or something."

"I was just thinking that if I quit my job…maybe, I could go and volunteer at Cloverdale…kinda pick up where Charlie left off, ya' know?"

"That's not a bad idea." I would definitely encourage her in that pursuit.

Tony got up to bring two more beers from the kitchen and came back, sitting down with a thump on the chair. "Personally, I think that you guys should wait and talk to your financial adviser before making any decisions."

We nodded our heads in acknowledgment. "I think you're right," I said taking another gulp of the cold beer.

Tony finished his beer and didn't stay around much longer after that. "You guys have a lot to figure out here, so I'm going to leave you to it. I'll give you a call soon."

With Tony gone, the house suddenly felt very empty. I refilled Mia's wine glass and got myself another beer. A glum silence fell over the house. We'd spent so much time with him in the past few days and now he was going back to his normal life. It was now a matter of deciding what we must do with ours.

I called to make an appointment with our financial adviser, and Mia and I met with him the following week. We'd made our decision where Mia was concerned—she had decided not to return to work. She contacted Marlene Dillman at Cloverdale, and they would be thrilled to have her there. As for me, I had taken this extended leave of absence from the police department to investigate Charlie's murder. But I ran into a roadblock, being cut off from the police department. Now, Chris wasn't taking any of my calls.

Three weeks later, I suddenly received a call from Tony on my cell.

"Cole," he said in a breathless voice, "I need you to get down here right now." It was very unusual for Tony to sound frantic about anything.

"What's going on, Tony?"

"Just get your ass down here. I don't know what to do."

"Okay. Where are you?"

"1423 Cherry Blossom. Do you know where that is?" he panted.

"Yea. That's in my sector. Tony what's going on?" I was very concerned at this point.

"Just please get out here as fast as you can," he begged.

I was already in the *Bronco* and headed that way by the time we were done talking. When I arrived at the address, I saw that the house was in a very bad shape. With flaking blue clapboard siding, desperately in need of a good painting. Most of the windows were broken and the screen door was half off the hinges. I saw Tony's BMW sedan parked in the driveway.

I saw Tony sitting in front of the house, while his crew was hanging around near some pickup trucks parked in the street.

I walked up to Tony. "What's up? Good God you look pale."

"Come in here, and you'll see why."

We entered the house. It smelled of mold and cat urine and yet there was the distinctive smell of something far worse than that. Half the walls in the front room were threadbare with peeling wallpaper curling around the edges.

"In here," Tony said, leading me to one of the bedrooms. The carpet was stained and threadbare and a mattress was laid on the floor in one corner. "Over there. In the corner." Tony pointed to a figure that lay like a clump of old clothes.

I walked closer to the lump, only to realize it was a small body that had been beaten and left to die in a corner.

"What the fuck is going on here?" Tony asked.

I stooped down to get a closer look and realized that the body, while beaten almost beyond recognition and despite the decomposition, was that of Lauren Stanford—the girl I'd taken that missing report on the night Charlie was murdered. It appeared that she'd been strangled, and there was a bullet wound at the center of her forehead.

"When did you find her? Did anybody touch anything in the house? In particular the body?" I asked, standing up straight.

The smell of decomposition from Lauren grew stronger as we talked.

"We've been here for a couple of days now, and we just found her here today. I don't think anyone touched her," Tony said visibly shaken. "We've mostly been working in the front part of the house, but that's about it. That's where we started working and one of the men found her today so I got everyone out and called you. Can we get out of here? I can't stand the smell."

"Yeah. Let's go outside and keep everyone out of the house. Since you all have been working on the house, they may need to take yours and your men's fingerprints for elimination." I escorted Tony to the front door, and we exited the house.

I called 911 from my cell, gave them the address, and told them what we'd found. They said they would dispatch a car and ambulance immediately.

"Just like Charlie," I heard Tony mumble under his breath.

"I know…a little too much like it."

In the distance, we could hear the sirens of the patrol cars and the ambulance growing louder. My heart sank as I was transported back to the night Charlie was murdered.

Two uniform cars arrived first, with an ambulance right behind them. Jeremiah Robinson was the first one out of the car, his tall dark imposing figure taking charge of the situation immediately. I met him at the end of the driveway and informed him of the situation.

"I don't know for sure, but I think it's Lauren Stanford, the girl whose missing report was filed. She was a runaway from Cloverdale. She's pretty beat up, but I do believe it's her."

His voice was low and authoritative as he turned to Tony and his men. "Did anyone touch anything at all inside?"

They all shook their heads, almost in unison.

Tony said, "We've all been working in the house but not in that room…until today."

"Did anyone touch the body?" Robinson yelled to the crew.

Again, vigorous head shakes from the men.

The other police officer had stepped out of his car and joined Robinson. His name was Joel Thompson. I had worked with him before. He was six feet tall and weighed about a hundred and fifty pounds. He wasn't overly muscular, but he could hold his own if it ever came to a fight.

Robinson turned to me and asked, "Where is she?"

I led him inside the house to the bedroom at the back, and he stooped down for a better look at the heap that once was a young girl. He immediately called for the E Squad Sergeant and Lieutenant to come to the scene and then called dispatch to have them send out the coroner and crime scene technicians.

"Who found the body?" Thompson asked, looking down at the decaying body.

"It was either Tony or one of his men."

"And they've been working in this house?" Robinson asked.

"Yeah. Tony rehabs old houses and sells them for a profit, so there's no telling whose fingerprints will be where."

"We'll have to take all their prints for elimination."

"Yeah. I've already warned them about that."

We went back to the front yard. "Alright, listen up everybody," Robinson's voice boomed through the street. "We need to write statements from all of you. This is Officer Joel Thompson, and he'll be asking you a few questions about what you saw, what you touched, all of that. I'd appreciate it if you'd answer his questions quickly and to the point. But make sure you're one hundred percent sure of your answers before you give them to him."

All the men just nodded and murmured their assent as Thompson walked up to the front.

Robinson turned to Thompson and told him to question all the workmen.

Both the Sergeant and Lieutenant of the E Squad showed up at the same time, asking the same questions as Robinson. They too went inside to take a look at the small figure huddled in the corner of the bedroom. I shouldn't have been surprised when the Chief and his Lieutenant showed up as well. A sudden surge of anger prompted me toward him. I wanted to rip his head off; I wanted to tear his balls off, and I wanted to make him eat them. I saw Tony in my peripheral, and he grabbed my arm and pulled me away from the Chief.

I heard him whisper, "No, Cole, not here." And I hated to admit it but he was right.

"Who's the man in charge of this rehab?" I heard Robinson's voice boom out over the neighborhood.

Raising his hand up, Tony said, "That would be me."

"What's your name, son?"

Son? Tony mouthed the word to me.

"Anthony DeMarco," he answered, straightening his back. Robinson's presence had that effect on people. Make them stand straight and be more polite. I always attributed it to his time with the Marines and his size.

"Okay, DeMarco, spell out your last name for me."

Tony obliged, and Robinson noted it down on his note pad.

"You the one that found the body?" Robinson asked.

"Yeah, I suppose I was. I was checking out the rest of the house when I found her. Most of my men were in the front side of the house…tearing it down…you know?"

"Do you realize your finding the body makes you the prime suspect? Do you know how long she's been here?"

"No, sir. We've been working here nearly a week now and she wasn't here when we first got here." I'd never heard Tony speak so formally. He had glanced at me on being called the prime suspect. "My crew can vouch for me…that I didn't kill her."

"Uh huh…so it could have been days then?" Robinson interrogated him.

"Well…no…when we first got to the house about a week ago, we went through the whole place to see what we needed to keep and what was to be disposed of, and she wasn't there then," Tony stuttered a bit as he spoke, clearly intimidated by Robinson.

"When did you go back there again, before today?"

Tony looked thoughtful and told Robinson, "I guess it was not again until today."

"And you didn't notice any strange odors coming from the place?"

"No…you know when you get to rehabbing houses, you find all kinds of dead animals inside them. So, the smells not all that unusual for us."

"I see." Robinson didn't sound or look pleased with that answer.

"Alright. You're dismissed." Tony walked away, giving me a look that clearly said, 'What' up with that guy?"

Robinson looked at me. "You on duty or what?"

"No, I'm on a leave of absence because of Charlie's murder." I couldn't help but wonder if he knew anything about that, and I wanted to ask him. But I knew right then was not a good time to open Pandora's Box. I needed to get some more facts and information.

"Okay. I think we can handle it from here," he said to me. "DeMarco…front and center."

I hadn't seen Tony move that fast in years. "Yes, sir?" he said to Robinson.

"Tell your men to leave for the day, as this place is now a crime scene, and you can't do anymore work in here for a while at least. Tell all your men that once they've given their statements, they need to stay where we can reach them if needed."

"Not a problem, Officer." For a minute, I thought Tony was about to salute him.

"I'm done with you too, Spencer. We know where to find you."

Without a word, I left and met Tony at the end of the driveway where he and his men had gathered.

"Shit, man. What's his deal?" one of the men said, making a repulsed face.

"He's an ex-Marine, Special Forces."

"He looks like a mean sonofabitch, I'll say that." another one added.

Tony sent all his men home for the day with their pay and decided it was time to start rebuilding Charlie's old condominium. He told his crew to start work on the condo the next day. He gave the men the address and handed the foreman the key. He instructed them to start tearing up the carpets and flooring, as all of it needed to be replaced. Then, he and I went out for drink at Whitaker's, which was a bar right by my house. When we went in, the place was dark and we needed time for our vision to adjust to the low lighting. I told Tony to grab a booth and got each of us a Bud on tap. I paid the bartender, left him a tip, and took the beers over to the table where Tony sat. I sat facing the door, a habit I'd developed from my time as a police officer. It was always good to know who's coming and going.

"So…" Tony said, and dropped it at that.

"So, what?" I was confused.

"Look, I know I'm no cop or anything, and I'm certainly no detective, but what did you think about those group of cops up there at the scene today?"

"I don't know, Tony. It's really hard to tell right now."

"What about that Robinson dude, huh? Do you think he's involved in all of this?"

"Now that would not surprise me in the least. I wouldn't trust him any farther than I could throw him. You saw how big he was."

"Yeah. I don't mind telling you he scared the shit outta me there."

"He seems to have that effect on a lot of people. And now, they're going to need someone from Cloverdale to identify the body."

"Not there, I hope," Tony gave an expression of exasperation.

"No. No. Down at the morgue. They'll clean her up as best they can and call someone over from Cloverdale to make the ID."

I had finished my beer and so had Tony. "You want another one?" Tony asked.

"Yeah, I think so." I started to get up, but Tony stopped me in my tracks.

"This one's on me."

He came back moments later with two ice cold mugs of beers and laid them on the table.

Tony took a long sip of his drink. "Sure feels good going down."

"Hey, you want anything to eat? I heard their hamburgers are really good."

"Nah," Tony said. "Seeing that dead girl and all today, I kinda lost my appetite."

"Yep, that does it to people."

We drank our beer in silence for a while, until Tony finally spoke up, inquiring about the money.

"I mean, I don't mean to get personal or anything, but I was just wondering…you know?"

"Well, I think Mia is going to quit her job and she's going to volunteer at Cloverdale like Charlie did. And we're thinking about moving into a bigger house. After that, we're going to invest most of it."

"You are gonna use DeMarco and Sons for your new house, yes?" he asked, his eyebrows raised a little.

"Of course. Who else!"

"Great. I'll tell my dad. We can start looking whenever you're ready."

"Yeah, we'll need some time here to get everything settled. I'll let you know, though."

We both finished our beers and were done for the day. We each went our separate ways after that. I went home and found Mia curled up on the couch. Crying.

Chapter 15

I RUSHED to the couch and tried to embrace Mia. She was curled up in a ball, and all I could do was to put my arms around her small little body and hold on. She had her head tucked between her knees.

"Baby…what's wrong? Did something happen while I was away?"

She mumbled something inaudibly.

"What, sweetheart? I can't hear you."

She sucked in a huge breath of air, lifted her head, and stared at me like I was a stranger who'd just come in from the street. "It's not you!" she proclaimed. Her hair was plastered to her wet cheeks, and I brushed it aside. She did not seem to mind my touch. "I'm sorry. I don't like to cry in front of you."

I squeezed her arm gently just to let her know that I was there for her. "What is it, darling?"

I handed her a box of Kleenexes, which she took willingly. She pulled out two or three at a go and began wiping her face. "I went down to the law firm to hand in my resignation. At first, they were reluctant to accept it, but I told them I really needed to do it, and that I would be following in Charlie's footsteps and volunteering at Cloverdale to work with the kids. They were really happy for me when I told them." She began to cry again and was somehow speaking between sobs. "And of course…I took Charlie's car down there…just to try it out, you know. I really like it…by the way." She paused to blow her nose and wipe away some tears. "And then, I went to Cloverdale…and talked to them about volunteering…and that I'm all set…I start Monday." She burst into tears again.

I was confused. So far, everything she'd told me was great news. "So, what's got you so upset then?"

"I just miss her so much. There are so many memories, and I'm afraid I'm not going to be as good as Charlie was at Cloverdale. What if I flop and all the kids hate me?"

"Sweetie, they're not going to hate you. They're gonna love you, just like they loved Charlie. You'll see."

"I just miss her so much. I can hardly bear it. My heart hurts. She's not here anymore to talk to. She was my friend. You know, I don't have any friends other than Charlie?"

"Don't be ridiculous. You have plenty of friends. You have me and Tony and maybe some of the gals you worked with."

"They won't call me, and you and Tony don't count. I need a girlfriend. Someone I can go shopping with or talk to on the phone or have lunch with."

"Well, maybe…you'll meet some people at Cloverdale, and you'll have some new friends."

"But I miss Charlie so much."

"So do I, sweetie; so do I."

"Yeah, but I don't see you sitting on the couch, bawling your eyes out. You don't cry. Men never cry."

"I cry," I said almost defensively, as if I were taking a stand on the issue.

"Oh yeah? When?"

"I cried at her funeral, and sometimes, when I'm driving

down the road all alone listening to my country music, it'll get me thinking of how much I miss Charlie too. And I cry again. So, you see. You're not the only one who cries," I tried to console her as best I could.

She blew her nose again and wiped up her face. Her eyes were red and swollen, and the tip of her nose was red as well. She asked in a small voice, "Do you think Tony cries?"

"Oh, I know Tony cries. He tries to put on this big act about being tough. But I know he cries. I've seen it in his eyes."

Mia let out a small chuckle at the thought of Tony crying. "It's really not funny, but…I just can't picture him crying."

"I know. Me too."

We snuggled on the couch for a while until Mia was feeling better, or at least, she'd stopped crying. I went to the bathroom and brought her a cool washcloth for her eyes and face, then went to the kitchen and poured a glass of wine for her and a bottle beer for myself. I settled back down, and she snuggled into me. I kissed her gently on the neck. She caressed my cheek with her soft finger tips as we kissed. A long soft willingly surrendered kiss. Our tongues intermingled with each other like we were playing some kind of game or performing a ritual of sorts. I slid my hand down to her shirt and began unbuttoning it, the desire to feel her breasts burning strong within. She pulled my shirt off over my head as we both lay down on the couch. I unclasped her bra and took off her shirt and bra in one swift motion. I felt my hands stroke both her ample breasts and bring them both together so I could kiss them both at the same time. As I bent down to kiss them, I felt a sudden impact intrude upon our private moments. And while I didn't know exactly what it was, the hair on the back of my neck stood. I grabbed Mia and rolled her onto the floor, my body covering her completely. I wrapped her in my arms.

"Stay down. Don't move!" I commanded her.

"What's going on?" she whispered in my ear.

"Shhhh…" I hushed her.

It came again. This time distinct. And without a doubt. Shots had been fired through our front window and into the house.

"Cole? What's happening? I'm scared…" Mia's voice was soft but trembling.

"I think someone just took a couple of shots at us. Stay down on the floor. We're safer down here."

I felt her cling onto my neck, holding on for dear life.

"I'm scared, Cole. Why would someone be shooting at us?"

"I don't know," I told her, and it was completely true. I kept going through the events of the day in my head, trying to remember what had happened that would make someone start shooting at us.

It was then that my cell rang. I looked at Mia; our faces were less than a quarter of an inch away from each other.

"You're not going to get that, are you?" Mia asked, a look of absolute terror shadowing her face.

"Stay here. Don't move. You'll be safe right here. Whatever you do, DO NOT stand up."

"You are actually going to get that stupid phone, aren't you?" Her voice was a mix of terror and indignation.

"I'm just going to crawl over and get it from the kitchen counter. I'm not going to stand up. And neither are you. I'll grab the phone and come right back."

"Oh my God. No! Cole. I'm so scared."

"I know, sweetie. Just hang on one moment."

I pulled my pants back on and crawled to the still ringing phone. It had gone to voice mail several times, only to ring again and again. I reached for the phone mid ring, grabbed it, and started crawling back toward Mia.

"Spencer," I said, picking up the call while moving. "Who is this?"

"Ah good. For a while, I didn't think you were going to answer your phone." I knew the voice, but fear was clouding my mind from placing it.

"I wasn't exactly in any position to answer the phone, seeing how I was being shot at. That was you, wasn't it?"

"Yes, you're a quick one, aren't you?" the voice on the other end taunted. It was deep, sarcastic, and rather annoying. It was then that I realized it was none other than Jeremiah Robinson.

"Yeah, I am. What the fuck do you want? Why are you shooting at us?" I could feel my blood boil as I reached Mia who was still lying on the floor.

"Let that be a lesson to you. Stay away from the investigation. And tell your little friend to keep his big ass out of it too."

"Hey," I yelled into the phone, "he called me when he found the girl, because he didn't know what to do. So I went out there. Don't dare threaten me and my family. And you leave Tony alone."

"Just let this be warning to you and your little friend to stay away. Have I made myself clear? Otherwise, I won't miss…because I don't miss."

And with that, the line went dead.

"Cole, who was that?" Mia was breathless, clutching her shirt and bra to her chest.

"Sonuvabitch!" I heard myself yelling.

"Cole." Mia grabbed my arm. "Who was that?"

"I don't know exactly, but I have a pretty good idea. Tony, I must call Tony."

As I was dialing Tony's number, Mia started dressing up. "What is going on, Cole? Tell me. I need to know."

Before I could answer Mia, Tony had picked up the phone. "DeMarco Construction."

"Tony…look it's me, Cole."

"Yeah, I know that I saw it on the caller ID. Are you okay? You sound pissed."

"No. Mia and I just got shot at through our front window. Listen, I need you to get over here with some plywood. We got shot at because of that little girl you found."

"What the fuck are you talking about?"

"Just get the hell over here."

"Okay, okay. I'll get the wood and be over in a bit."

I hung up on Tony and turned to Mia, who had decided it was now safe to sit up on the floor. There were questions etched all over her face. "What the hell just happened, Cole?"

"Tony found that dead girl in one of his rehab houses today. She's the one I took the missing report on the night Charlie was killed."

"So? I don't understand. Why are they shooting our house up?"

"Well, when Tony found the girl, he called me, and I went there. We called the cops and…Do you remember Jeremiah Robinson—that really tall black cop with the bald head?"

"Yeah. What does he have to do with this?"

"He was the officer-in-charge at the scene this morning, and he saw me there. I guess he thought I was investigating Charlie's murder. So, he took a few shots at us to warn us off from the investigation."

"Are you sure it was him?"

"Yeah, I'm pretty sure," I said nodding my head. "And here, look at this…he used a burner phone." I showed her that there was no caller ID associated with the call.

Tony arrived in his work van about half an hour after my call. We both checked the front window and saw two bullet holes. We tried to follow the line of the bullets, but it's not as simple as they show it to be on television. We then checked the opposite wall of the living room and saw where the bullets had penetrated the wall leading to the kitchen.

"It looks like they got stuck in your wall here," Tony said, "but I'll be damned if we can find them that simply. We'd have to tear down the wall to find them."

"Oh no you don't," Mia interrupted, putting in her two cents. "It bad enough we're being shot at but to tear our house apart for two lousy fucking bullets? No fucking way." Rarely did Mia say the word 'fuck' much less use it twice in a sentence. She was scared. And she was upset.

I tried to hold her. "We're not going to tear down anything. We're going to board up this window and fix these holes in the wall and we'll figure out what to do from there."

I could feel her pushing me away, holding back from me as though she didn't want me touching her. "Oh no you don't," she said, her voice high pitched, with hints of hysteria. "You may be used to being shot at, but I'm not. I don't like this. I don't like this one bit." And with that, she shoved me away with her hands.

I grabbed her by the arms and forced her to look up at me. "Mia," I heard myself yell, "I need you to get a hold of yourself. Your being hysterical is not helping matters."

"Hysterical…?" she yelled back at me. "Of course, I'm hysterical…we've just been shot at. In our own damn house. In our own living room. That too while we were…" She suddenly remembered Tony's presence in the room. "Well, you know what!" she huffed.

She was starting to calm down and I let go of her arms, holding her close to me. I could feel her body melt into mine. She was still shaking from the fear but at least her hysteria had decreased quite a bit.

"We need to call the police," Mia said into my chest.

"We can't do that. Especially, if they're the ones behind this. I think it was that Robinson fellow. He was a sharp shooter with the Marines Special Forces. We call the police, we could be opening a whole can of worms that we don't want to," I told her.

"Then what are we going to do? We can't live like this," Mia said. "Maybe, you can call your friend from the FBI. He may be able to help us."

"We'll see." I led her to the couch to sit down. "Let's just relax for a few minutes.

Tony brought her a fresh glass of wine and two beers, one for each of us. "Come on," he said, "let's all take some time and get over the shock."

I noticed Mia looking over at him with one eyebrow raised. "What? Did you just get shot at too?"

"No. I'd be upset too if I had been, but it's time to let cooler heads prevail and figure out what we're going to do next," Tony told her.

"You're right. I'm sorry, Tony." Mia took a big sip of her wine. "I'm just not use to this being-shot-at business."

To help ease her mind, I said, "To be perfectly honest with you, neither am I. Look, sweetheart, just 'cause I'm a cop, doesn't mean I get shot at every day or even get shot at all. In fact, I've never even fired my weapon on the street the whole time I've been on the force. Hell, the only time I ever fire my gun is at the range for practice or when I had to qualify."

She wrinkled her nose a little at me, like a child, and asked, "Really?"

"Yeah. Really. This scared the hell out of me too. You're not alone there."

"Well then, what are we going to do? You're gonna be investigating the murder, and they're going to take pot shots at us the whole time?"

"No. That's not going to happen again. We'll just have to be very careful from now on."

Tony finally spoke up after chugging down his beer. "First thing I wanna do is put up a board on that window and take a look at those two holes in the wall. I wanna see if we can see in there and maybe get the bullet out or something."

"Are you okay with that?" I asked Mia. When she nodded her head in agreement, I told Tony I'd help him.

"Now will you call your FBI friend?" I heard Mia ask as we were walking out to Tony's truck to get the plywood.

"Maybe," I said and walked out the back door behind Tony.

~~~

Chapter 16

IT DIDN'T take Tony and I very long to get the window boarded up. He said he could get the window replaced for us in no time. In fact, considering all the money we had just inherited, Mia and I decided to get all the windows around the house changed.

"Can we get bullet-proof glass?" she asked, giggling just a bit. She'd been drinking wine the whole time Tony and I were working on the window.

Tony chuckled. "Yes, but it's very expensive."

After that, we went over to the two bullet holes in the wall. Tony had a flashlight, which he directed into the holes, and told me to go to the kitchen and check the cabinet to see if I could see his light. I couldn't, which meant that the bullets had not penetrated through to the cabinets. I wasn't sure if I should be grateful or worried, since the shots were meant for us. I came back to the living room and found Tony looking through the second hole.

"Let me get my pen-light. Maybe, I'll be able to see better that way," he said.

While Tony was out to his truck, Mia refilled her wine glass and sat back down on the couch. "So?" she said, with a very large smile.

"So?" I repeated back to her. She let out another giggle.

"So, are you going to call your FBI friend now?" She took a large gulp of the wine.

"I may. Just to let him know what's going on and have him come out and look at the wall. And I think you've had just about enough wine for one day."

This made her laugh to absolutely no end. "Here's the deal…" She burst into peals of laughter again. "…this girl and her husband are shot at in the privacy of their own home…" More laughing. "…while in the process of trying to make wild passionate love…" Uncontrolled laughing. "…and he says I've had too much wine for the day?" This time she rolled over on the couch laughing. "You know, it's not every woman who can claim that she's been shot at while trying to have sex with her husband on the couch."

I looked over at her and couldn't help but giggle at the sight. She'd had a hard day and she deserved to get a little drunk.

"Oh…Hi, Tony…" Mia said, straightening up, as Tony walked in through the back door. "How much of that did you hear?" Mia asked with a snicker.

"Don't worry about it. Your secret's safe with me." And he, too, let out a chuckle.

He put the pen-light up to the wall where the bullet had gone in. "I think I see it. Geez, you'd think you'd have a bigger hole." And, instantly, Tony realized what he'd said.

Mia broke into fits of laughter again. Falling down on the couch again.

"At least she's a happy drunk," I shrugged. Turning to Tony, I asked, "Do you think we can get them out?"

"I don't know. Let me see what I have in my truck." And with that, Tony was gone once more.

Once Upon a Charlie

When Tony came back, he had a screwdriver and a pair of rubber-grip needle nose pliers with him. "I figure if I can see it, I can use this screwdriver to widen the hole a little." He put the screw driver in the hole and twisted it around to make the hole big enough to accommodate the pliers. I watched as he worked. After the screwdriver, he stuck the pliers into the hole, had to work on it a bit, and finally, he pulled out the bullet. He held it up with the pliers as it if were the Crown Jewels. "I got it!" he announced.

He put the bullet in my hand while he worked on the other bullet hole. And again, he pulled out the same kind of bullet and handed it to me.

Mia bent over and looked at the two bullets in the palm of my hand. "That's it?" She looked incredulous.

"What do you mean 'that's it?' Yes, that's it. Those are the two bullets shot at us."

"Oh yeah?" Mia asked, taking the bullets out of my hand and looking at them in wonder. "Wow. It's amazing how small it is and how deadly it can be in the wrong hands. And they definitely were in the wrong hands today. If you know what I mean." She giggled again. "I think I'll keep them for posterity. I am a marked woman," she said, placing her hand to her chest in an effort to be dramatic, then fell backwards onto the couch.

"Well, you better give me those," I told her. "We'll see how you feel about being a marked woman in the morning."

"Oh my God…look at the holes in the wall! Tony, did you do that?" Mia's eyes widened.

"It's okay, Mia. I'm gonna fix them right now, and with a little paint, no one'll never know they were there."

Mia looked over from the holes in the wall to me and then back again. "He's really going to fix them?" she asked

"Yep, he's going to fix them right now. He's got some putty, and we still have paint in the garage from when I first painted the living room. Why don't you take a couple of aspirin, drink a bunch of water, take this cold washcloth, and go lie down in bed for a while," I suggested as sweetly as possible.

"You're right. I'm no good here. Maybe I'll feel better in the morning."

I think you will. I escorted her to the bedroom, gave her the aspirin and water, and rinsed the washcloth. I managed to get her in her pajamas and tucked her into bed, safe and sound. I then went back out to the living room where Tony was still fixing the walls.

"I can't tell you how much I appreciate this," I told him.

"Hey, is Mia gonna be alright with everything that happened?"

"I guess we'll see in the morning."

~~~

I woke up early thanks to the restless night I had, and when I got out of bed, Mia was still fast asleep. I had at least slept till six thirty, so I had a fresh pot of coffee waiting for me. I moved all the coffee fixings over to the table and poured myself a mug. I knew Mia liked her coffee with cream and sugar. I couldn't help but check the wall of the living room, and you could barely tell anything had happened. I had placed the bullets in a safe place, just in case I decided to call my friend at the FBI. All I had for him at the moment was two bullets and a lot of suspicions. I didn't want to bother him until I had something more concrete, and yet, there was this nagging feeling that maybe he could help us. I checked the clock on the kitchen wall, and it showed that it was a quarter past seven.

"Too soon to call yet," I thought aloud to myself. In the meantime, I sat at the table and stirred my coffee aimlessly, looking at the black twirling abyss that sat in my mug.

At eight o'clock, I heard a shuffling coming from the hall and I knew Mia was up.

I grabbed her coffee mug from the cabinet and poured her some coffee as well as a glass of water, and I got some aspirin out just in case.

"Hi baby," she said in a hoarse voice and kissed me on the head. "Is that for me?"

"Yep. How you feeling?"

She was in her fuzzy pink robe and her pink slippers. Her eyes were nearly crossed and she was a bit unsteady, so I helped her into her chair.

"Oh my head…it hurts…" she said, crossing her arms on the table. She stuck her head on her arms.

"Here. Take this and you'll feel better once you get some coffee inside you."

"What I need is a shower. When I woke up, my mouth felt like I had eaten a stuffed animal while sleeping. But I'll have that coffee first. Thanks for getting all this ready for me."

Her hair was a tangled mess, but I knew once she showered, she'd be back to her old self.

"I'm sorry I acted like that last night. Especially with Tony here. But…I was so scared and confused…I didn't know what to think."

"That's fine. And don't worry about Tony. He got our wall all fixed up, so that's not an issue."

She lifted her head up from the table. "The issue is, what are we going to do about this? I mean if you and Tony are going to keep investigating Charlie's murder, are we going to get shot at all the time?"

"No. I don't think so. I honestly think that was only to warn me off, because I was at the crime scene where they found Lauren's body. I think they were trying to make a statement."

"A very loud and dangerous statement. Will you please call your friend at the FBI now? Have him come over for dinner. I'll cook something really nice, and you can tell him what's going on. Maybe, he can help us."

I took a deep breath and let out a sigh. "Okay. I'll invite him over. We'll tell him what we've got, but there isn't anything he can do to help us. We have no proof at all. And that's exactly what he's going to tell us."

"But I'd feel so much better if you'd at least let him know."

"Okay, sweetie." I ruffled her hair.

"Oh my God…Cole, I'm supposed to start volunteering at Cloverdale on Monday. Do you think I should back out? I'd hate to do that, but what if I am in any danger there?"

"You should be fine there. Don't worry about it," I told her, trying to convince myself as much as her.

When Mia left to shower, I cleaned up the coffee dishes and called Daniel Bentley at the FBI, inviting him for dinner on Saturday. He was happy to receive the invitation, as his wife was out of town and a good home-cooked meal probably sounded very inviting to him.

~~~

Once Upon a Charlie

It was Friday. Mia had made a dash for the grocery store to get the ingredients for our dinner with Daniel. In the meantime, Tony called and told me that a friend of his would come by to take a look at our windows if I was home. I told him I would be.

"Don't worry about the cost, because I get them wholesale, so you won't have to pay an arm and leg for them."

"That's great. Thanks Tony!" I informed him I'd be home for the rest of the day.

Tony's friend showed up around three that afternoon and measured all the windows and gave us an estimate. He gave me Tony's wholesale price and said he'd have the windows the following Monday and could begin installation the same day. I thanked him and then called up Tony to express my gratitude for his help.

I gave Daniel a call to make sure the plan was still on. He replied in the affirmative, so I sat down and opened myself a beer, waiting for Mia to get home with the groceries. We unloaded them, she got herself a glass of wine, and the we sat on the couch, snuggling for a while.

"Be careful with that stuff," I jokingly warned her. "You remember what happened the last time you got hold of wine."

She laughed out loud, not because she was drunk, but simply because she was happy again. Her laughter was as beautiful as spring breeze over fresh flowers and I really needed to hear that.

We feasted on hard salami and cheese and crackers as a substitute for our dinner. We ate in the living room and relaxed on the couch, cozied up next to each other.

"Say, why don't we go to the bedroom and finish what we started last night?" I suggested raising my eyebrows up and down, suggestively.

It took no convincing on her part to follow suit. We retired to the bedroom and lay across the bed. We couldn't get each other's clothes off fast enough, but before long, our bodies were an entangled mass of limbs, deep abandoning kisses taking all of my focus. I kissed her neck and sucked on her earlobe, slowly moving down to her ample breasts. They were soft and warm, and I squeezed them together and kissed each one, sucking each of the nipples softly and gently. I felt her back arch. I knew she was enjoying it. I slowly made my way down to her hips where I lost myself in the wonders of Mia. I kissed my way back up to her face and felt the heat between her legs with my fingers and found that sweet spot she loves so much. When she had finally climaxed, I rolled over on top of her and entered her. It was warm and soothing yet my breath came hard and fast. I couldn't get enough, and by the sounds of it, neither could Mia. When we finally finished, we lay in that position catching our breath, sweat pouring off each of us.

"Oh, my God, Cole…I love what you do to me."

Still on top and inside of her, I placed each of my hands on her cheeks and kissed her again. Another long drawn out kiss. We lay that way for a while until we were ready to get up.

"I don't want to get up," she said to me.

"Me neither. But we have to come up for air sometime."

She started laughing and I rolled off her. We laid on our backs enjoying the coolness after the heat and passion that inevitably arises from making love.

I was the first to get up and she was right behind me. We washed up and she grabbed her pink night shirt and robe, while I toweled off in the bathroom.

"Do you want another beer?" she asked.

"Yeah. I think I could use a cold one after that."

~~~

The following night, Mia set the table with the fine china and the good silverware.

"Cloth napkins and everything!" I exclaimed, while she peeled potatoes in the kitchen. I had slid in my arms around her waist.

"Hey, it's not every day that you get to have your local FBI agent over for dinner," she said with a laugh.

"Make that Special Agent In Charge, Daniel Bentley." I kissed her on her head.

"Don't you start something you can't finish, buster," she said to me, turning around to give me a kiss and squeezing out of my arms. "He's going to be here soon."

Daniel arrived just after three in the afternoon. His dark brown hair was in perfect order and parted on the left as always. His hair was always neatly trimmed just above the ears and the collar. His thin straight nose offset his deep blue eyes, which seemed to drive women crazy. But Daniel paid no heed to that, as he was happily married. We had drinks all around. Daniel preferred scotch on the rocks, and while I rarely drank hard liquor, I had one myself. Mia always had wine when we entertained.

"So, I gather this isn't just a social call?" Daniel said taking a sip of his scotch.

"What gave it away?" I asked with a nervous chuckle.

"Well, the fact that you rarely invite me to dinner…and the plywood on the windows were a dead giveaway." He chuckled.

"Yeah. We're having a bit of a problem, but I don't know how much you'll be able to help. Oh, that reminds me. Tony was able to pull the slugs out of the wall." I got up to retrieve them from the safe and passed them to Daniel. I told Daniel a brief synopsis of what was going on and what had led to the plywood on the windows.

He examined them carefully. "I'm really sorry about your sister. She was such a sweet woman," he said as he inspected the bullets. "Looks like a .223 Remington to me. You say there's a sharp shooter on the force?"

"Yeah. His name is Jeremiah Robinson. He was in the Marines Special Forces and was apparently one of the sharp shooters."

We watched as Daniel wrote down his name.

We told him what was going on with the police department and with Cloverdale. Mia and I each took turns telling him what one of us may have forgotten or left out.

"So, you think this has something to do with Charlie's murder, then…" Daniel said more as a statement than a question.

"Oh definitely," I said to him. "I know it does, because they keep telling me to stay out of the investigation"

"Well, that's no real surprise, especially since your family…but it looks like they meant it when they said you could get hurt," he said, pointing at the plywood on the windows.

When dinner was ready, we continued with our conversation at the kitchen table as we ate.

"So, for whatever reason, you're being targeted, because you're trying to investigate Charlie's murder," Daniel said finishing up his meal, "and now someone is taking potshots at you guys and you don't know why. Other than your investigation of Charlie's murder."

"That's about it in a nutshell. I don't mind telling you, those shots scared the shit out of us."

"Hell, who could blame you. And we can't get anything out of the kids," Daniel muttered, thinking out loud.

"I'll tell you what, why don't you give me the names of these guys that you know are involved, and I'll do some checking on them. I'll also send these bullets off to Quantico and have them run a ballistics test. Although, without the gun, we're kinda screwed."

"Yeah, I know," I said, trying not to feel let down.

"I'm afraid we're high on circumstantial evidence but low on actual evidence. Plus, I'll need someone with authority to call us in."

"Yeah, and since the Chief, Lieutenant, and Captain are involved, that could be pretty difficult. Also, who's going to take the word of a rehab kid over the Chief of Police?"

Daniel nodded.

In spite of it all, we ended the evening on a happier note. Mia had bought a cheesecake for desert, and we sat around talking and finished off the wine Mia was having. After Daniel left, I helped Mia do the dishes and we went to bed.

~~~

We had a quiet two weeks after that. Mia had started her volunteer position at Cloverdale and was loving it, and our new windows had been installed. During that time, I had also gone to see Dr. Costa about Lauren Stanford.

I had walked in and told the front desk why I was there. Dr. Costa herself came out to let me in and we went directly to her office.

"I bet I know why you're here," she said with a sly grin.

"Yep. You got it. I was just wondering when the autopsy was going to be done on the Lauren Stanford girl?"

"Done…except for the test results. The tox screening and all that. No forcible rape. No bruising in the groin area. Of course, if you saw her, you'd know she was beaten badly. The people from Cloverdale had a hard time recognizing her, because it was so bad."

"Sonuvabitch," I said shaking my head. "You got it done already? That was fast."

"Hey Big Chief yells, little ME runs. Plus, they wanted the cause of death as soon as possible."

"And?"

"Same as Charlie—beaten to a pulp, strangled, and a .22 shot through the center of her forehead. That's two now. Do I see a pattern emerging here?"

"Good God, I hope not."

We chatted a bit. I told her I was on indefinite leave from the police department and asked if she would keep our conversation only to the two of us. She agreed.

That night, Mia and I got into bed, and after a long day, we both fell asleep rather quickly. For the first time in a while, we were both feeling safe and free from harm.

At around one thirty in the morning, I heard a noise from the living room that sounding like shattering glass. Right behind it, came another crash. I immediately leaped out of bed and went to check on the noise, only to find our living room was on fire. I ran back to the bedroom, woke Mia up, and dragged her out of bed. I found her robe and slippers and flung them at her. I grabbed a pair of jeans and a T-shirt for myself.

"Get up. The living room is on fire," I commanded.

Her immediate instinct was to head for the living room, but I grabbed her from behind and told her it was engulfed in flames. I opened the bedroom window and let Mia go out first. It was a bit of a drop, but she'd made it safely. I was right behind her. We ran toward the front of the house. Flames licked at the roof and spread across the entire front part of the house.

In the distance, I could hear sirens. Apparently, someone had called the fire department.

"Cole. What just happened?" Mia was horrified and the reflection of the flames on her face and eyes made it that much worse.

"I don't honestly know." I told her as I watched our house crumble. Our front porch reduced to flames and ash. By this time, the flames were coming out the doorway. Three large trucks arrived, and the firemen got to work immediately. I watched as they poured water over our house and through our windows and doors. But the flames kept coming. Licking our roof like a lizard. Licking at its prey.

"Oh my God, Cole…our house…our little house is burning away," Mia said tears flowing down her cheeks.

Chapter 17

THE FIRE Chief made his way over to us, as a crowd had begun to gather. Two police cars arrived as well.

"Do you have any idea what happened here? Were you cooking something? Burning candles? Or maybe smoking?"

The Fire Chief was a big burly guy. His name tag read B. Riddick.

"No sir," I answered him, as I continued to watch the flames roar through the roof of our house. "We were in bed, sleeping. We had no candles and neither of us smoke, so I can't help you there."

"It's okay, son" he patted me on the shoulder with a heavy gloved hand.

He moved away and began barking out orders to his men working the fire.

The two patrol officers who responded were not from my squad, so I wasn't very familiar with them. They came up to me and started asking the same questions the Fire Chief had. And they received the same answers from me.

I paid no heed to them, since I didn't know if they were in on the whole Cloverdale thing or not. I was polite and answered their questions.

That whole time, Mia had a death grip on my arm as we stood and watched.

"What are we gonna do?" she asked with sheer desperation in her voice.

Mia had broken into tears and cried into my arm for a while. "Look," I told her. "It's the Red Cross. They'll help us out."

The Red Cross allowed us to use their phone to call Tony, who said he's be right over and told us we could stay with him for a while until we got this mess straightened out.

It took well over two hours for the Fire Department to get the fire under control and put out most of the flames. There were still hot spots, but the Fire Chief said that was to be expected.

He walked over to Mia and me, with something in his hand.

"Here's your culprit…Molotov cocktail. First, they threw a brick to break the window and then the cocktail right behind it. See these scrapings along the glass pieces we found?"

Mia and I leaned close to see what he was talking about.

The Fire Chief continued, "These cuts along the pieces of glass mean that someone knew what they were doing and wanted to make sure the bottle broke so that the accelerant from the bottle got into your living room. They weren't messing around with this one. Whoever did this knows a lot about how to create a good hot fire. And with your house as old as it is, it didn't take much to spread."

"Can we go in and get some of our stuff?" Mia asked, half hidden behind my arm.

"I suppose. I'll have one of my men take you in there. He needs to go in with you because of the hot spots I mentioned. But I am pretty much sure that there will be very little stuff in there that's salvageable. It's either going to be smoke damaged or water damaged. We're going to send these pieces of glass and the brick to the Arson Investigation Team."

The Fire Chief was true to his word and allowed us to look around the house. One of his men followed us through the house and pointed out the hot spots, so we didn't step on any of them. It smelled like charred wood and plastic. It irritated the nose. We checked each room, and the Fire Chief was right, there was nothing left to recover.

"Maybe, when we come back tomorrow, we'll be able to see things a little better," I tried to console both Mia and myself.

By the time we came out, Tony had arrived. We filled him in on the details that the Fire Chief had given us and I made sure that the Fire Chief knew where to reach us, since our phones burned in the fire. I gave them Tony's number, and the three of us turned to leave the charred and shattered building we once called home.

We were silent all the way to Tony's.

When we got there, Mia was the first to speak, "Tony, can I please have something to drink. My mouth tastes like a fireplace?"

"Sure. Cole, you want a beer?"

"Yeah," I could really use one.

"I'll have one too," Mia said.

In that single moment, everything stopped. The room fell quiet.

"You really want a beer?" Tony asked. "I mean I have some wine if…"

"No. I don't think wine's gonna cut it with this one," Mia said accepting a cold bottle of Bud Lite.

He handed me one and took one for himself.

We went to the breakfast nook and sat at the table. It was a beautiful redwood table with eight cushioned chairs around it. The woodwork around the table had a scrolled design, which showed a touch of Charlie's work in it. In the center of the table lay a delicate blue dish filled with butterscotch candies.

Tony looked down at his beer and then at us again. "I don't know what you've gotten into here, but apparently someone really doesn't want you investigating Charlie's murder. I mean to go to such extremes?"

"I know," I said. "I just wish I knew what was so important that they want us out of the way so bad. First, they shoot through our front window and now this?"

Tony shook his head back and forth several times. "I sure wish I could tell you bud."

Mia and I were covered in soot from our walk through the house. "Do you think…maybe we can wash up somewhere…take a shower to get this soot off us?" I asked him.

"I only have the half bath down here, but there's a full bath upstairs in the hall, first door on your right, and a full bath in the master bedroom. Mia, I still have some of Charlie's clothes here, I'm sure we can find something for you to wear to sleep in and maybe to get dressed in tomorrow morning." He paused for a moment and looked at me. "I'm afraid I don't have much that's gonna fit you, Cole. You're a little…uhh, taller than I am."

Mia piped up, "Don't worry about it. I'll find something of Charlie's to wear tomorrow, and I'll go shopping to get us each something to start replacing our wardrobe."

"I think I have a robe that will fit you," Tony told me. "It was always a little big on me."

"That'll work," I told him gratefully. "And maybe if you have a t-shirt I can sleep in, that would be great."

"Yeah, no problem. I'll get that all together while you're taking your showers, and I'll see you back here after some while."

Both Mia and Tony disappeared at the same time to the second floor. Tony was able to find both a nightgown and a robe for Mia and a robe and T-shirt for me.

While Mia showered, Tony and I finished our beers at the table where Mia's beer sat idle.

"I didn't even think about the cars. I don't even know if they survived the fire or not."

"Well, Mia had the *Mustang* in the street in front of the house, so the only thing you'll have to worry about is the *Bronco,*" Tony said.

"Well, that's at least one saving grace. I guess we can pick up Mia's car tomorrow. In the daylight, we'll probably be able to see what kind of damage was done."

Tony brought back two more beers from the kitchen, when I heard Mia descending down the stairs. She was drying her hair in a towel and was wearing a peach-colored silk robe with a hint of orange blossoms on it.

"Thanks, Tony," she said, taking her seat back at the table. "I feel so much cleaner. My God, you never really realize how dirty you get after a fire like that." There was a sadness in her eyes and a hint of a tear forming in her left eye.

I kissed Mia on the head. "Well, I guess it's my turn," I said and headed for the stairs.

"I put that T-shirt on the bed for you in the bedroom right next to the bathroom."

"Thanks Tony…for everything. Really."

Mia gave a resounding thanks as well and I was gone, headed for the shower. The water at the bottom of the tub was black when I first rinsed off, and I couldn't help but wonder if anything was left of the house at all. When the water finally ran clear, I walked out of the shower and found the T-shirt and robe that Tony had left for me. Fortunately, my boxers weren't too dirty to put back on for the night, and come tomorrow, Mia would get us some new stuff before we went to the house. I made my way back downstairs and Mia was on her second beer. Tony had provided us with clean toothbrushes and toothpaste, and it felt so good to have a clean mouth again. We each finished our beers and finally called it a night after thanking Tony with all our heart for his help. He showed us to one of the spare bedrooms next to the bathroom we had showered in. Mia and I melted into the warmth of the comfortable bed and soft fluffy pillows and just lay there and held each other in a long silence. It was as if we were both hanging on to the same life boat, and yet we still felt like we were sinking. Mia finally opened up and cried into my chest. I, too, couldn't help but let a few tears escape.

~~~

The following morning brought sunshine seeping in to the entire house. I had never really realized how wide-open Tony's house was and how many windows there were. Most of the time, we'd been to Tony's, we'd been there at night, so I never actually realized how bright it could be. By the time we got down to the kitchen, Tony was up and had coffee and scrambled eggs with cheese and toast all ready for us.

"Mornin' guys," Tony said still standing at the stove. "I hope you were able to get some sleep."

"Yeah," I told him. "That bed was great."

"I love your pillows," Mia added, as Tony brought breakfast over to the table. "They're so soft and comfy."

"Thanks, guys. Charlie actually picked out most of the stuff for the bedrooms."

Mia looked around the room and the house. "Charlie is everywhere in this house, you know that?"

"Yeah, she did most of the decorating…oh, what the hell…she did all the decorating!"

"Well, it's just beautiful. What a wonderful way to remember her," Mia said, gazing around the room.

"Yeah…it's good and it's bad…" Tony trailed off. "In some ways, it just makes me miss her more."

We all nodded in agreement. "I'm sorry, Tony. I didn't mean to bring back painful memories for you like that," Mia apologized.

Tony waved his hand in front of his face as though shooing an imaginary fly. "Ahh, it's okay. Don't worry about it. I'm settling back in. When she died, I hated to be here, and I was going to sell the whole house, lock, stock and barrel, but then I realized there was no way I could let go of all of her memories like that." Despite his attempt at cheering himself, Tony sounded sad and even a bit depressed.

We finished our breakfast in silence. Mia insisted on doing the dishes as a way to thank Tony for going through all the trouble to make us breakfast. She didn't mind it either, since there was a dishwasher, which we never had.

"So, what do you guys want to do first?" Tony asked.

"Well, I think if you don't mind, you could take Mia out to the house to pick up the car. And then she can go shopping. When she gets home, we can go back to the house and have a look at what all's left…if anything."

Since I had no clothes, I stayed back while Tony ran Mia to the house to pick up the *Mustang*. I utilized my time by washing our clothes from the previous night. It took several washes, but I was able to get them clean enough to put them in the dryer.

All things considered, it only took Mia a couple of hours to shop for the clothes we needed. It's really amazing how much we needed when it came to replacing our entire wardrobe. She bought us each several pairs of jeans and shirts, some T-shirts, boxers, and socks, and panties and bras for her. She also got us each a pair of tennis shoes. Once we were dressed, we climbed into Tony's car and headed toward what was left of our old house.

As we turned down our street, I could see the charred skeletal remains of the place we once lived in. The pillars that held up the front porch were reduced to ashes, and the front porch seemed to have imploded upon itself. There was yellow 'Crime Scene' tape surrounding our house. So many times had I seen that yellow tape, but it had always been obscure and unrelated to me. The last time I saw that tape was at Charlie's. Twice now, it was hitting home for us, and it was tearing me up inside.

All of us got out of the car slowly. Tony was the first to get out. He looked from the house and back to us, as we slowly stepped out of the safety of his BMW. We stood in the front yard and simply stared at the destruction. Mia's hand went immediately to her gaping mouth, yet no words were spoken.

"Holy shit," I heard Tony say in a quiet voice.

"Well," I said, taking Mia by the hand, "I guess we need to go through there."

I started to lead her to what was once our front door, but she held back. "Are you sure we can go in there…what with that 'Crime Scene' tape and all?" Her brow was furrowed and there was a fear of the unknown in her eyes.

"Yeah. It's okay. The fire department put that up, because it's an arson fire and they're investigating it."

"And what about the police department?" she asked still reluctant to go inside. "Well, they'll do their investigation, but they should go by what the fire department investigators have to say. We can go in though."

I turned to face her and placed my hands on her wet cheeks. She'd been crying, and I hadn't noticed. I felt horrible and pulled her close to me. She wrapped her arms around my waist and sobbed into my new shirt. "It's okay, sweetie. We don't have to do this today. We can come back another time."

I heard her sniffle and she looked up. "No." Her voice was a little hoarse from crying. "I want to do this today or I'll never do it."

"Okay, then…if you're sure." I held her cheeks in my hands and wiped away her tears. "Whenever you're ready."

She nodded. "I'm as ready as I'm ever going to be."

The three of us treaded slowly through the wreckage of the house. There was water everywhere, still dripping from the rafters. We started in the living room, which was a complete disaster. There was a shell of what once may have been our furniture. But it was black and wet and smelled of burnt out embers. We made our way to the kitchen; again, there was nothing left in it. What the fire hadn't damaged, the water had. Everything was covered with soot and embers or wet from the water dripping everywhere. It wasn't until we reached the bedroom that we all gasped.

"Holy shit," I heard Tony say, only this time his words were loud and clear.

Tony and I stood at the doorway and watched Mia make her way around the skeleton of what was once our bed. It sat askew on the box spring—black and dripping from the water poured upon it last night. It was hard to believe that Mia and I had made love in that very bed the night before. And now, it was all dark and black and shrouded with ugliness. Tony and I finally entered the bedroom and walked up to the dressers. We were able to open the drawers, but most of the things in them weren't salvageable. In the meantime, Mia inspected the closet and got the same results—black, charred, and wet clothes that would never be worn again. As I walked across the room, I felt a crack under my foot and looked down.

"Oh my God," I said, bending down to pick up the cracked item. It was a picture of Mia and me from our wedding day, and for some unexplained reasons, it was in near-perfect condition. The frame and the glass that held it were broken but the picture inside was intact.

Mia made her way slowly to me, afraid of what I had found. I held it up for her and she took it from my hand, staring at it as though it were the first time she had ever seen our wedding picture. Tony joined us as we looked over Mia's shoulder at the picture.

"Oh, Cole," she said, on the verge of tears again. "In all this…this…carnage…the only thing that survived is our wedding picture." She held the picture against her chest and began to sob uncontrollably.

~~~

Chapter 18

THE NEXT few months went by rather quickly. After a great deal of discussion with Mia and some serious thought put into it, I decided I wasn't going to quit my job. I considered going to the Mayor, as I did not believe he was involved in the situation nor did he know about it.

In the meantime, Mia kept volunteering at Cloverdale and told me Michelle was making progress but it was going very slowly. I spent most of my time trying to replace as many of the things that we had lost in the fire as possible. I needed to replace our cell phones, daily clothes, and so many miscellaneous items, we had to keep a list and scratch them off as things went. Mia and I made plans to go shopping to replace the rest of our clothes. Even though the *Bronco* was sitting on the side of the house, there was damage to the trunk, roof, and hood from flying debris. Tony talked me into looking at BMWs to replace the *Bronco*. So, Tony and I spent some time running around to BMW dealerships and found a metallic plum BMW *X1* Crossover fully loaded with tan leather interior and heated seats. We talked to the salesman and got the pricing worked out. We told him that my wife and I would be back that evening for her stamp of approval. I couldn't wait for Mia to see it. That night, I didn't even give her a chance to get inside the doorway when she came home, and we headed for the dealership. She was absolutely thrilled with it, so we finalized the deal. The salesman already had it detailed and ready for us. We took a ride out to nowhere just to see how it worked. Mia didn't want to drive it just yet, because she thought it was too big for her. As we drove around the back roads and the highways, I noticed a gun metal Ford *Escape* pass us several times but didn't give it much thought. When I mentioned it to Mia, she said she hadn't noticed it.

Over the next few days, Tony took us to several of his rehab houses to see if we'd be interested in them. None of them were exactly what we wanted, so we decided to look at new homes. We finally settled on a new spacious three-bedroom house, with a fireplace in both the master bedroom and the family room. Most importantly, there was an attached three car garage, big enough for both our cars and storage space.

"Now that we have a new home, we can finish our shopping, because we'll have a place to put everything in," Mia said one night while we were eating dinner, "and now, we go furniture shopping."

Tony offered us some of his furniture, as Charlie had selected them. We politely turned down his offer, because we were hesitant about robbing him of Charlie's furniture. It was all he had left of her—memories and furniture. We had both noticed that Tony seemed despondent, but neither of us brought it up.

Mia seemed excited about shopping for new furniture though. "Maybe we can do that tomorrow?" she suggested.

"Sure. Why don't we take off, first thing in the morning, and see what we can find?"

Once Upon a Charlie

Tony asked us again, "Are you sure you don't want some of Charlie's furniture?"

"I did really like her things. How about I take a look at some of her things after we move in to the new house," Mia said, hoping it would cheer him up some.

It only took two weeks for us to close on the house. By now, the hot days of summer were already upon us. Once we closed, we picked out colors for all the rooms and Tony had his men come in and paint the whole house for us. The carpet was beige in the bedrooms, and that ran down the hallway and covered the stairs. Hardwood floors covered the downstairs floor. And Mia picked out some beautiful oriental rugs for all the rooms. Tony thought it would be best if we installed an alarm system with a panic button because of what happened to our house the last time. Tony's crew installed our alarm system and we were finally ready to move into our new home.

Over the next few weeks, all of our furniture was delivered to the house and we were able to put all of our newly purchased items away. We said our goodbyes to Tony we thanked him profusely for his hospitality. As we approached our new home, I saw the same Ford *Escape* driving up our street. I found myself on alert, as I had seen the car several times by then while Mia and I were out shopping.

After we were settled in, we invited Tony over for dinner to see the final results. While he was happy with the invitation, he seemed lonely and discontent as ever.

"You did good here. You're just as talented as Charlie, Mia," Tony said, looking around the place. "The place seems so warm and welcoming."

After dinner, we sat around the table, having a few drinks and talking.

"The guys are finished on the condo. I haven't been up there lately. Maybe when we get done here, we can stop by and have a look around the place," Tony said to Mia, taking a sip of his scotch and soda.

"I'd love to," Mia said. The offer had brightened her face.

"So, have you given any thought to what you're going to do with it?" I asked out of sheer curiosity.

"I'm thinking of furnishing it and then renting it out to someone," he said.

"Rental properties are always a good investment," Mia said.

"Of course, I'll need your help getting it decorated though," he said to Mia.

"No problem," she responded, the excitement at the prospect of decorating another place clearly written on her face.

"Look, I still have to go to the police, and maybe, they'll be ready to release at least her artwork," I said.

"Sounds good to me," Tony said as if it were an abstract idea.

Finally, Mia managed to approach the elephant in the room. "You doing okay, Tony? You kinda seem down in the dumps lately."

"I'm fine," he responded, but his face betrayed his sadness and his eyes seemed somewhat lifeless.

After we finished our drinks, we went by the condo to see what Tony's men had done. And the place looked fantastic. All the walls were painted, and he had replaced the carpet with hardwood floors and the kitchen was brought up to date.

"Tony, your guys did a great job." I said walking around the place. It was a far cry from the wreckage we had seen the first time we went in after the police investigation.

"What do you think, Mia? You think you can decorate this place and make it half decent for renting?" Tony asked.

"Oh yeah. I've already got plenty of ideas running through my head from decorating our house. It'll be fantastic. I promise you."

"Just let me know if you need anything, and I'll get my guys on it right away."

"Thanks, Tony. I'll do that."

"No. Thank you guys for the dinner and everything. I'd be lost without you two. You're all I have left since Charlie died. I really do appreciate it." He looked at the floor as he spoked. "The house just isn't the same now. With you guys gone and all."

"Well, we have to thank you for taking us in and doing everything you did to help us after the fire," I said to Tony, patting his shoulder.

"I have to work at Cloverdale tomorrow, but I'll swing by afterward and work on some ideas and start getting the furniture all planned out. I won't be as good as Charlie, but at least I'll try to make it close."

We bid farewell to each other and went to our respective homes.

We pulled into the garage and entered the house through the connecting door into a mud room.

"I think I know what's bothering Tony," Mia said, when we stepped into the living room. "It's September, and it's getting close to when their wedding date was."

I hadn't even given that a thought, but she was right. "Listen, why don't we take him out to dinner on that night to kinda cheer him up or something. At least, he'll be with family and won't be in that big house alone."

"That's a great idea," Mia agreed.

"Why don't we take him to that place in Kirkwood called Citizen Kane's. It's supposed to be really nice."

"That sounds exactly like what Tony needs.

Since we were both exhausted, we went straight to bed. We cuddled for a while. Mia had her head on my shoulder, she stroked my chest. I could feel myself relax immediately. I rolled over and kissed her on the nose making her smile. I couldn't help but run my hands across her hips, kissing her as she kissed me back. Her skin was soft as velvet. It wasn't long before we were entangled in each other, breaths coming in deep gasps as we made love. When we were through, we lay together, connected in a way only Mia and I could be. I held her in my arms, and before long, we were both fast asleep.

~~~

The next morning, she asked me if I was still planning on going to meet Chris. I told her I had some running to do, but I'd do it the next day. We sat and had our coffee as usual. The view was so open and beautiful. The bay windows in the family room overlooked trees and a small lake that was just outside of Palisades.

"I love the brightness in the house," Mia said, looking around the living room and kitchen.

"I know. I'm still trying to get used to it all."

"So, when was their wedding date set for?" I asked Mia, knowing full well that she would definitely remember.

"It was set for the twenty fourth, which is this Saturday."

"That sounds good to me. Are you going to call Tony?"

"Yeah, I'll make the reservations and call Tony. I sure hope we can cheer him up a bit."

Mia bit her lower lip for a moment, pondering over something. "I have an idea. Why don't we make the reservations for four, and they can have a place setting for Charlie, so she can be with us in spirit on the day. I've seen people do that at holidays; when someone dies, they set an empty place for them. Do you think that would bother Tony?"

"I don't know. Why don't you go ahead and make the reservations for four, but I won't tell him about it. And if it does bother him, we can always have them take the plate away."

"Sounds like a plan then."

"I think I'll put off going to the condo until after the dinner, since it's just two days from now," Mia said, almost disappointed.

"You can go any time you want to."

"I'd rather wait until after the dinner was over."

I told her I supported her whichever way she decided to choose. When we finished with our coffee, I took care of the dishes while Mia showered and got ready for Cloverdale.

I called Tony and invited him to dinner on Saturday, and I could swear there was almost a sigh of relief in his voice. I thought to myself that he really did dread facing that date alone. As I placed my phone on the counter, I looked out the front of the house and saw a Ford *Escape* drive down the street once again. Again, I tried to get the plate but couldn't. I was wondering if I should tell Mia and Tony about it, as I'd seen it at his place too.

~~~

Chapter 19

ON SATURDAY, we picked up Tony at six thirty for our seven thirty reservation. The conversation in the car was light with an occasional laugh here and there. When we hit Lindbergh and Highway 270, I checked my mirror and noticed the Ford behind us. Having seen it several times as I rode around town and seeing it driving down our street, I was usually on high alert now. Fortunately, the traffic was heavy for a Saturday night, but as we continued on, I noticed that when I changed lanes, so did the Ford.

"Heads up, Tony," I remarked.

I could see the confusion on his and Mia's face. "What's up, Cole?" Tony asked.

"Check the side mirror. There's a gun metal Ford *Escape,* and I think he's been following us." I saw Tony check his side mirror from the corner of my eye.

Mia immediately turned to look out the back windshield. "I've seen this car around town and I wasn't sure if he was following me or not. This is just too much of a coincidence for me. Mia, why don't you just get down for now. We've already been shot at once, and I don't know who this dude is," I told her.

Mia complied. As we reached the Lindbergh Tunnel, the Ford was still following us but gaining ground.

"I'm trying to get the license plate but I've not had any luck," Tony said, still checking his side mirror.

"Yeah, I can't get it either," I told him.

The Ford was two cars behind us as we went through the tunnel. I knew once we reached Kirkwood, I could shake him, because there were many one-way streets and I could wrap around the side streets to lose him. I hit the accelerator and sped my way through the Tunnel. He matched my speed.

"Who is it?" I heard Mia ask from the back seat.

"I can't be sure, but if I'm not mistaken, I'm thinking it's Jeremiah Robinson," I told her. "That's the guy who shot at us."

"Oh my god," Mia said, panic creeping into her voice.

"I know, sweetie. That's why I want you to stay down. I don't know what he wants or what he's doing."

Just north of Manchester Road, Lindbergh turned to South Kirkwood Road. The Ford was still two cars behind us, so I sped up even more and made a drastic right onto a street called West Monroe and then made a left onto South Harrison. I checked my mirror and the Ford was no longer behind us but I didn't know if he was still with us. I took a hard right on to Woodbine Avenue; then made a left into an ally just off Woodbine and watched as the Ford passed us by, headed back toward South Kirkwood. We sat in silence and waited for him to return. After waiting fifteen minutes or so, he did not reappear. So, we proceeded on to West Clinton and made a right into the parking lot behind the restaurant. We were all a little shaky and none of us were anxious to get out, but both Tony and I checked the street as we got out and there were no signs of the Ford.

"Huh," Tony said, running a shaky hand through his hair. "That was scary. What do you think he wants?"

I helped Mia out of the back seat. "Let's just get inside where he can't see us," she said nearly in tears.

"I wonder what he wants or what he planned to do if he did catch up with us," Tony said with raised eyebrows.

"I have no idea. I'm just glad we lost him," I said to both of them.

The restaurant sat in an area where many of the old houses had been turned into businesses. Citizen Kane's was an old house converted into restaurant. It was three stories high and had a large wire sculpture of a cow in front of it. The house had light green siding and white handrails for the steps to the entrance. When we entered the place, it amazed us. There was a bar to the left of the entrance, and the tables were set with white linen with black folded napkins. There was a small alcove on the ground floor, where they would seat us to allow us some privacy.

When they were ready for us, the hostess showed us to the table, and Tony saw the four place settings. "What's going on here, guys?"

"Well," I explained, "this would have been your wedding day, and we didn't want to leave Charlie out. It's a customary thing that some people do when someone dies—they have a place setting for them."

Tony looked at us tears in his eyes and hugged both me and Mia separately. "Oh God, that's the sweetest thing anyone's ever done for me." His tears streamed down his face and he reached in his pocket, pulling out a handkerchief to wipe them away.

We finally sat down and got settled. Tony's eyes kept darting toward the empty plate.

"You know we can have them take that away. It doesn't have to stay there all through dinner," Mia offered him an out.

"No. You guys are right. This day was as much for Charlie as it was for me, so let's leave it."

When the waitress came to take our drink orders, she asked if we wanted the extra place setting removed. We told her no, so she left it untouched. We all ordered our drinks. The dinner clatter was muffled, as we were in the alcove.

"I guess you've noticed how I've been miserable lately," Tony said, wiping away more tears. "It's just that…it's been hard. I feel like a piece of me is missing and now…" he gestured to the empty place setting "…it's kinda like you gave that back to me."

I saw tears in Mia's eyes as Tony spoke. "We didn't mean to upset you."

"No, no. This is really great. It kinda makes me feel like she's still with us."

"She'll always be with us. You know that Tony," Mia said.

I let a few tears run down my cheeks.

"Look at us," Tony said, gaining sudden composure. "Let's make this the celebration it was meant to be. To Charlie!" He raised his glass and we all clinked and took a sip.

The rest of the dinner conversation were stories about Charlie and her little idiosyncrasies and we spent most of the night laughing and having a good time. When the wine came, we raised another toast to both Tony and Charlie. And that filled our night. I paid the dinner bill and left a generous tip, since the place was so busy and we took up a long time at the table.

As we left the restaurant, we all kept an eye out for the Ford, but it was nowhere in sight. We all climbed into the car and headed back to Tony's. He invited us in for a nightcap, which we accepted. None of us wanted the night to end.

Both Tony and I had scotch on the rocks, while Mia drank some wine.

We sat in the living room and talked some more about Charlie, and Mia told Tony of some ideas she had about the condo. He thought her ideas sounded pretty good, and she promised to go there on Monday to give the place a look over.

"I really wish you would take some of Charlie's stuff with you. I know she'd want you to have some of it," Tony said, looking around at Charlie's creations spread around his house.

"I'll take a look and see," Mia gave in.

"I have this beautiful credenza in my office that you can have. Charlie said it was an antique, but I don't use it at all. I don't even think there's anything kept in there. And there's also an antique chair that would look really good in your bedroom's sitting area."

"Okay, okay…call it the wine or just the wonderful gesture, but we'll take them. But they're going in our house and not the condo. I want to be able to appreciate them, and besides, tenants don't necessarily take good care of stuff," Mia said, throwing her arms up in surrender.

We went upstairs and looked at the pieces of furniture, and Mia fell in love with both. "We'll take them both. The credenza can sit behind our couch, and the chair will go in the sitting room like you said."

We went back downstairs and returned to our drinks, sitting and talking for a while longer. It had been a trying day for the all of us, and we were all ready to retire for the night. Tony walked us to the front door and turned on his front porch light. We all caught a glimpse of the Ford *Escape* sitting in front of Tony's house. He immediately left when he saw us coming out of the house.

"Well, if he's here to hurt us, now would have been the chance, so apparently he doesn't want to kill us," Tony said with a hesitant chuckle.

"Yet," I told him. "Just keep an eye out for him, because he knows where you live for sure now."

"I've got the same alarm system that you guys have, so if he breaks in, I'll immediately know it."

Mia kissed and hugged Tony goodbye and we got into the car to head home.

"God that was a great night…except for the whole Ford thing," Mia said to me.

"Yeah, it really was. Reminiscing about Charlie and all that. I think we really helped get Tony out of the funk he was in. And who could blame him with it being the day they would've been wed and all. I think this night did more good for him than anything else we could have done. And your idea of the extra place setting really touched things off nicely."

"Now if only we can get rid of that stupid Ford," sighed Mia.

"Well, you can relax for a little bit at least," I told Mia, "he's not following us now."

~~~

Chapter 20

THE FOLLOWING day, Mia and I spent our time just hanging around in our house. We both kept an eye out for any car that went down our street. Fortunately, there was no Ford *Escape* passing by. We spoke Tony to make arrangements for picking up the two pieces of furniture we had selected. He had two of his men drop them off in their big trucks, and the men helped us place the credenza behind the couch. The credenza was three feet long and of mahogany color. It had two side-by-side drawers and stood on four wooden legs. There were two panels under the drawers for storing bottles of liquor or anything else we wanted. As for the chair, they easily carried it up to the sitting room, and Mia was not shy in instructing them about where to set it. The chair was powder blue with a soft seat. It had a wing back with armrests and buttons sewn onto the fabric. It was framed in a light mahogany from the top to bottom, including the chair legs. It not only matched the room color, but it was also a perfect chair to curl up and read in. After the furniture had arrived, I called Tony and thanked him for giving them to us and for having them delivered. I spoke highly of his men, and there was pride in his voice.

Monday morning brought beautiful sunshine, and the brilliant colors of the trees were suddenly apparent, as fall had begun to show. Mia and I talked about the dinner, revisiting the stories about Charlie. This was the first time Mia was able to talk about Charlie without crying.

"Will you go to the police department to talk to Chris about Charlie's stuff today?" Mia asked, pouring herself coffee.

"I think I'll wait until tomorrow to do that. I have some running to do, and then, I want to maybe have lunch with Tony. Make sure he's still okay with all this."

"That sounds like a really lovely idea. Don't forget I'll be going over to the condo to try visualizing some decorating ideas for it after I leave Cloverdale today. I'll probably get there around four or so."

"I'm glad you reminded me, otherwise I would have worried myself sick over you not coming home. Maybe, I'll even stop by while you're there."

"I'd love the company." Mia finished up her coffee, and I cleaned the dishes and prepared the pot for brewing the next day.

Mia had already showered and was dressed by the time I finished fiddling around the kitchen. Before she left, I checked the street for the Ford and it wasn't there. I warned her to keep an eye out for it, and she promised to do so. I also made sure she called me when she got to Cloverdale just for my peace of mind. Being the speed freak she is, she called me ten minutes later to let me know she'd reached safely and had not seen the Ford.

I called Tony, and we decided to have lunch at Whitaker's where we met at noon. We each ordered a burger with the works and a Bud Lite on tap.

"I can't begin to tell you how much I appreciate what you guys did for me Saturday night. It meant the world to me,"

Tony said taking a swig of his beer, leaving some suds on his upper lip, which he quickly wiped away with a napkin.

"It was actually Mia's idea," I told him.

"Well make sure you thank her for me. It really helped me so much in getting past Charlie's death. It's still hard, but somehow, now, I feel closer to her, whereas before, she was just gone. It's almost like you gave her back to me."

Our food arrived and we dug in. "Mia's going to the condo after she leaves Cloverdale to have a look around and find some decorating ideas today."

"I know she'll do a great job. I mean, look at what she did to your place in such a short period. You know she always talks about how great Charlie was at decorating and all, but she's just as good. I really can't wait to see what she does with the place."

"Yeah, she underestimates herself a lot, but she really is good at that stuff. It's a talent, I tell you."

"Well if it is a talent, Mia has it too," Tony said finishing up his burger and fries.

When the plates were cleared, Tony and I sat and had a couple of more beers and talked. It just felt nice to talk to him again, like old times.

Tony asked, "Have you seen any more of that Ford around lately?"

"Nope. But I told Mia to watch out for it and be careful. She said she didn't see it on the way to Cloverdale this morning, so I'm thinking that's a good sign."

"Yeah, but always be hyper-vigilant out there," Tony warned.

"Already am buddy…already am!"

We didn't leave the pub until a little after four, and I knew Mia was headed for the condo, so I headed there myself while Tony went home. It took me a while to get there, because traffic was tied up due to an accident. I checked all the mirrors, constantly looking out for the Ford that never reappeared. When I finally pulled into the condo, I saw Mia's car parked in Charlie's old parking space, and it made my heart leap. I still missed Charlie dearly, and it just seemed to me that things would never be the same without her. I climbed up the stairs, two at a time, and heard yelling and screaming coming from somewhere. As I made my way up the stairs, I realized it was Mia who was yelling and screaming. The door was ajar, there was a man dressed in all black and a hooded cap, throwing Mia around like a rag doll.

"Tell me bitch!" was all I heard against her cries.

I bolted toward them and grabbed the man by collar of his shirt, pulled him off her, and threw a right upper cross. I'm not sure where it landed, but he let out a gasp of pain, or maybe of surprise at my being there. While I had a hold of him, I brought my knee up to where his solar-plexus should be and kicked him a few times. He managed to tear away from my grip, and he dashed out the door. My immediate instinct was to follow, but I had to see Mia first. I needed to know she was okay. She was my top priority. She lay in the fetal position crying and bleeding.

"God, baby, are you alright? Can you hear me?"

"Cole?" she asked in barely a whisper. Her left eye was nearly swollen shut and her right eye was showing signs of bruising. Blood was oozing from her nose like a faucet. I took off my shirt and gave it to her to help staunch the bleeding. Her lips were bruised, broken, and bleeding as well.

"We need to get you to the doctor," I told her. She was sitting up now and I could see there were bruises all over her.

"No, we can't. They'll want to make a police report and we can't do that," she tried to speak through her sobs and the pain.

"That's not important anymore. You need to be seen by a doctor."

"No ambulance. You take me." It was difficult to understand, as her voice was muffled under my shirt, but I knew what she was saying.

"Okay. I'll take you."

I picked her up and she groaned with pain. "It hurts…" Tears streamed down her face and mixed with the blood from her nose.

"Sweetheart, you just got the shit beat out of you, of course it's gonna hurt. How'd that guy get in here and what the hell did he want?" I could feel anger my rearing its ugly head as I carried Mia down the stairs and into the BMW as gently as I could.

"I heard a knock on the door and thought it was you, so I opened it. Stupid me…I didn't check the peephole," she said, trying to talk through the shirt.

When we arrived at the DePaul Hospital emergency room, they immediately attended to her in view of all the blood that had now covered most of my shirt.

"What happened here?" a nurse in blue scrubs asked as she led a gurney over to where we were. I placed Mia gently on the gurney, and once again, she went back to the fetal position. She lay there weeping like a small child, and I stood there helplessly, wanting to make it all go away.

"She got beat up pretty bad. She was working in a condo, and someone got in and was beating the crap out of her. I got there just in time."

"And who exactly are you?" I felt my gut grow tighter with anger. Mia needed assistance, and she was delaying that.

"I'm her husband. I found her there being beaten to a pulp by the guy."

"Well, I'm sorry but you'll have to go to the waiting room and wait for us to examine her and see what we find."

"NO!" I yelled, "I'm her husband and she'll want me with her."

"I'm sorry, sir. But in the case of assault victims, all family members must wait in the waiting room like everyone else." Then she swished her fingers, shooing me away. She took the gurney and headed back behind a curtain. Resigning to the fact that I wasn't going to be permitted in there, I went to the waiting room and called Tony and told him what happened.

"I'll be there in a jiffy," he said and hung up the phone.

He arrived at the waiting room some fifteen minutes later. There were a quite a few people sitting in the waiting room, but he had no problem finding me.

"Thanks for coming," I told him.

"Was the Ford in the parking lot when you got there?" he asked.

"No. I would've seen it. Plus, the guy was definitely not Jeremiah Robinson…this guy was…white."

I got out my note pad and started writing everything I could remember about the guy. *White/male/maybe five feet five or six inches tall/brown hair/brown eyes.*

"So, how'd this guy get in, and how'd he know she was there?" Tony asked, leaning forward with his arms resting on his knees. He sat at the edge of his chair.

"She said she heard a knock at the door and thought it was me and opened the door without checking through the peephole first." I told him trying to hold down my anger.

"What do you suppose he wanted?"

"I don't know. I heard him ask her what she knew, but that's about as far as I got, because then I grabbed him and pulled him off of her. I tried to get the ski mask off, but he slipped away from me and ran out the door. As much as I wanted to follow him, I needed to make sure Mia was alright."

"That's understandable."

It was well over three hours before someone finally called my name from behind the curtain. "Cole Spencer."

I stood and raised my hand like a school kid. "That's me."

"You can come in now."

Tony followed me to the nurse. She led us down several curtain-drawn beds and a few that were open but with no one inside. She pulled back one of the curtains, and I saw Mia sitting up on a gurney. Her left eye had swollen shut, and the right eye was bruised but open. She had cotton stuffed in her nose and several stitches on her lip.

I ran over to her and held her gently, careful not to hurt her. "Are you okay?"

Her voice sounded nasal due to the cotton stuffed inside her nose, but she managed to say that she was fine and that there were no broken bones. She didn't have a concussion either, which was all good news as far as I was concerned. Not so much for Mia, but for me, it was a huge relief.

"Hi, Tony. Thanks for coming down," Mia tried to say as clearly as possible despite the cotton in her nose.

"Hey, Mia."

"Are you up to telling me what happened?" I asked her, gently stroking her hand. She had an IV in place.

"I thought it was you. Someone knocked on the door, and I thought you didn't have your key, so I opened the door and he came charging at me. He kept asking me what I knew, but I didn't know what he was talking about. I kept trying to tell him I didn't know anything, but he just kept hitting me left and right."

"Did you get a good look at him at all?"

"Not with the ski mask on. All I know is that he has brown eyes and he's white around where his eyes were."

"Well, we know it wasn't Jeremiah Robinson, because he's black. This must have something to do with the investigation. But what? Anyway, I'm going to start driving you to and from places now. You're not safe anymore."

At that point, the nurse came in and told me that because this was an assault, a police report would need to be filed. I explained to her that I was a police officer and would take care of it. She wasn't happy, but after a little convincing and showing her my badge, she finally agreed. She wrote my badge number in the file just to follow through and cover her ass.

"Once the doctor comes in, I'm sure he'll clear you for discharge," the nurse said, removing the IV from Mia's hand.

As soon as the nurse left, Mia took out the cotton from her nose. The bleeding had stopped and it was uncomfortable she told me.

"They think you did this to me," she said sounding like herself again.

"What? They thought I beat you up?"

"Yeah, they asked me all kinds of questions like if I feel safe at home and if you did this to me and if you have a temper or ever hit me…stuff like that. I guess I passed the test, because they let you in here."

"Well, that's a good thing. I suppose it's their job to ask all that, because there are so many wives who end up in the emergency room, battered by their husbands."

"I suppose," Mia said, sounding tired. "When is the doctor going to get here," she whined.

"I'm sure he'll be here soon."

It took about half an hour for the doctor to make his way to Mia. He said she had several bruises on her stomach and face, but her nose was not broken. No broken ribs and no concussion. Relief. He told her that it would take several weeks for the swelling in the eyes to subside, but there was no permanent damage done in all. He also said that she could have a family physician remove the stitches in her lips in about two weeks. He gave her a prescription for pain and then discharged her, moving on to the next patient.

She handed me back the bloody shirt. "Sorry about your shirt," she said, sounding genuinely sorry.

"Hey, it's just a shirt. As long as you're okay, that's all that matters."

"I'll be okay," she said and tried to get up. "Wow…that really hurts."

"I'll get you a wheelchair. That'll make it easier for you. You're going to be really sore for a while."

I left to find a wheelchair, and then, I helped her into it. It was a slow going, but we made it. I wheeled her to the car and lifted her into the seat. Each move came with a renewed groan.

"Don't worry, sweetheart, I'm going to get those prescription meds for the pain, and that'll help a lot."

We stopped at a Walgreen's on the way home, and I went in and got the medicines while she waited in the car. Once we were home, I gave her the recommended dosage with a glass of water and managed to get her up the stairs and into the bedroom. I helped her into her nightshirt. I tucked her into bed, and she was asleep before I was even out the door.

Chapter 21

THE FOLLOWING morning, Mia was really sore, so I helped her down the stairs for our morning coffee ritual.

"Whose big idea was it to buy a two story, anyway?" she rolled her eyes and laughed, squinting from the pain.

"I believe that was you, darling. Do you want me to carry you?"

We both chuckled, well as much as Mia could chuckle anyway.

"No, that would hurt even more."

I escorted her to the table where our coffee awaited. The bruising on her eye was starting to turn a deep black and blue, and her nose was swollen as well.

"How you feeling?" I asked her tenderly.

"Sore." Her voice was raspy; she wasn't quite awake yet.

"You need another painkiller?" I asked her.

"I will later. Once I've had some coffee."

"You can stay in bed or on the couch all day. Just sleep and relax."

"Are you leaving me?" There was panic on her face, her eyes widened, and for a moment, I thought she was about to cry.

"I'm not leaving yet. All I'm going to do is get your pain pills. Later, I'm have to run down to the police department and talk to Chris about Charlie's stuff. If you want, I can have Tony come and sit with you."

"That would be nice, but I'll need to shower and get dressed and all first."

I couldn't help but laugh. "Only a woman would want to shower and get dressed after what you just went through."

She slapped my arm. "Stop making fun of me. I just don't feel clean. And I don't feel right siting around in my jammies with Tony here."

"Okay. We'll get you in the shower and dressed. Then, I can set you up on the couch where you can relax all day. And don't even think of going over to Cloverdale."

"Did not even cross my mind!" she rolled her eyes at me again.

"Good. Whenever you're ready, we'll get you cleaned up and I'll give Tony a call."

There was a strange hesitation on her face, as if she wanted to ask something but was afraid to.

"What is it?"

"Well…" she started, "…do you think that was the killer?" I could see the fear flash on her face.

"No," I told her. Then I told her about my conversation with Tony the previous night and she looked relieved.

We talked for a little while longer, but I could tell she was running out of steam, so I helped her to the shower and then helped her get into jeans and a T-shirt. She wore slippers for the day. I had already called Tony, and by the time we went back downstairs, he was there waiting for us. I carried her pillow and an afghan to the couch and made sure she was comfortably tucked in. I left Mia the pain pills for when she would be there with Tony.

"How you doing, Mia?" Tony asked plopping down on one of the side chairs.

"Oh…well…I hurt."

"Yeah, I bet you do."

"Will it bother you if I watch some TV?" he asked Mia.

"Nope, not at all."

I handed Tony the remote and gathered my things together. "This shouldn't take too long. And remember to set the alarm when I'm gone."

As I left through the garage door, I heard Tony lock it and set the alarm.

I climbed into my new car and took a moment to enjoy the sweet smell of the new car seats and interiors. I opened the garage door and headed for the police department. When I reached it, I went straight to the detective's bureau to talk to Chris and see if any of Charlie's stuff was ready to be released. I found him at his desk, wading through paperwork.

"Hey, Chris," I took a seat next to his desk. "What's going on?"

"Cole." The surprise on his face was apparent, as I noticed a rather large bruise on his left cheek. He seemed to be moving a little slowly and carefully, not unlike Mia. My heart sank.

"Wow, where'd you get that shiner?" I asked.

"Ah, you know how it is. I got into a fight with some guy on the street and came out with this beauty. I'm good though. We got him. He's behind bars now." His eyes failed to meet mine.

"I see," was all I could think of to say. "Street fight, huh?"

"Yeah. You know how it goes. Guy cops an attitude, and before you know it, you're going at it."

"Uh huh," I muttered.

"So whatcha' doing here anyway?" he enquired.

"Well, I came to find out if any of Charlie's stuff is ready to be released yet."

He turned to the boxes behind him. "Yeah, all the pictures you can definitely have and most of this other stuff. I don't see what we'll need it for."

"What about her laptop?"

"We're not ready to release that yet, but you can have all the rest of this stuff," Chris said motioning toward the boxes.

"Great. If I can, I'll just take the boxes to my car and load them up."

"Sure. I'd give you a hand, but I'm still a little stiff from the fight. Come back and see me when you get them all loaded."

"No problem. I got them."

I went over and started gathering the boxes. There were six boxes and I managed to get them all in the car with ease. It took several trips, but I did notice that Chris was watching my every move the entire time.

As I was leaving, I saw Chris outside, in the parking lot, smoking a cigarette by my car. "Nice car," he said to me. He placed his arm around my shoulder and looked at me. "Listen Cole. I'm gonna give you some advice here, man. Stay out of this investigation. It's dangerous and you could get hurt or killed."

"Oh really…" I let my words trail off, as I headed toward the driver's side door.

"I mean it, Cole. You don't know what you're getting into here. Please stay out of it. You know me, I'm your best friend and I'm only looking out for you here."

"Sure…" I gave him a pat on the back and climbed into my car.

The new car smell did wonders to help me relax. I turned on ignition, feeling eerily unsettled and worried about what Chris could've meant by what he said. Obviously, he was not as trustworthy as I had originally thought. I put the car in gear and drove toward my new house with Charlie's boxes in my car.

When I got home, Mia had just woken up from a nap. Her eye was healing, as some of the bruising had started turning green and yellow, but she was stiff and sore. Tony and I unloaded the boxes from the car and placed them on the floor beside the couch, so that Mia could help us go through them. There were several pieces of artwork that we divided up for us, Tony, and the condo. Mia had spent a lot of time going through interior decoration magazines, looking for ideas to decorate the condo.

Inside one of boxes, there was some jewelry that had belonged to Charlie, and as per the will, Mia kept them for herself now. Charlie had great taste in fashion, her jewelry being no exception. We found a few notes about some of the kids at Cloverdale, one in particular about Lauren Stanford. The paper was from Charlie's personal letterhead and said:

"…There's something wrong with Lauren but I can't seem to reach her. She's withdrawn and quiet. Yet, she still participates in the reading session. I'll keep trying…"

I was wondering why Chris had allowed us to see this. There were other notes similar to this one. It's as if Charlie had known something was wrong but couldn't quite place her finger on it. I placed the note on the table and noticed a phone number on the back of it but pushed it aside.

"So, what do you make of this?" I asked both Mia and Tony.

"I don't know, but I'm surprised Chris let us have them." I wanted to tell them that I believed Chris may have been the one who attacked Mia, but since I wasn't completely sure, I said nothing. Once again, I began to question Chris' loyalties and exactly where they were.

"You think he wanted us to find it?" Tony asked.

I looked through the notes again. "I honestly can't say what Chris's intentions are."

"Do you think that maybe Charlie knew something, and Chris wants to send us a message about it?"

"I wish I could tell you."

Tony and I each had a beer, but with all the pain medication, Mia couldn't have any alcohol. She took a few more pain pills, and before long, she was peacefully passed out on the couch. Tony and I moved to the dining room to drink our beer at the table, and I noticed the phone number on the back of the note again. This time, I dialed the number.

The phone rang and a woman answered. Her voice was somewhat wary. "Hello…?"

"Hello. My name is Cole Spencer, and I found your phone number among my sister Charlie's belongings. I was wondering if you knew her, maybe?"

The woman immediately hung up on me. I stared at the phone, bewildered, not knowing what exactly I had said to make her hang up on me.

Tony asked me who it was, and I told him I had no idea, because the woman hung up on me before I could ask. I asked her if she knew Charlie and she hung up.

"Huh?" was all he could say and looked as confused as I felt.

We sat quietly at the table and finished our beer. While we stacked everything back in the boxes, the memory of the phone call rang in my mind like a gong. Tony looked over at Mia who was still sleeping on the couch.

"So, how did Mia do today while I was gone?" I asked Tony.

"She spent most of the time sleeping while you were gone," Tony told me. "So, what happened at the police department?"

"Not much. Chris was at his desk, and I picked up the boxes and loaded them in the car. I have to be honest with you Tony, he had a shiner on his cheek and wasn't moving very well. He claims it was from a street fight, but I'm not sure I believe it."

"You think he's the one who beat up Mia?"

"I wish I could tell you; first he has all these bruises, and then, he acts like he has something to hide. I honestly don't know what to think. We'll need to make sure she's not being followed, so I'll be taking her to and from Cloverdale once she is fit to go back."

"Well, you know I'll do what I can. And with the alarm, at least you know she'll be safe at home."

"Yeah…hey, thanks for doing all that. The panic button makes me feel a lot less panicky."

As Tony and I talked, I heard Mia moaning, and I wasn't sure if it was from the pain and soreness, or whether she was having a bad dream. I went to the couch and knelt beside her, caressing her head.

She immediately sat bolt upright, instantly letting out a powerful wince of pain. "Oh God, Cole. I'm so glad it's you. I was having this nightmare that it was all happening all over again."

"Well, it's not, and Tony and I are here to make sure you're okay." I laid her back down as gently as I could and asked her if she needed more pain medication.

"No. That stuff makes me too loopy, and I think I just want to go to bed and get some sleep."

And with that, Tony and I helped her up the stairs and got her tucked into bed. "Will you come in and lay with me?"

The pitiful look on her face told it all, as tears escaped from her dark eyes. "Yeah. I'll be back in a minute."

Tony and I went back downstairs and said our goodbyes. I cleared away the beer bottles and headed for bed myself. I had to admit I was worn out as well.

As I climbed into bed, Mia reached for me. "Mmmm…that's better."

I held her as tenderly as I could while she laid her head on my shoulder, and then, we were both asleep.

~~~

Chapter 22

TONY SHOWED up at our house around eleven thirty, giving Mia and me ample time to shower, dress, and get ready for the day. Mia was moving a little easier now that her bruises had started healing, but we still showered together if for nothing else but safety's sake.

We sat at the kitchen table, drinking our coffee and eating some scrambled eggs and bacon I had made for breakfast, which Tony equally indulged in. When all of us were done, I cleaned up the dishes and put the dishwasher on cycle.

I still had the two pictures of the girls and had placed them on the table. Once again, we all looked at them in turns, wondering what it really meant. Lauren had already been found dead but what about the other girl? Was it possible to save her from whatever was going on? Was it even possible for us to find out what was going on? Since Lauren had been found dead in the abandoned house, there was no real point in trying to track her down. Our only other lead was the telephone number on that sheet amongst Charlie's belongings and that woman had hung up on me. We were at a total loss.

It was just after one in the afternoon when my cell phone rang and gave us all a start, as we all lost in our own thoughts, pretty much zoned out. It was lying on the counter, so I had to get up and look at the caller ID that showed it was an

'Unknown name.' I didn't recognize the number. I generally don't answer such calls, but I felt compelled to answer this one for some reason.

"Hello? This is Cole Spencer," I spoke into the phone.

There was a very long pause and I knew there was someone there, as I could hear faint breathing from the other end. I was getting ready to hang up when a woman's voice came through the line and said, "Hello. Don't ask me who I am, because I'm not going to tell you."

"Okay," I answered. "What's this about?"

"You called me the other day, and I wasn't ready to talk, but now I'm willing to tell you what I know. And it isn't pretty."

"Okay…" I let her lead the conversation from that point on.

"Here's the rules. I will give you the information you need but don't ever try to contact me. This is a burner phone, which I'll dispose of it as soon as this call has ended. I've been sworn to secrecy for what it's worth, but now that murder is involved, that changes everything."

"I understand." What choice did I have? She apparently knew something I needed to know, so I had to play by rules and wait for the information.

"Your sister Charlie was killed recently, am I correct?" The hair on the back of my neck stood up, a chill running down my spine.

"Yes, that's right. How did you know?"

"Oh, I know a great deal that can help you find her killer, but you must listen carefully as this is the only call you will ever receive from me."

"I understand."

At this point, I had attracted the attention of both Mia and Tony. As I spoke to the woman, I began pacing between the kitchen and the living room.

At first, I was beginning to think that his was some kind of a sick joke but that changed as she went on. "She volunteered at Cloverdale, didn't she." It was more a statement than a question.

"Yes…yes, she did. What does that have to do with her murder?"

"I will give you the information you need to help you with your investigation."

"What secret do you have?" My head was reeling by now, so I sat down at the table.

"You see, the Chief of Police, Edward Denault, his Personal Assistant, Lieutenant Kenneth Dintzman, and Captain Randolph Eaton are working with the Headmaster, Wilson Puckett at Cloverdale to sneak children out at nighttime…and then, they take them to cheap hotels and…shall we say…'have their way with them,' if you catch my meaning? They make sure to leave no marks or bruising on the children, so it can't be traced back to them."

"How long has this been going on?"

"Oh my goodness, for years now. It started before Denault was even appointed Chief of Police. They pay this Wilson Puckett a thousand dollars per child to take them out of Cloverdale. There are others who do this, but I know for certain that the Denault, Dintzman, and Eaton are a part of it. And a major part at that. You see, they promise to take the kids out for ice cream or a pizza or something, and then once they've…you know…they actually do take them for their promised treat, and that keeps the kids quiet. They also threaten the kids that if they tell anyone about what's going on, they'll come back and kill them. So, you see, they put the fear of God into these poor little kids."

"Do you know who else is involved in this thing?"

By this time, I had both Tony and Mia standing close to me trying to listen in, but her voice was so soft, they couldn't hear a word.

"No…not by name. But I do know others are involved. So, I strongly suggest that you trust no one there, because you don't know how deep this goes. What's more, they have no qualms with killing anyone who may get in their way.

It was my turn to be silent for a minute. I needed time to think. Time to digest what she was telling me.

"Are you still there?" she asked.

"Yes. Yes, I am. Let me ask you something, if I take this to the Feds or the Prosecuting Attorney and get warrants, would you be willing to come and testify at the trial as a witness?"

"No."

Straight up…just a flat no.

"Can I ask why?"

"I told you at the beginning that I was sworn to secrecy, and I cannot and will not come back to testify or they will kill me as well. You'll have to find another way. But just beware, you don't know who your real enemies are. So, trust no one. No one at all."

And with that, the line went dead.

I got up from the table and started pacing up and down the house, between the kitchen and the living room, Tony and Mia in suit.

"So?" Mia asked. "Who was it?"

I told her and Tony what the woman had said and spelled out what was going on at Cloverdale. It made me wonder about Chris…was that why he was acting so strange with me? Did he know all this too?

"So, what are you going to do?" Tony asked.

"Technically, I should inform the Feds, but I don't have any proof to give them. I don't even know if this lady is for real or not. She didn't give me her name or anything."

"You could call Daniel Bentley," Mia suggested.

"I'm not sure how to go about getting Daniel involved. Normally, the FBI has to be asked in before they can investigate a police department, and unfortunately, all the big shots here are the ones we'd need to have them called in."

"Looks like we're on our own now, bud," Tony said.

We all went into the living room to talk it all out, and we thought it over and over again in all of our heads but came up with nothing more than we had before the phone call came in.

Finally, Tony grabbed both of us a bottle of beer and got Mia some wine, and we sat in the living room in silence and stared into different objects respectively; the outer spaces of our minds filling with all this new information. Mia made us some sandwiches for lunch, which went down well but didn't really solve anything.

"So, who do you think this woman was?" Tony asked, taking a large gulp of his beer.

"I wish I could tell you. She seemed to know a lot about what was going on, so she should be someone who is in on it. Or maybe was."

"And you're sure it wasn't a crank call?"

"Yeah, I'm sure. She sounded too sure of herself, and she knew of things we didn't."

Mia finally spoke up, "Maybe she's one of the wives of the big shots and knows what's going on because of that?"

We all stopped to think about it and considered it a good possibility.

"That's quite possible. But could you live with a man who did that to small children?" I asked Mia.

"Me? Personally no. I'd leave him in a heartbeat." She shivered at the thought of it.

"Well, I know Dintzman is divorced, so maybe it was his ex-wife."

"Yeah," Tony said, "and the condition of the divorce was her silence. If he's willing to kill little kids, imagine what he'd do to her."

"I'm with you two on this one. I'd put my bets on that. But why would she call me?"

"Well, you called her first the day we were going through Charlie's stuff, and maybe her courage got the best of her, and she decided to call back finally."

"Either way, I'm glad she did. Now, we need to tell Marlene at Cloverdale, so she can hopefully stop this whole chain of events that's transpiring."

"That would certainly explain Michelle's reaction to your being a police officer. Maybe she thought you were there to kill her, or something else," Mia shuddered.

"I agree. We need to head this off at the pass, so to speak."

We all agreed to go see Marlene in person, as this was not the type of news she would want to hear over the phone. I called and left a message for Marlene to call me, but they said she would be in meetings all day. I left a message for her and told her it was of the utmost importance that we see her first thing in the morning. The girl took the message, but I was still uneasy that this would be going on between now and then.

In the meantime, we ordered Chinese food and had it delivered for dinner. We all sat at the table and discussed the matter until all of our heads were spinning with overbearing thoughts.

It was around nine o'clock when Tony finally left Mia and me alone in the big house. I set the alarm, but my stomach was still queasy from my recent knowledge. Mia felt much the same way. We headed up the stairs silently, making our way to the bedroom. We said little to each other, as we had pretty much said all there was to say on the issue for the moment.

Leaving the outside world behind, I held her close to me, her head lain against my chest, and it felt good and right. We removed our clothes silently, both thinking of the same thing. As we climbed into bed, I took her in my arms as we lay on our sides and kissed each other deep and long. I could still smell the lavender shampoo and the cocoa butter soap she used. I wanted to inhale her. To hold her. So that the comfort of her soft skin would protect me from the outside world. My hands caressed her breasts and I slowly made my way in between her hips. All the while kissing each other. Barely coming up for air. We made love in a flood of passion and emotions that consumed our every thought. Her breath was warm against mine and mine against hers. It was what we both needed. Afterward, we held each other. Our sanity lay deep within the recesses of our love and in the quiet of that evening, we both drifted off to a soothing sleep.

~~~

Chapter 23

BEFORE WE had a chance to call Marlene the next day, we received a frantic call from her. "Cole, I'm so glad I could reach you. Do you remember Michelle…Michelle Waterman?"

"Yes, I do. The little girl we tried to talk to. What's up?"

"She's missing, Cole." The panic in her voice grew with each passing word, like a pot of boiling water.

"What do you mean she's missing?"

"I went to her dorm room, and she just wasn't there. I searched everywhere and simply can't find her. This isn't like her. She never leaves her room."

"We'll be right over."

I called Tony, telling him to meet us at Cloverdale and why.

I explained what was going on to Mia, and I could tell by the look on her face that anxiety had taken over. "Cole, she was in no condition to go out. She was still pretty withdrawn and scared."

"I know. Let's get over there and talk to Marlene and see what's going on."

We jumped in the car and headed for Cloverdale. Fortunately, it was only a ten-minute drive, and I probably broke all land speed records to get there.

Marlene was waiting for us in the lobby. "I'm so glad you're here."

"When was the last time you saw her?" I asked, feeling the police officer emerging from within me.

"Just last night. She came down for dinner with the rest of us, and then we read a little in her room before I put her to bed. When I went there this morning, she was gone." She looked at Mia. "Oh gosh, I've been so upset about Michelle that I didn't even ask you how you are doing," she said.

"I'm fine," Mia said. "The most important thing now is that we find Michelle."

I told Marlene about the phone call we received the previous night.

"Have you filed a missing persons report on her yet?" I then asked.

"No. And now, with what you've told me, I'm afraid to call them. Isn't that a shame? To be afraid to call your own police department," Marlene responded.

By this time, Tony had arrived, and we filled him in on the details.

"What about her room? Can we see her dorm room?" Mia asked. "Maybe it'll provide some clues or something."

We went to her dorm room. The bed was unmade. The sheets were thrown on the floor like a misshapened ghost had left it behind. The blanket was on the floor in a heap, as it too had been pulled off the bed.

"Well, it looks like she didn't go willingly," I said, approaching the bed. "I don't want to touch anything just in case we need to call the police in, but it honestly doesn't look too good. It looks like she was taken by force."

"That's exactly what I thought when I saw the room. Someone had to let them in. What'll we do?" Marlene asked, shock and horror clearly written across her face. She was still hysterical and had begun to cry. "She was just starting to come out of her shell and now this."

"God, Cole. What does this mean? Do you think the person who beat me up is responsible for this?" Mia asked, surveying the room. Tears had started flowing from her eyes as well.

"I don't honestly know. We don't even know who beat you up, much less who did this. But I'll say this, she was definitely taken by force."

"Oh my God," Marlene said and placed her hands over her face, covering her nose. Tears dripped down her cheeks like a waterfall. Like it wasn't going to stop anytime soon.

"How are we ever going to find her?"

"I'm not sure, but I have a few ideas. Tony and I can go search for her. In the meantime, what's her last name?"

"Waterman. Michelle Waterman," Marlene said between sobs. "She's not capable of being out there like this. What are you gonna do?"

"We're going to go look for her. Mia, you stay here with Marlene in case she shows up. If she does, call me right away. In the meantime, Tony and I will be looking for her."

"Thank you," Marlene said, grabbing my arm and squeezing it.

"Also, keep searching the grounds. This is a big place, so she may still be here." I told them.

We returned to the lobby, and Marlene gave us a picture of Michelle that I placed in my pocket. I kissed Mia goodbye and gave Marlene a comforting hug.

I climbed into Tony's car and we took off. We weren't sure where we would find her, but we headed toward the cheap hotels in the area, since that was the Chief, Lieutenant, and Captain's favorite place to take the kids.

After looking in on several cheap hotels, we pulled into the parking lot of a rundown Holiday Inn.

"I'm sorry Cole, but I'm not holding onto much hope here," Tony said, pulling into the parking lot.

"To be honest, neither am I."

We parked the car near the office and went inside. The man at the front desk was dressed in a uniform. He was tall and thin. He looked like he'd been working there for some time now. He appeared to be in his late fifties, with a long unshaven face. He had a small mustache and his hair was balding. He looked at us with dark gray eyes.

"We're looking for a little girl," and I showed the man Michelle's picture. "She's missing from Cloverdale."

"Yeah. I saw her earlier this morning. She was with a cop…Lieutenant, I think he was. Anyway, he had a white shirt and some bars on his collar and a bunch of stars. I figured it was safe…him being a cop and all. I see him and that Chief of Police here all the time with these young girls."

"Are they still here?"

"Naw…he left a couple of hours ago, but the girl wasn't with him."

"Can you tell me what room they were in? I need to see it. It's very important."

"Hey, no. Who are you anyway? I have to live up to the whole privacy act thing, you know," he said in a huffy manner.

"I'm a police officer, and this girl is missing from Cloverdale, and there are several people worried about her." I showed him my badge. He stared at it, as if it were shiny new penny.

"Cloverdale, huh? That's that rehabilitation center over by the river bluff, isn't it?"

"Yeah, that's the one. So, can we see the room?" I was running real low on patience.

"Well technically, I shouldn't, but since the Lieutenant already left, I'll let you in. Besides, the maids gotta clean it anyway. Here's the key. Room 128. And I'd appreciate if you'd keep this between you and me."

"No problem, but I think you'd better come down and open the door for us," I told him.

The three of us made our way to room 128. It was on the bottom floor and near the end of the corridor with many doors leading to the other rooms.

I looked over at Tony. "Ready?"

"What, we've been looking all afternoon for this girl. I'm more than ready."

The manager opened the door and did it slowly.

"Michelle?" I called out her name in case she wasn't decent. God knows what must've happened between her and the Lieutenant.

When I got no answer, I knocked again and the door opened a little wider. "Michelle. Are you in here?"

It took a moment for us to notice the foot sticking out of a clump on the bedsheets. She was almost completely covered with a blanket. I approached the bed. "Michelle? Remember me. I'm Cole, that police officer who came to talk to you."

There was no movement from under the blanket. No sound. The eerie silence in the room was deafening. Finally, I couldn't take it any longer and lifted the edge of the blanket. She lay there in the fetal position, beaten to a pulp. Her eyes were black and blue, and her face was swollen. There were finger marks on her throat. I saw a bullet hole square in her forehead.

I saw Tony turn away and heard the manager back in to the wall.

"I guess we'll have to call the police now," Tony said.

"Yep. No avoiding it now," I agreed

I asked the manager to close and lock the door.

We went to the front desk, so the manager could call the police. Before he could call the police, I told the manager we needed to talk.

"The police don't know I'm investigating this. And it needs to stay like that!" I told him.

"What do I tell the police?" the desk manager asked, his face filled with confusion.

"Tell them the Lieutenant left without the girl, and you were concerned about her welfare and went to check on her. When you opened the door, you found the girl like that and called the police," I told him. "Just tell them how it happened but leave the two of us out of it."

"I'm not in such good standing with them, and I think it would be best to keep my name out of it right now," I explained.

"Gotcha," he said pointing his finger at me, making a gun with his hand.

"With the Lieutenant involved in this, it is very important that no one knows that we were here."

"Are you investigating the police?" the hotel manager asked.

I replied, "We can't talk about that right now."

"Okay, then. Nobody else was here," the manager said.

"I'm very grateful for that." I gave the man a hundred dollars for his time, and Tony and I headed back to Cloverdale.

I thought of calling ahead, but this was not news to be communicated over the phone.

When we reached Cloverdale, Marlene and Mia were both waiting in the lobby for us.

"So, did you find her?" Marlene asked, an ounce of hope in her voice and her face.

"I'm afraid so," I said. "It's not good."

"NO…" Marlene screamed and Mia wrapped her arms around her.

"Why don't you take her to her office, and I'll meet you there."

We followed Mia and Marlene back to her office. "She was just a baby…" Marlene said through inconsolable sobs. She had her arms crossed on her desk with her head down on them.

"I'm so sorry," I said but my words felt empty and hollow, knowing full well that nothing would help.

Mia and Marlene were crying and comforting each other.

"Look. The local police have been called, but I think it's time to call the FBI. I had the hotel manager call it in to the local police, so our names are still out of it. But I think we can now catch these guys. Leaving the girl behind was a big mistake."

Marlene looked up, her cheeks stained with tears and running mascara. I handed her a Kleenex and she rubbed the black makeup off.

"How? How are we gonna catch them?" she asked me, almost pleading.

"I know some people who can help." My words caught Mia's attention, and I could tell she knew exactly what I was talking about.

"Tony and I have a phone call to make, and we'll be in touch. If the police show up, don't let them know Tony and I have been involved. Mia, will you stay with Marlene until I get back?"

"Sure," she said, the tears still rolling down her cheeks too. The two of them standing there with tears running down their cheeks was a brutal statement of how quickly beauty could turn so cold.

~~~

Chapter 24

TONY AND I went back to my house, and I made a call to Daniel Bentley.

"If you can't trust the police, we'll just take it higher," I told Tony as the phone rang.

He answered on the third ring. "Bentley."

"Daniel, it's me, Cole."

"Hey man, what's up?"

I told him what had happened with Michelle at the Holiday Inn and how I was able to leave my name out of it.

"What? This is a kidnapping, so it falls under Federal Jurisdiction. Is this guy willing to testify that the Lieutenant brought her in there?"

"To tell you the truth, I didn't get into that with him."

"Tell you what I'll do. We'll go out there and talk to the guy and see what he has to say. I'll meet you there…say, four o'clock?"

"That works for us. I'm bringing my friend Tony with me, if that's okay with you."

"Sure, no problem."

It was only two in the afternoon. Tony and I sat down in the living room and opened a couple of cold ones.

"So, you think this is it? This is what we're looking at in order to get these guys?" Tony asked, making himself comfortable on the couch. He crossed his foot over his knee and put an arm on the back of the couch.

"Daniel said it's a kidnapping, which falls under Federal Jurisdiction. We can't prove that the Lieutenant was the one to kill her, but it's a start. He wants to know if the desk clerk will testify."

"Testify?" Tony took his hand and wiped it down his face as if washing it. "He didn't seem the type."

"I know. Maybe, once Daniel gets there and talks to him, he'll persuade him to talk some."

We sat and mulled over the entire ordeal in our heads, till we both had splitting headaches. We left around three thirty, headed for the Holiday Inn. Once there, we waited for Daniel. Punctual as ever, he was there at four o'clock sharp. He got out of his black Lincoln town car and met us in front of the office.

"Okay. First, let's go over this again, so I have fresh in my head what we're doing. And so I ask the right questions here," he said turning to me. He was dressed in a dark blue Haggar suit with a three-button coat. He wore a white shirt and a blue tie to match his suit. The tie had red and white stripes on it. He still had on his sunglasses, making him look exactly like an FBI man you would expect to see in action.

"Well, you know about Charlie's murder, beaten, strangled, and shot through the forehead with a .22. And remember, we had coffee with one of Charlie's old neighbors, a Mrs. Mower? She remembered seeing a black male around Charlie's apartment the night she was murdered."

"I knew Charlie was murdered, but I didn't know about the neighbor." I told him about our visit to Mrs. Mower.

"Well, then, there was that little girl, Lauren Stanford…she was found dead in one of the houses that Tony here was rehabbing."

"Okay," Daniel said. Even though we couldn't see his eyes, I knew he was taking this all in.

"Then, someone followed Mia over to Charlie's old condo that Tony had asked her to decorate. So, someone followed her over there and beat her up."

"Holy shit. I didn't know about that. Is she okay?"

"Yeah, she's fine now. But they did a number on her, and well she is having nightmares."

"Well, that's to be expected. Okay, so go on."

"Okay, the little girl we found today is the last one I know about."

"Do you think there may be others?" Daniel asked.

"I really don't know. These kids runaway from Cloverdale all the time. And I think I know why now. You remember me telling you about that anonymous phone call?"

He put his hands in his pants pockets and nodded.

"Well, a few months ago, Marlene Dillman called me, and Mia and I went over to help her with this girl who was totally withdrawn. Her name was Michelle Waterman and she was hunched over in the corner of her bed. She wouldn't talk to the child psychologist on duty there, and she just wouldn't come out of her shell. Then, just as she was starting to come back around, we received a call from Marlene this morning that Michelle was missing. We went to her dorm room, and I'll be honest with you Daniel, it did not look like she left on her own accord."

"What makes you think that?"

"The bed was all askew. The sheets torn off the bed. That's when Tony and I started looking for her, and this is where we found her. She was beaten. Her face was a mess and she was strangled. There's a bullet wound through her forehead. Looks like a .22 to me. I didn't question the front desk guy too much. I just had him call the police. I was afraid if I did, they would retaliate against me like they did with Mia."

"Okay. Why don't we go talk to this guy and see what he has to say? I can't give any guarantees, but we'll see."

We entered the lobby, and the same desk clerk was behind the counter.

Daniel was the first to speak. "I am Special Agent in Charge Daniel Bentley," he said, flashing his FBI credentials.

The man at the front desk stood up straight. "Yes sir," he said in a shaky voice.

"I understand a little girl was murdered here," Daniel went on. "Room 128?"

"Yes sir," the clerk answered. I could see his hands were trembling.

"What do you know about it?" Daniel interrogated.

"N-nn-noo-ott-t much," the clerk stuttered.

"Why don't you tell me what you know then?" Daniel said, trying to calm the man's nerves.

"Well, this police Lieutenant came in with her and asked for a room. I didn't think anything of it, because he'd been here before with other little girls," the clerk's voice was becoming clearer now.

I looked at Tony, and we each raised our eyebrows at the same time.

"Really? How often does he bring little girls here?" Daniel

asked, his voice filled with intrigue.

"I don't know. I don't keep track. You see he and the Chief of Police, and this Captain pay me not to record their visits and pay me a little extra…tip as they say."

Daniel took off his sunglasses and placed them in his inner coat pocket. "A tip huh? And just how much is this 'tip'?"

"I don't know…couple of hundreds plus payment for the room." The desk clerk started sweating profusely and took out a handkerchief and wiped his brow.

"I see. And did you see anyone else go into that room, while the little girl and the Lieutenant were in there?"

"Ummm…yeah, this big black guy…oops…African American…I mean."

"And what did he look like?"

"Oh…he was tall and bald and really big. I mean really, really big."

"And how long was he in there for?"

"Gee, I don't know. But the Lieutenant left right after the big guy got here."

"Okay, now let me get this straight…You said that both the Chief and the Lieutenant and the Captain put up at your hotel and bring little girls here?"

"Yeah, but I figured it was okay, because they're the high-level police officers and all. I figured the kids would be safe and all…being with the police. You know what I mean?"

"Yes. Unfortunately, I do. So, they've each been here before. Do you know how often?"

"Not really. There are other desk clerks, and I heard they skip around to a lot of different hotels in this area."

"I see. May we see the room?"

There was a very long pause. "Well, you see the police are already here, and they told me not to let anyone in."

"They did, huh? Well, let me tell you something Mr.—I'm sorry I didn't get your name."

"Stewart…Brandon Stewart." The clerk wiped his brow with his handkerchief again.

"Well, Brandon Stewart, FBI trumps Palisades Police every time. This is a kidnapping case, and it falls under our jurisdiction."

A look of shock cast over Brandon's face. "Am I in any trouble here?"

"Just give me the key."

Brandon handed him the key, and we took off for room 128.

Crime scene investigators were crawling through the room like ants in an ant farm.

"Ladies and gentleman," Daniel said in his commanding work voice. "I'm Special Agent in Charge, Daniel Bentley with the FBI." He once again flashed his credentials. "I'd appreciate it if you'd stop whatever you're doing for the moment and tell me where Michelle Waterman's body is."

One brave soul spoke quietly, "She's been taken to the morgue already."

"I see. I want you to all put down everything you have in your hands and stop what you're doing. Then, please leave the room. No evidence is to leave the crime scene," Daniel announced.

"But…" the technician let the words trail off.

"I'll take care of the Chief and the Lieutenant. As of now, the FBI is taking over this investigation." Daniel then made a call to the St. Louis County Police Department to have them lock down the room and send their Forensic Team.

Turning to the Palisades Police Forensics Team, he said, "I want you all to stay just outside the door, so that we can preserve the chain of evidence when the St. Louis County Forensic Team arrives."

Within minutes, the two St. Louis County Police officers arrived and locked down the room. Daniel also requested for one of the St. Louis County officers to be sent to the Medical Examiner's office where Michelle Waterman had been taken and to inform them that the FBI was taking over the investigation.

He walked out of the door without another word, leaving some very surprised looks on the technician's faces.

We returned to the lobby to speak with Brandon Stewart, who was sitting on a stool, recovering from our earlier talk.

"Hello Mr.— uh, Bentley…?" he said, the quiver returning to his voice.

"Agent Bentley," Daniel corrected the man.

"Sure. Sure. Am I in any trouble here?"

"I'll need you to step out of that desk for a moment," Daniel waited patiently for the man to come to the front of the counter.

"Mr. Stewart, I think we need to have a little talk down at the police station." Then Daniel turned to me. "Cole why don't you stay here with Mr. Stewart, while I arrange some transportation for him to be brought down to the police department.

"Wait…wait a minute. Am I under arrest here?"

"Right now, you're a 'Person of Interest,'" Daniel said.

Daniel wasted no time in calling St. Louis County dispatch and telling them what we had on our hands. He asked for it to not be broadcast on the radio. Just call a car and have them come by the Holiday Inn.

It didn't take long for the car to arrive, and Daniel ushered Mr. Stewart into the car. He told the officer to place him in an interrogation room at Palisades Police Department and to stay with him. The officer nodded and took off just as the St. Louis County Crime Scene Unit arrived.

"Gentlemen, shall we proceed to the room," Daniel said.

While walking down the long sidewalk to the room, we immediately spotted the two St. Louis County officers guarding the room as well as the group of Palisades Crime Scene Technicians waiting outside the door for further instructions from Daniel.

Daniel turned to the Palisades technicians and told them to return to the room and sign any and all evidence they collected over to the St. Louis County Crime Scene Unit in keeping with the Chain of Evidence protocol. He further advised the Palisades Technicians to go down to the St. Louis County Police Department to make their formal statement.

We went back inside the room, and once again, Daniel pulled out his credentials and said, "This is a kidnapping, which falls under FBI Jurisdiction, so we will be handling the case from this point onward. All crime scene evidence will be processed at the St. Louis County Crime Lab with copies sent to Quantico, Virginia."

- No one said a word, and they left in silence.

"As for you two, I'll meet you at the station." And with that, Daniel left the room.

He went to the hotel reception and told the replacement clerk that room 128 would be out of service until further notice.

Tony and I climbed into his car and headed to Palisades Police Department, each of us wondering what lay in store for us there.

"Shit's gonna hit the fan now, buddy," Tony said, grinning from ear to ear.

"Yep. You betcha!" was all I could say. And excited as I was, I felt a gnawing in my stomach. Somehow, I knew this was only the beginning.

Chapter 25

DANIEL WAS not idle during our drive over. By the time we got to the station, the place was crawling with FBI Agents. The Chief, Lieutenant, and Captain were in custody and waiting in separate interrogation rooms. The agents had stripped them of their guns as well as their dignity. Since Tony was neither a police officer nor an Agent, he had to wait in a room between the two interrogation rooms. The mayor, on hearing of these happenings, appointed Sergeant Rogers as acting Chief of Police, until someone from St. Louis County Police could find a suitable replacement.

They started with Brandon Stewart, and Daniel allowed me to sit in on the interrogation. Two agents dressed in similar suits took chairs opposite Brandon. The second agent had sandy blond hair, parted on the side, his face all angles. His nose sloped slightly yet flared at the nostrils. His eyes, although bright blue, had a look of ruthlessness. Daniel introduced him to us as Special Agent Landon Moore.

Brandon's hands were trembling, and he was sweating like a pig. Sweat dripped off his nose and onto the table. He wiped it with his sleeve and ran a handkerchief over his forehead. "Do I need an attorney?" he asked, his voice trembling.

"Do you want an attorney?" Daniel asked.

"I…I don't know. Do I need one?" Stewart asked again, nervousness clearly marring his face.

"Well that's up to you," Daniel began. "Right now, we just need to ask you a few questions about what's been going on in that hotel. There's a chance you could be an accessory to child pornography, kidnapping, and possibly murder. But I'm sure we can work out some sort of a deal with the Federal Prosecutor."

"What…" The man began to cry. "I didn't know what they were doing…I swear…and I didn't help murder no one!"

"Well it's five years on Accessory to Child Pornography, and Life on the Murder charge, with possibly the death penalty, depending on how helpful you are to us in this investigation."

"I'll help…I'll help…I can't go to jail. They'll kill me in there."

SA Moore spoke up. "Either way, you're doing time buddy, but we can get your sentence reduced if you're willing to testify against the Chief, Lieutenant, and Captain."

"So, now tell me: how well did you get a look at the black male that came into the room?" Daniel asked.

"I got a pretty good look, I suppose," he was starting to gain some composure, but his body would still probably hit a 3.0 on the Richter Scale.

SA Moore nodded his head. Both agents had notepads out in front of them and were jotting down notes as they went. I stood in the corner and watched as my heart raced.

"Can you pick him out of a photo line-up?"

"Yeah…sure…I can do that."

SA Moore got up and left the room. In the meantime, Daniel continued.

"We can probably get you off on probation, no time served on the Accessory to Child Pornography, Kidnapping charge, and the murder, first degree, we can probably get you off, since you didn't know what was happening in there," Daniel said.

The man began to cry harder. "I'll do it. I'll do anything you say. I can't afford no fancy defense attorney, and I honestly had no idea of what they were doing."

When SA Moore reentered the room, he had a photo line-up in his hands. There were six squares, each containing a picture of a bald black male resembling Jeremiah Robinson. He laid the lineup on the table and turned it to face Brandon. "I want you to take your time and look at each of these men and tell me if any of them is the person you saw going into that room today," SA Moore ordered authoritatively.

Brandon stared hard and long at each picture of the lineup. He placed his finger on each picture as if he might lose his place while reading a book. He shook his head several times as he surveyed each picture. He went over each picture again, each time pointing at the pictures.

"Yep…there he is," Brandon finally proclaimed, "right there."

He placed his finger on Jeremiah Robinson's picture.

"You're sure it's him?" Daniel said like he were talking to a child.

"Yes. I remember how big his neck was. It was huge and thick, and he had massive arms and shoulders," Brandon said, backing off from the pictures.

Daniel handed the photo lineup to the SA Moore. "Go pick him up."

Daniel then handed over a yellow legal pad to Brandon Stewart. "Write out what you know and what happened, and then sign it at the bottom. I want you to write out everything. Spare no details. Who was there…who brought children into the rooms…who paid you tips and how much…everything. From beginning to end. Then I need you to sign it at the bottom." He gave Brandon no choice in the matter. "Are you willing to testify to all this in court?" Daniel asked.

"Yeah…sure…whatever you need, I'll do it," Brandon said, grabbing the pen and paper.

"Okay. Make sure to put in your contact information there as well."

Daniel and I left the room.

"We got them. We will be requesting the St. Louis County Police to take over the police duties for the city until we complete our investigation. I have arrest warrants and search warrants in the process of being completed, so we can pick up Wilson Puckett, since the former Chief, Lieutenant, and Captain have all implicated themselves in the involvement, it's just a matter of paperwork now."

SA Moore returned with Jeremiah Robinson, cuffed and his belt removed.

"Make sure he doesn't have a 'drop gun' in his ankle holster," I warned them.

SA Moore looked at me, as though I'd been dropped on my head. "Look, pal. This isn't my first drive by…as they say. I did check, and strangely enough, I found a .22 in his ankle holster. We're sending it out for a ballistics match along with everything else."

Tony hadn't come out of the room, so I went in to tell him it was okay to come out.

Daniel looked at me and said, "Listen, between you, me, and that door over there, we really don't have anything to charge this Stewart guy on. But we needed his statement and witness ID for the record."

"Well, how're you gonna get him on the stand if you got nothing to hold him on?" Tony asked.

"We have his statement," Moore said, "and we can hold him as a material witness. We still have the Chief, Lieutenant, Captain, and that Robinson guy to deal with. It's gonna be a very long night."

Just then, my phone rang. It was Mia. I excused myself, going around the corner to take the call.

"Hi babe," I answered.

"Oh my God, Cole. What the hell is going on? There are two county cops standing in front of Wilson Puckett's office. The place is swarming with FBI Agents."

"Looks like we got 'em sweetie. We literally caught them with their pants down."

"Holy shit! What's going on over there?"

"Pretty much the same. We got both FBI and St. Louis County out here taking out boxes. And from what I understand, St. Louis County Police is now patrolling Palisades."

"Jesus Christ, Cole. Are you okay?"

"Yeah. Tony and I are talking with two FBI agents. Daniel and his partner Landon Moore. It's finally over, sweetie. We can relax and take it easy. No more being scared. No more people shooting at us in our own home. No more being followed. We're safe again."

Mia gave a loud sigh of relief. "I'm so relieved. And I'm so happy for you. But what about Charlie? Did you find out about that?"

"No. Not yet but I intend to. They have Denault, Dintzman, Eaton, and Robinson in custody, and you just said that the county police are watching Wilson Puckett. So, it's gonna be a long night for Daniel and his partners. I'll be leaving here soon and will have Daniel call me when he finishes up. I have a feeling that Charlie found out about the child pornography thing, and that's what got her killed. They've still got to interview the three blind mice, but I'll make sure to find out about Charlie".

"Don't you want to stay for the interview of Denault, Dintzman, Eaton, and Robinson at least?" Mia asked.

"I don't know. We'll see. Let me talk to Daniel, and I'll call you back before we head out. I love you, Mia."

"I love you too."

We blew kisses over the phone and I hung up.

When I returned to Daniel and SA Moore, I asked Daniel if he'd be interviewing Denault about Charlie's death.

"Absolutely. In fact, there are agents in there right now dealing with Denault, Dintzman, and Eaton. And we have someone interviewing Robinson as well. SA Timothy Peckard and SA Jesse Bateman are interrogating Denault if you want to watch."

"Sure. I do. I've waited a long time for this," I told him. He led us to the interrogation room where the defunct chief sat. Tony went into the viewing room as I entered the room where Denault sat. He was handcuffed to the table and became enraged at the sight of me.

"YOU! YOU DID THIS!" he screamed, trying to get up from his chair.

Daniel placed a hand on Denault's shoulder and pushed him back on to the chair. He fell back with a thud.

"I won't talk as long as he's here," Denault said reluctantly.

"Just answer me one question and I'll go," I told him, trying to remain as rational as possible.

The arrest had certainly taken its toll on the fat old guy. Gravity had forced his jowls down further, and his double chin, now visible without his tie, was red and chafed from the years of stuffing it under his collar. His eyes drooped, and for a fraction of a second, I thought I saw a speck of tear form in the corner of his eye. I held no sympathies for this man who had hurt so many without ever giving it a second thought. A true psychopath in front of me. I was relieved to see justice being served. The bright lights in the room gave his already ruddy complexion an even redder hue. Anger seethed through him, and I swore I could see steam wafting up from the top of his head.

"I'm not talking to you," he said and spit toward me. Fortunately, he missed as I was still standing by the door. He never really had good aim to begin with.

I stepped up to the table and placed my hands flat on it beside him. I knew I was within spitting range now, but I didn't care. Mia was right. I had to know about Charlie before I left the station.

He refused to look at me. "Listen to me, you sonuvabitch. You WILL talk to me. Right here. Right now. You and me in front of these agents."

The man didn't flinch. He sat staring at the center of the table.

"Listen you motherfucker…tell me what happened to Charlie. Why'd you kill her?"

A delta of veins began to pop out on the balding spots on his head. "I didn't kill nobody. It was that damn Robinson."

Ever so slowly, he turned to me and spoke through clenched teeth, "Like you, she just couldn't mind her own business. She had to go digging around and found out what was going on. She had to go. Don't you see? She had to be eliminated."

"YOU SET HER UP!" I said in a rage. "You had me called to the station to take that missing report on that girl from Cloverdale, so you guys could beat the shit out of her and kill her!"

In his silence, I found his reply.

I reached out to strangle the bastard, but Daniel and the other agents in the room held me back.

The small speckle of a man now laughed at me and my anger. "You see…" he said as he laughed, "…you just couldn't leave it alone either, could you?"

Daniel and the other agents pulled me out of the room. "Look at you," I said to Denault, "you're such a miserable little excuse of a person that I can't even begin to pity you." And with that, I was out the door.

Tony was in the hall waiting for me. He had tears in his eyes. I said, "Tony. I'm so sorry. I didn't…"

"No. I want to thank you. Don't you see…we can finally put this behind us. We can finally put this whole thing to rest," Tony said.

I found myself crying too. I felt an arm on my shoulder. It was Daniel.

"Why don't you two go home now. It's really over for you, and we're going to be here a while." For an FBI agent, his voice was soft and soothing. I guess he dealt with all kinds of people, and we were just a couple more. "Cole, I'll stop by tomorrow and give you an update, but I'm pretty sure we got Child Pornography, Kidnapping, and Accessory to First Degree Murder on Denault, Dintzman, and Eaton. And possibly Puckett. With the exception of Jeremiah Robinson. He's going down for at least three counts of Murder First for killing those kids. As for Charlie, that must be handled on a local level, but I'll make sure the paperwork gets pushed on that. I'm hell bent on getting a conviction on all of them, for one thing or another. I don't think we're going to have any problem getting the defunct chief, the lieutenant and captain to roll over on him. I'll let you know though."

"Thanks for everything, Daniel. I can't tell you how much I appreciate it," I said, drying up my tears.

"Hey, it's what I do." We shook hands, and he thumped Tony gently on the back. "You take care of each other now. And invite me over to your new house for dinner."

"You betcha'. And this time, it won't be business."

Tony and I walked out of the police station and headed to Cloverdale to pick up Mia. We went toward the front door. The place was swarming with brown uniforms and men in suits carrying out boxes. It was like watching bees in action around a beehive, as they packed and moved boxes from inside to the trucks awaiting outside.

I found Mia in Marlene's office. She grabbed me around the neck and was still crying. Marlene was crying too.

"Tell me again what happened."

I told them both the story, which only made them cry more.

"How are we ever going to put this place back together?" Marlene asked with a breathless sob.

"You'll get your files back as soon as they've interviewed the kids," I told her.

"Do they really have to interview the kids?" Tears streamed down her cheeks. She held a Kleenex to her eyes in a vain attempt to stop them from escaping.

"I'm afraid they will, but they have Child Psychologists who deal with children all the time. So, I wouldn't worry too much about it." I went over and held Marlene in my arms as she cried on my shoulder. I told her that it was all over now and no more kids would be hurt or killed. That gave her a little relief. And she was able to gain some of her composure again.

She stood back and gave me a tearful smile. "You're right. We'll manage. We always have and always will." She turned to Mia and asked, "Are you still planning on working here?"

"Oh yeah. I love it here. If you'll have me, I'll be here."

"Well, since we seem to have lost our Headmaster, he'll need to be replaced…and I think that the Board is going to give me that position. Although, I think I'll call myself the Director of Administration. And my first official act as Director of Administration could be to hire you on full or part time. Your choice."

There was an immediate look of surprise on Mia's face. "Of course, I'll accept the position. But I'd prefer part time if that's okay. Maybe three days a week…And if I change my mind, can I go full time later?"

"Of course, my dear. We'll work out all the arrangements next week when this mess is cleaned up," she said, referring to the police and FBI agents moving their stuff. "I'd like you to start as soon as possible to help get the kids stabilized again."

"No problem. I'll be here, first thing, Monday morning. Say, nine-ish?"

"That's fine by me."

Marlene and Mia hugged so hard, I thought they might break each other. But both those ladies were made of stronger stuff than many men I knew.

The three of us climbed into our respective cars and headed home. The ride was solemn. The silence in the car was palatable. And I couldn't help but wonder what Tony must've been thinking. Each of us lost in our own thoughts and issues. But tomorrow promised to be brighter and happier, just knowing that we were going to be safe once again. Us. And the kids at Cloverdale.

Chapter 26

WE CAME in directly through the mud room in to the living room. Tony parked in the driveway and came up to the front door. I offered Tony a beer, but he turned it down.

"Maybe later. I think, right now, I kinda want to be alone. I think I'll go see Charlie and tell her all about it. I need for her to know what's going on." His head was down—sorrow wrapped around him like an old army blanket.

We said our goodbyes. Inside, I poured Mia a glass of wine and got myself a cold beer. We went to the living room and made ourselves cozy on the couch.

"So, you're going back to work, huh?" I asked, a sly look on my face.

"Yeah, I guess I am," she said, smiling back naughtily. "So, do you feel like you have closure on Charlie now?"

I thought about it for a minute. "I suppose I do. I guess all along, I figured that she'd found out what was going on. It was just a matter of proving it. And it took Daniel to help us do so. But we got the job done and…yeah…I do feel a whole lot better about it all."

"Yeah. Me too. Poor Tony though."

"I know. I feel really bad for him. We stirred up a lot of old and painful memories for him."

"You think he'll be okay?" she asked.

"Yeah…in the long run, I think he will."

We sat in silence for a while and drank, once again, lost in our own thoughts, when a knock at the front door startled us both.

"That can't be Daniel already," I said. Mia followed me to the door, anxious to hear the news.

I opened the door, and it was immediately jerked from my hands and flung open, hitting the wall behind it. "You miserable sonuvabitch. You bloody motherfucker."

I looked down and saw the man in front of me was holding a gun to my chest. Since Mia had fallen when he flung the door open, I reached out to try and help her up but was barred by the presence of the gun pointed at us.

"Get up you little bitch, or perhaps, you need me to beat you up again," he said, pointing the gun at her. I immediately turned to help Mia to her feet, and she stood half-hidden behind me and clutched my arm tight.

"Chris…what the hell's going on here?" I couldn't believe my best friend and old partner was behaving this way.

"Who were you expecting…your FBI friend 'Special Agent in Charge' Daniel Bentley?" he spoke through clenched teeth.

"Look Chris, put down the gun and let's talk about this. What's wrong with you?"

"What's wrong with me? WHAT'S WRONG WITH ME?"

"Are you drunk?" I asked, my eye glued to his gun, trying to remember where I had left mine.

"DRUNK? You want to know if I'm drunk." His words were slurred, but he was steady with the gun in his hand. The line between anger and drunkenness was a thin one sometimes. "I've had a few. So what? I see you two are having a few of your own?" He posed it as a question more than a statement. "Celebrating your victory over all of us?"

"Look, why don't we all sit down and talk about this rationally?"

"RATIONALLY? YOU WANT TO TALK THIS OVER RATIONALLY?" his voice screamed and echoed through our usually quiet home.

"What the hell happened, Chris?"

"What the hell happened? You want to know what happened? I'll tell you what happened…I'm out of a job…that's what happened. After I was interrogated by your FBI friend SPECIAL AGENT IN CHARGE, DANIEL BENTLEY! For three and a half fucking hours. That's what happened. And that doesn't include the two hours I had to sit in the interrogation room before they came in."

"Look, I had no control over all that. I was long gone when that happened. I didn't give him your name…I never even mentioned you to them."

"Well you didn't have to my friend…buddy…old partner…You want to know what they told me? They told me they were going to charge me with Child Pornography and Accessory to Murder First…"

"Chris, that's ridiculous. You didn't do any of that. Why would they charge you for that?"

"Because you're a mother fucking sonuvabitch, that's why. I told you to leave your nose out of it, but you didn't. You just kept on pushing and pushing, and now we're all fucked over."

Now, it was my turn to be angry. "So, you knew about the kids and Charlie's murder and you didn't tell me?"

"I didn't know jackshit. They just think I did, because I was the lead investigator on the case. Those Feds just figured, hey, if I was investigating, I knew all about it. But I DIDN'T! I DIDN'T KNOW SHIT!" he yelled up at our large open ceiling.

"So, I went out had a couple of drinks…they took my gun away, you know…so I wouldn't do anything stupid…well there's stupid for you. I obviously had another one, didn't I? And…if I'm going to prison for Murder One, I've got nothin' to lose by killing you two first. As long as they're gonna kill me, they may as well do it for a REAL reason…You mother fuckin' sonuvabitch."

"Look Chris, why don't you put that gun down? They can't charge you with murder…you didn't do anything. It was Jeremiah Robinson who did all that."

"That motherfucker is one mean sonuvabitch."

I had tried distracting him long enough. I thought I might make a move for the gun. But if he fired at me, the bullet would go right through me and into Mia. I couldn't take that chance.

"Don't even think about making a move for my gun. I'll kill you both right now. I just want to see you sweat a little…like I did waiting for the Feds to come and accuse me of something I didn't do."

I could hear Mia gasp behind me, and I knew she was scared and crying. "Aww, what's the matter little lady? Afraid to die, are you? Afraid it's gonna hurt? Just like when I beat the shit out of you the other day? Well, hell yes, it's gonna hurt. He hurt me, I hurt you, I figure that way, we're even. And then…I get the pleasure of killing him too," he jeered.

Again, another gasp. "OH God Cole, I'm so scared," Mia whispered in my ear.

"I know. Me too." Her hand dug into my arm harder.

"And now ladies and gentlemen, if we could have the little lady step out from behind curtain number two…" Chris said in his best Monty Hall impression.

"No…I'm not going," she said stubbornly.

"Then I'll just come around him and bring you out myself," Chris said, attempting to approach Mia, but I gave him a right cross. The gun flew out of his hands, across the dining room, and landed under the table out of reach for both of us.

Chris and I scurried toward the gun, but he got there just seconds before me. We all stood, like people at a church service.

"That's it man…buddy…old partner…old best friend…Today is your turn to die."

"I don't think so," I heard a voice booming from the mudroom. Two shots were fired, and Chris was flung down backwards, blood flowing from his chest. The sound of the gunshots rang in our ears and echoed through the house like a church bell ringing in its tower. My ears buzzed at the loudness of the shots.

"Tony!" Mia said and ran to him. She wrapped her arms around him and held him. "I've never been so glad to see you all my life."

I went to Tony, and I too couldn't resist giving him a big hug. "Wow…I don't know where you came from, but I'm glad to see you too buddy."

"How'd you know?" Mia asked, hugging him again.

"I saw it through the front window. I couldn't hear what was being said. But I knew you guys were in trouble."

I ran over and hit the PANIC button to call for the police.

Four St. Louis County Police officers and an ambulance arrived at our house within three minutes. The medics immediately attended to Chris and tried to resuscitate him, but to no avail. We explained the situation, and crime scene investigators were called in. They told us that in view of everything going on at the police department, we could come down tomorrow to make our formal statements. Based on our statements, they did not consider the house as a crime scene, so we were able to stay in our home.

Once everything had been cleared away, I got Tony a beer, and we all headed to the living room to sit back and relax.

"Now, we're all safe and sound," Mia said.

We all nodded in agreement, held up our glasses, and took a sip of our drinks to celebrate.

"So," Tony said, "tell me about this Marlene Dillman. Is she married?"

"Nope," Mia said with a sly smile, "…and she's not seeing anyone either."

"So…do you think?" Tony let the question trail off.

"Oh, I know she would. She's already asked about you," Mia said.

Tony sat back in the armchair and smiled his biggest smile I'd seen in months.

And then, we all laughed until we cried. But these were tears of joy and relief.

~~~

Chapter 27

DANIEL FINALLY showed up at our house late in the afternoon the following day. He had not gotten any sleep all night, but still looked as though he'd come from a good night's sleep. In truth, his bloodshot eyes were the only thing that gave away his fatigue.

I offered him a drink, but he refused. "I still have stuff to do, and technically, I'm still on duty."

"Well, at least come in and sit down for a while," I invited him into the living room.

"I'll take you up on that one."

Mia asked, "Have you gotten any sleep?"

"Not yet. Hopefully soon, though." He looked around the house and noticed the blood on the carpet. "I heard what happened here last night. I'm really sorry about your friend."

I looked at the blood myself, which was now a deep maroon and matted on our carpeting. "I guess we weren't as close as I thought. He knew about Charlie the whole time and never bothered to tell me. He just kept telling me to stay away from the investigation or I'd get hurt or killed."

"Well, he may have been right, what with that Robinson guy. That man is all crazy," Daniel said, rubbing the bridge of his nose.

"I just wanted to let you know that Denault, Dintzman, and Eaton all implicated Puckett, and Robinson's going away for life. They're all going to testify against each other in court. It's like rolling bread dough. One's rolling over on the other who's rolling on the other and on down the line. But as for Robinson, I don't think we'll have much problem getting him life and probably the death penalty. Most juries are not sympathetic towards child murderers."

"That's true. What's gonna happen to Denault, Dintzman, and Eaton?" I asked.

"Well, they'll do some time, because they're all going to plead guilty on the child porn thing. That carries three to five years with time off for good behavior…but then again, I'd be surprised if any of them make it through their jail times. If you think juries are hard on child molesters and killers, wait till they get to prison. There are some bad dudes in there, and they'll beat them to shit. They'll have to be isolated."

"Well, it serves them right," Mia said. "They're all a bunch of psychopaths anyway."

"Do you want something to eat?" I asked.

"No. I'm fine. In fact, I need to get back to the police department and get some paperwork done. As far as your sister, Charlie, is concerned, Robinson's going down for that one too. So, justice will be served," Daniel said, giving me a pat on the back.

Mia gave him a warm hug and thanked him for his help.

When Daniel was gone, we closed and locked the door behind him and set the alarm.

"Justice has been served." I said repeating after Daniel. And it felt good to say it.

~~~

About the Author

Karen Wilkinson worked as a 911 Dispatcher, Court Runner, Legal Secretary and Auxiliary Police Officer. She lives and writes in St. Louis, Missouri.

Acknowledgements

I would like to thank the many people who helped me with my research for writing this book. First, I would like to thank my husband Thomas (Tom) Wilkinson for helping me with my research, editing, and putting in many hours of work with me on this book. I'd also like to thank my brother Gary Patzke for all his assistance in helping me with the writing program and for helping me complete this book. I'd also like to thank William Lau who taught me about guns and ballistics, in particular. I'd also like to thank my nephew, Zachary Jerman, who served in the Special Forces for the United States Marine Corps. He also taught me about guns and the way Marines Special Forces work. I'd like to thank my friend Dave Sussman who explained to me about how police dispatch centers operate. I'd also like to thank Anna Lee and Attorney Gregg Stade at Advisor Inc. for explaining how trust funds and wills are done. I'd like to express my gratitude Kathy at the Medical Examiner's office for answering my questions about how autopsies are performed and for directing me to the proper web pages I needed to go through for further research and Evelyn Estegno for her wonderful work on designing the book cover. I'd also like to thank my cousin, Sandy Patzke Bulgrin and the people at PaperTrue, for helping me in the editing process.